DARKSPACE CALAMITY

A RELIC KNIGHTS NOVEL

CHRISTOPHER BODAN

FHP

Future House Publishing

Darkspace Calamity

Published by Future House Publishing LLC under license from Soda Pop
Miniatures LLC. All rights reserved. No part of this book may be reproduced
in any form or by any means without the written permission of Future House
Publishing at rights@futurehousepublishing.com.

Relic Knights created by Chris Birkenhagen, John Cadice, and Dietrich
Stella.
Based on an original story and characters written by Dietrich Stella.

ISBN: 978-1-944452-90-2

Developmental editing by Emma Hoggan
Copy editing by CreelaBelle Howard
Proofreading by Kayla Echols
Interior Design by Emma Hoggan

For my father, who always said, "Do what makes you happy." And to J, who always said, "Write me stories."

CHAPTER 1

Tranquil Wind starliner, outbound from Daeveron

*T*he stars are going out.

Malya blinked and refocused her eyes. She found herself staring up through the transparent roof of the United Stars boarding gallery. The thought had risen unbidden in her mind and pulled her from the pleasant enjoyment of the swirl and rumble of the busy spaceport all around her. Hundreds of people from dozens of species clustered in small knots or formed loose, hopeful lines at passenger gates and boarding ramps. The milling traffic was directed by brisk and efficient staff in the uniforms of various starlines. Her friend Betty stood just behind her, checking ID and itinerary documents. Malya soaked in the wonderful, banal normality of it all.

Their light has gone. The esper that gave them form and motion is gone.

She frowned. Someone had said that to her, once, and she couldn't remember who or understand why she remembered it now. She glanced around at the crowd, as if a stranger might volunteer the answer, and saw only Betty and the boarding queue for the *Tranquil Wind* forming swiftly in front of her. She looked back up through the transparent roof at the gathering clouds and the rose-tinted blue sky. Out there, somewhere beyond her sight and Daeveron's double rings, she thought, the stars still shone.

Except they didn't, not all of them. Not anymore.

Mr. Tomn had pointed out the wide, brilliant carpet of shining stars from the view ports of dozens of starships. Her cypher always pointed to the vast, black swaths of sky next. "They used to be full of stars, of galaxies, of so many people," he had said more than once. She shook her head. Not now. Not on her vacation.

But she couldn't stop. Her mind flashed to the esper crystals growing so thickly that they choked the life from whole worlds, of Darkspace creeping closer and eating the stars one by one. She closed her eyes and pushed the thoughts down, but she knew that she could not forget, not really, not for long.

She ground her teeth and fought back to the present. She smiled humorlessly and scrubbed her face with firm fingers. "I definitely need this time off," she muttered. "I'm tripping over my own mind." She adjusted her cape so that its hood fell a bit further down over her face. The whole point was to avoid getting recognized.

She nearly jumped to the roof when Betty tapped her on the shoulder. "Whoa. Easy there," the small mechanic said. "You okay? You looked like you wandered off for a minute."

"Yeah. Yeah," Malya said. "I'm good. Just—tired."

"Well, pay attention." Betty smiled and pointed past Malya's shoulder.

Malya turned and saw that the line had firmed up in front of them, and she trotted to close the gap. She glanced around a bit sheepishly and then looked down. Just ahead of her stood a tonnerian family. The large matriarch's feline features twisted in annoyed concentration as she tried to juggle luggage and boarding passes and identity papers and four children. They seemed almost completely focused on each other, except for one young girl at the back. She had turned to watch Malya hurry toward them.

The girl had adorable dark stripes running down the fur around her eyes and over her muzzle. Her perked ears twitched around curiously, waving their red-dusted tufts. She had huge brown eyes—tonnerians often did at that age—and they opened as wide as they could to stare at Malya.

Malya stared back for a moment and then smiled and winked. The girl blinked and her mouth dropped open. Malya's smile widened. The girl glanced over her shoulder at the distracted woman.

When the girl turned back to Malya, she shuffled closer. "Are you Princess Malya?" she asked in a low voice. Her tail twined and loosened unconsciously at the small of her back.

Malya almost couldn't hear the girl over the chatter of the crowd and crew. She leaned down. "Maybe."

The girl sniffed. "I saw you race once, on holovid. You didn't win."

Malya heard a muffled snort. She glanced back to see Betty covering her smirk and tactfully looking away.

Malya shrugged at the little girl. "Sometimes you don't win, sometimes you do. That's why you run the race, to find out."

The girl scratched at the fur around her right ear. "My dad says you almost always win. I like that."

Malya chuckled. "So do I, but it doesn't mean as much if you don't lose sometimes. What's really important is that you come out ahead in the end and have a good time doing it." She tapped the girl's shoulder. "Are you going all the way to Catermane?"

"No," the girl said, looking around. "We're going to Fornor to see my aunt." She looked back before Malya could answer. "Are you going to Catermane?"

"Yes."

"Mom says that Catermane is full of witches and troublemakers."

Malya laughed softly. "Well, then, it sounds like I'll like it there. We're going for a festival."

"Are you—" The girl stopped as her mother turned around and noticed her.

"Kollia, what are you doing? I'm so sorry, miss. She's sometimes a, little, um, too, ah, friendly . . ." The woman's voice stumbled and broke off.

Malya stood and saw recognition dawn on the other woman. Malya smiled, put her finger over her lips, and winked. Then she pulled her hood back up so that it fell over her face and covered her distinctive sky-blue and blonde hair. "No problem," she said as warmly as she could. The line had started to move when the woman turned for her daughter, and Malya pointed at the gap opening up. "We better get going."

"I—um, yes." She fumbled a bit, and Malya picked up the handle of some of the family's loose luggage and started forward. "Um, thank you. I—I hope she wasn't bothering you."

"Not a bit," Malya said brightly. "Have fun on Fornor."

"We will. I—How did . . . ?" The crew whisked her aboard before she could finish.

Malya smiled and waved.

Betty stepped up to hand off her own luggage. "Well that was uncommonly kind of you." She swatted Malya's shoulder.

"You know me. Always happy to meet a fan."

Betty eyed her. "Especially if they're not demanding that you sign everything they shove in your face. Still, you're in a funny mood."

"Am I?" Malya asked, trying to sound amused but not quite getting there.

Betty nodded, less amused than the princess had hoped for.

Malya sighed and tried to ignore the knot forming gently in her stomach. "Well, maybe. I just want to get this whole thing started." Her smile turned wry. "Which seems strange, I guess. Hurry up and relax." She strode up the ramp and handed her boarding pass to the attendant at the top. "Where's Rin?"

Betty shrugged. "Last I saw, she was arguing with the cargo crew about something."

"Of course she is." Malya sighed and looked up. She saw a small, fur-covered face glancing over a rail down at her. Malya waved and smiled. "I didn't think I'd be recognized quite so soon."

"You're hopeless," Betty replied, turning over her own papers. "You're one of the most famous racers in a generation on the most famous racing circuit in the galaxy. Nobody else has her face plastered over as many billboards, brochures, or holodisplays." She shook her head. "This just makes me extra glad that we booked private cabins for this trip."

Malya sighed and followed the steward down the corridor. "Me too, I guess. I really need some quiet time."

"Clearly." Some quality in Betty's voice turned Malya's head, and she saw her friend stepping aside and flagging down another steward. "That just makes me think of something," Betty said. "You go get settled. I'm going to check on the pit crew."

"They're fine," Malya called as the small woman trotted away. "They're—Oh, forget it." She shrugged and shook her head before turning back to the steward. "After you, good sir."

The man nodded and started off smartly. Malya strolled after him, mostly gazing out the long armor glass viewing port beside her. The occasional reflections from holodisplays caught her eye, but she resolutely ignored them. She snagged a drink from a tray as they breezed past and then spent an awkward few moments trying to find a place to leave the empty glass. It felt like they had walked through half the ship before the steward finally tapped a wall control and gestured her inside the sliding door.

Malya gasped at the luxurious interior of the first-class cabin. It put her in mind—in the most pleasant way—of the better guest rooms in her parents' palace on Ulyxis, the ones made up to impress visitors without seeming ostentatious or garish. She almost bounced through the door into the long, luxurious room. Bright, textured pelex wall panels slowly shifted colors like waves flowing over her. A faint scent of crisp air and salt water settled over her, and heat came from a warm, flickering light on a floor panel at the far end, suggesting a fire.

After a quick glance at the open door, Malya unhooked her cape and freed her hair, so long bound with pins that it felt like straw. With no one watching, she felt free to finally relax her control a bit. Flashes of blue, green, and pink energy appeared almost instantly, drifting around her head and fingers like dust motes dancing in sunlight. Before she started winning anything like decent money, she had spent cycles poking her nose into the seedier parts of the galaxy or the low-rent sections of Cerci. She ran her fingers lightly over the cool flexisteel and patterned garowood bar. This wasn't half bad. For all the purses she had won and endorsements she had earned, she had never thought to spend her money on furnishings. She wondered briefly if she should.

The esper that floated past her eyes started moving to a space over the bar. The motes swirled and flowed together, and her cypher materialized from the air with an almost audible pop. He regarded the room with a mixture of pleasure and anticipation that she suspected matched her own. Mr. Tomn barely topped two feet high, and his off-white fur and pink markings combined with his bright eyes made him look like nothing so much as an animate stuffed animal. She knew better, of course. She could feel the esper, the raw power of creation, flowing from him along their connection. Flesh, blood, and fur he might be, but he was a creature formed directly from the raw building block of creation and bonded to her as closely as her lungs or limbs. She scratched behind his long, floppy ears.

He also, she knew, had his own ideas and agenda. She stepped back and turned a dubious expression on him. "Have you been talking in my head?"

He raised an eyebrow. "If you have to ask . . ."

She rolled her eyes. "Fine. Okay."

"Not that you couldn't use a talking-to."

Malya frowned. "Not now. I hear enough doom and gloom without you piling on."

"Most people can only watch the doom and gloom, princess. You can actually do something about it." He wiggled his nose, which detracted somewhat from the gravity of his words.

"Don't start." It came out more sharply than she intended, but she let it stand.

"Such is the life of a Knight."

"A life I didn't choose, thank you very much."

"But a life you have, nevertheless," Mr. Tomn said matter-of-factly. His voice turned more serious, more imploring. "The universe grows dark. A century ago, you could look at the sky and see the light still traveling from stars that died a billion cycles before. That light should have shone for a billion cycles more, but it's gone now. The esper that powered that light has been drained from the universe. You've seen this."

"Yes," she nearly shouted. "Yes. I've seen it. And I've seen that there's nothing I can do about it."

"That's not true," he shot back. "And you know that too." He crossed his arms and turned away, pouting.

"So you always say. But you know what else you say?" She glared at him. "Not yet. For all the questing we've done, for all the firefights and fistfights, you still say not yet. Why?"

He looked a little embarrassed. "The Source hasn't appeared, but I'm afraid that when it does, there won't be much time. Something is interfering."

"And that sort of vague nonsense—" Malya cut off her own words and simply fumed. "Look. If and when there's something I can actually do to help, I'll try. You know that."

Mr. Tomn nodded diffidently, but Malya held his gaze until he acknowledged her more firmly.

"But for now, I need some rest. We've been running nonstop for cycles. Between racing, whatever cockamamie scheme you cook up on any given day, and the gaggle of goons we seem to attract, I haven't had a moment's peace in a long time." She arched her eyebrow and lightened her tone as an olive branch. "You're a trouble magnet, you know. All cyphers are."

Mr. Tomn snorted. "You don't need the help, princess."

"So," she said after a beat, her eyes half-lidded, "are you going to give me a hard time for kicking back a bit?"

Mr. Tomn made a show of gravely considering the question but could not hold back his grin. He took a running leap from the bar and landed on the padded bench seat beneath the armor glass viewport. He flopped over onto his back. "Nope. You're right. We've earned it." He glanced at her. "But only for a little while. Something tells me we need to take this trip anyway."

Malya decided that was the best she was going to get from him and nodded firmly. "Good."

She knelt on the deep upholstery beside him and stared out the windows at the dock crews loading the last of the luggage and cargo into the ship. She could not stop smiling. The journey stretched out before her like a clear road on a bright day. She heard people almost arguing in the hall, approaching, and she cocked her head to listen.

She recognized Betty almost at once and then giggled lightly when she identified Rin's firm, rich voice complaining.

"No, I don't see why they had to take it."

"You don't see why a civilian passenger ship wants you to stow a high-powered sniper rifle in the secure cargo hold?" Betty asked. Malya could almost hear the small mechanic rolling her eyes.

"It's my carry-on," Rin said sourly.

"No, it's not," Malya called without turning. "We told you that." She watched the dock crews below them, searching.

"It fits and everything," Rin replied, exasperated. "I measured it."

"I don't even know why you brought that thing." Betty's voice had gotten a little shrill, but the tightness around her eyes looked more anxious than angry.

"First," Rin replied, "that 'thing' is called Rudy, and you know it. Second, you brought that huge wrench of yours. When did you think you might need that?"

"The princess is performing, right? I thought I might, you know, need to do my job."

Malya could feel the satisfaction rolling off of Rin. "Exactly."

"We're going to Catermane, the very heart and soul of the Doctrine. We'll be in the center of Doctrine space, surrounded by wizards and other esper-wielders dedicated to making sure we stay safe and happy. If you ever feel like you have to do your 'job', then something's gone horribly wrong."

"It's a dangerous galaxy," Rin mused.

"Sure, but we won't have to worry about that when we get there, and until then," she gestured around her. "Where exactly did you think you were going to use a sniper rifle on this ship? Besides," she said, turning brittle, "if Lug has to stay down there, then so does your Rudy."

"It's not the same," the tall woman said. "He doesn't fit in the passenger sections, and he knows it. He volunteered."

Malya turned slightly to see Rin flop into an overstuffed chair, her strawberry blonde hair completely covering its back. Two ceiling panels slid back in response and large holodisplays swung down from each.

"Yeah. Yeah," Betty replied, her voice sinking. She settled onto the corner of the bench seat and wrung her hands gently. "He did."

Both displays automatically brightened and started playing the same news feeds as the others on the ship, all discussing the Darkspace Calamity. Malya frowned at them for a few seconds before Rin found the control panel in the chair's armrest and shut them off. Betty did not seem to notice.

Malya's excitement dimmed a bit as she watched Betty's anxious sadness over Lug. No one expected the chee to ride in the cargo bay; she had seen other members of the sentient machine race all over, just on her short trip to the cabin. Even an industrial model like Lug could find room in the better sections, but he had immediately claimed a space as cargo as soon as she had announced this trip.

"He's okay," Rin said. "He said so, remember? He's in one of his moods where he doesn't really want to socialize with anyone. You know how he gets. Besides, he's got a datajack and the specs for the new model year racers. He's going to be fine."

"For three weeks?"

"It's not quite that long to Catermane," Malya said, trying to lighten the mood with her cheerful tone.

"It would've been faster if we went straight from Cerci."

"Sure," the princess replied, "but I wanted to keep a low profile and get some quiet time, remember? Give me a chance to forget about things for a while." She smiled over at Mr. Tomn, who remained stretched out with his eyes shut. "At least as much as I can forget."

No cypher bonded to a sentient without a greater purpose, someone had told her once. She wished she could remember who. The stories said that Knights, sentients bonded with a cypher, all had a destiny, some part to play in the coming Calamity. Mr. Tomn sat up suddenly and looked in her eyes.

She blinked and turned to Betty. "Did the pit crew get settled?"

"Yeah, they're all tucked in down on first class," Betty said, accepting the distraction. "I'm not sure most of 'em quite know how to behave there, but nobody's complaining about you springing for the good tickets."

Malya smiled and turned back to the window. A little chill fell over her shoulders and settled in her stomach. Out the window, she saw a cargo mover with the last of the large items for the hold. The heavy, nondescript crate it carried bore only the diplomatic seal of Ulyxis and could have contained any official cargo—but it did not. Malya could feel her relic Sedaris folded up and packed away in there, and she yearned for it with something that felt like hunger.

She had dug that magnificent machine from the crumbling wreck of a ruin on Vordexis Major two months after her third Prime win. Injured, pursued by assassins, and hopelessly lost, Mr. Tomn had guided her to a sacred place. There he had poured a torrent of esper into her. He had shown her a truth of the universe, a truth of passion and joy and creation through pure speed, and it had coalesced into her relic Sedaris. She would need it, he'd said; need its incredible swiftness, its strong frame, and its long blade. Now, she felt soft and vulnerable without it. She pushed aside the impulse to summon it, to force the esper to materialize the racer in front of her. It took quite an effort.

Malya swallowed and shook her head. "Well, we're all out of our comfort zone right now." She settled into the seat. "It'll do us all good to get away for a bit."

"You've been saying that for weeks," Rin said. "What is it you're trying to get away from, exactly—the fame, the celebrity? It's not the racing; you live for that."

"It's the—" Malya paused, trying to find alternates to the words that leapt to mind; saying them out loud would make the whole impulse seem wrong. "It's the responsibility," she said, and realized too late that she meant exactly that. "To—Ah, to everyone. About everything. The fans, the promoters, the organizers, the sponsors. I feel like I owe everybody some of my time and energy, and I don't have any left for, you know, just enjoying what I've got. I guess."

"Well, I'm all for a little R'n'R," Betty said, visibly trying to relax, "but we've only got so much time, you know? The galaxy doesn't stop turning just 'cause you're dizzy."

"No, but I'd still like a chance to catch my breath." She shrugged and forced a chuckle. "I mean, you win the Cerci Prime all three times in the same year, I think you should get to savor that, right?" Her eyes unfocused for a moment, and she thought she could see dead stars. "Need to think about what's next and not think about other things."

Betty frowned, and Rin cast a dubious look at the princess. Mr. Tomn watched her expectantly.

She frowned at him and sighed. "Look, we're committed to celebrating the Festival of Scrolls on Catermane. We're going to perform, relax, and have a good time. We're on this ship for three weeks, and then we've got a couple of weeks back to Cerci. We'll be rested, refreshed, and then we'll figure out what's going to happen next." She glared at Mr. Tomn.

"Time for rest and reflection is a luxury not often granted to a Knight," the cypher said, unmoved.

"Well, then let's enjoy it while it lasts." She looked up. "Rin, call room service. I figure we've got to kill a few hours before mister mouth here," she nodded to her cypher, "can break us into the secure cargo hold."

Both of the women brightened up. "Yes ma'am," Rin said and reached for the intercom.

CHAPTER 2

Corsair ship *Black Spot,* wildspace

Golden Vance sat in the *Black Spot's* command chair and brooded. He unconsciously flexed the stained and pitted manipulators of his industrial-grade cybernetic arm as his thoughts rolled and darkened. What good was the life of a free and independent corsair, he wondered, if he still had to jump and come calling at someone else's whim? Who was Kate, and especially Harker, to call him here to this black nowhere? And what did it say about him that he answered?

Outside the armored viewport of his ship's bridge, the stars and shifting wonders of wildspace drifted past unnoticed. The call would come soon, he knew; Harker was never late when he called a conference. The thought of speaking to that arrogant, imperious, aristocratic pig drove Vance to grind his teeth and break furniture with his claw. He looked forward to seeing Calico Kate only slightly less. Worse, Harker likely wouldn't have dragged them out to this empty corner of space if he didn't have word of a prize. Vance had seen no prize worth the taking for over two standard weeks, and the urge for violence crawled up his back like a spider. Just seeing Harker's smug face would gall, but owing the man for a chance at plunder would rankle like nothing else. Vance couldn't decide which he hated more.

Something else tugged at him, though; something beyond having to deal with Harker and Kate. He kept poking at the corners of his grimy mind to find it, fix it, put a name on it, but always it eluded him. He could not call it foreboding, though it had a touch of that. He had never been given to prophecy or uncanny insight even after the esper chose him. Nevertheless, he had a feeling, like an itch in his mind. Something was coming. He wondered if it would finally make him rich.

A soft gold and violet light rose behind him and spread across his patched cape and, now empty, mug.

He frowned further. "Don't hover, little fish. Come forward or go away."

A second later, the scaled form of Minnow, his mermaid-like cypher, drifted over his left shoulder and into view. She seemed anxious; well, more anxious than usual. Vance wondered at that for a second but then decided it fit with the impending . . . something . . . that he felt. She was always too bloody sensitive. He grew impatient with her instantly.

"My Knight," she began, and broke off at the sight of his sneer. She rallied, though, and tried again. "Captain, I—"

"Quiet," he said. It came out as a low growl. "When I've need of you, I'll ask. Until then, be silent."

Minnow hesitated, as if she might speak anyway, but slumped her shoulders instead. Her gaze fell to the floor, and she drifted to his left just out of sight.

The low whistle of the comm signal cut across the bridge. Vance's second-in-command stepped over to the communications station and then moved toward him. "Captain," the grizzled man said, touching his cap, "they're here. That's Kate what just signaled, and scans show that Harker's just coming out of slip space now."

Vance nodded, sliding easily into the official captain role. "Thank you, Mr. Skreev. Put her through, and let's get this over with."

He strode toward the center of the bridge as the overhead holodisplay sputtered to life. A shaky image of a young woman with red-gold hair, an eye patch, and a cavalier attitude formed above him and gradually gained resolution. Calico Kate, the self-styled Queen of the Star Nebula Corsairs, stared down at him. He could have spit. She'd done well enough from their little 'business arrangement,' no doubt. Vance had yet to decide if he'd done well enough. Perhaps he'd find out today.

He stepped up to the edge of the holoprojector's floor inserts, where the optics could pick him up and render his image to Kate. "Captain," he said as evenly as he could manage.

"Golden," Kate replied, in an almost sprightly manner. "How are you faring this lovely day in the void?"

He shrugged. No reason to play her games. "Well enough. Better, once I find out why we've come all the way out to nowhere."

"Aye," she replied in her rich, rolling tones. Her expression slipped more serious. "And Harker can explain his haste as well."

"Of course," came a cultured, smooth voice over the link.

Vance gritted his teeth again as the third pirate captain's face resolved in the air.

"Apologies for the unusual nature of this meeting, but it's a rare opportunity and the situation is fluid." Harker glanced down at something the others could not see and data files began appearing on the displays below them. "This is the *Tranquil Wind*, pride of the United Stars starline, and bound from Daeveron to Catermane on this course." He glanced at something to his left. "Indeed, they should be dropping out of slip space in the next few moments to recharge."

Kate rubbed her chin, thoughtfully regarding the passenger ship's image on the display. "Hmm. Big and fat, true enough. And while I don't mind relieving some dirt-huggers of their pretties, it's not as though this is a Merchant's Guild bulk hauler." She fixed her gaze on Harker. "You could take this fish yourself, I think. While I appreciate you sharing, why did you feel the need for all of us here?"

Harker grinned, and Vance wanted to hit him. "Because I have word that Malya Ulyxani, Crown Princess of Ulyxis, three-time Cerci Prime champion, and—lest we forget—famed Relic Knight, is traveling incognito aboard this very ship."

Vance's jaw dropped open. This was it. This was what he had felt coming; he knew it. His vision shrank to the starliner's image, and he fancied he could see a glow within it. He realized a second later that Kate was talking again, and he had to struggle to hear her.

"Are you sure, Harker?" The pirate queen had turned all

business.

Harker nodded. "Yes. I have a very well-placed source whom I have tasked specifically with this. It's long been rumored that Malya leaves Cerci secretly, sometimes for extended periods." He shrugged. "She is a Knight, after all, and that means a life of strange journeys and danger. This we can all attest to." As if on cue, Harker's parrot cypher Caesar landed on his shoulder, just barely in the image. He had the good grace to look embarrassed. "Yes, yes. We remember you exist. Shoo." He gently pushed the cypher out of the image. Harker straightened up and cleared his throat.

Vance wanted to smack the ghost of a smile off of the man's face.

"In any case, I have kept watch for her to take one of these unannounced trips, and now I've managed to get her itinerary and course."

"How good is your man?" Vance demanded. "Is he reliable?"

"For what I paid him, he'd better be," Harker said. "But more than that, his reputation for this kind of thing is impeccable. As you've said, this ship is hardly worth the trouble for all three of us, and I wouldn't have involved you or Captain Kate if I didn't trust the report."

Vance growled. "That's a rich prize, princess or no, and you'll not keep me from it—us from it," he corrected. "We share booty, as we've agreed, and I'll hold you to that bargain. Personally."

"Of course," Harker said airily. Vance's frown deepened. Harker should have come back with some contrived, upper-class insults; he always had. His simple dismissal of the threat raised Vance's hackles.

"Well, it's a fun prize all the same," Kate said. "Right then, we'll hit 'em when they appear. We can't waste time on this one; if the princess is aboard, it's likely that the paladins or some other authority will hop to her aid the second the distress signal goes out. So look sharp. Vance, breach aft between the passenger sections and the cargo hold. Keep the passengers from running." She fixed him with a stern look. "Passengers first, then cargo."

Vance grumbled but nodded. He would just see, he decided, how things went. He'd likely have to improvise.

"Harker, take the starboard side forward of the passengers and push aft," Kate continued. "I'll take port and aim for the bridge. I'll join you once I've secured that. Remember, we need the princess unharmed or at least intact."

"That's no easy task," Vance said, "considering she's a Knight."

"You want easy, go back to snatching purses," Kate said with a biting smile. "You want rich, you take her alive."

"Aye, aye," Vance replied. She seemed to hesitate at his easy acceptance, and he scowled so she would not suspect that he had any ideas other than following orders.

"Right. Hop to, everyone," Kate said and cut her link. Vance turned away without a word to Harker, and the display fuzzed out behind him.

Schematics of the *Tranquil Wind* replaced the images of the pirate captains in the air over the bridge. Diagram information blinked into life describing the ship's features and construction, and a green glowing tag appeared over the passenger section. Vance studied it for a moment with an experienced eye and finally nodded. "That's our boarding point," he said. "Helm, come about when they appear and make for that section, port side. We'll beat Harker to anything worth having. Mr. Skreev!"

"Aye, captain," the man called, saluting.

"Gather the hands at the boarding airlocks." He could not help grinning at the thought of the coming fight. "Tell 'em we've throats to cut." Mr. Skreev shared his captain's smile and hurried off. A second later, the general quarters signal sounded through the ship, and Vance strode out to get his weapons.

Malya sat back and enjoyed the view from the top deck of the *Tranquil Wind's* smaller food court. The dining area looked like a scoop taken out of the ship's midsection four decks high, with dancing colors, shifting holoprojections, and currently, a cool sea breeze wafting through to entertain and relax the guests. The three women had a private table at the railing of the top deck. From here, they could look out through the vast open space, seeing just the edges of the next two scooped decks, and all the way down to the bottom level. The noise fascinated Malya. The ship did an excellent job of muffling the roar of so many people, but she could still follow the low rumble of conversations, laughter, and shrieking children. It sounded like the crowd at a mid-tier track before the flag dropped.

Rin had insisted on a good vantage point, and Malya didn't blame her. The sniper pulled her second-favorite scope from the long pocket on her vest and began idly scanning the visible parts of the lower decks. Only Rin had actually extricated anything from storage, but just being able to visit Lug improved Betty's mood immensely. Similarly, laying a hand on Sedaris now and then made Malya feel immeasurably better.

From a discrete spot under the table, Mr. Tomn touched Malya's leg, and she smiled down at him. He held up his paws. She rolled her eyes and dutifully dropped half of her sweet muffin to him. The cypher chewed away happily. His presence helped, but it did not stop the nagging feeling in the back of her mind.

She glanced over her shoulder at the displays. Three different projectors showed three different news feeds, all discussing the Darkspace Calamity. One described how astronomers could find no other galaxies than this one. The second lamented that the Doctrine's codifiers could not detect even lingering traces of the esper energies that once bound the lost stars to existence. The last reported that corsair and noh raids had increased dramatically over the last two cycles and that panic and chaos were sweeping across the Last Galaxy.

Malya frowned. "Even here," she said quietly as she turned away, "technically on vacation, we can't relax. You have to stay out of sight. I have to keep my head down." She closed her eyes. "And we can't get away from that."

Mr. Tomn looked at her and cocked his head, as if waiting for her to continue, and she realized that she could not have honestly said if she was talking to her cypher or not.

"And there's nothing we can do about it," she muttered.

"That's not true," Mr. Tomn said.

Malya blinked, startled by the firmness in his voice, but Rin glanced over before she could say anything.

"What did you say?" the sniper asked. Malya saw Rin regarding her through the riflescope.

"I didn't say anything. What are you doing?"

"I can see every pore on your nose."

Malya laughed sharply. "Great. Thanks. That makes me feel better." Rin turned back to studying lower deck.

"I heard you," Betty said. Malya started. She turned to see that the mechanic had not lowered her dog-eared copy of Crew Boss Monthly. She had leaned over the table, though, and pitched her voice low. "And I heard him, too."

"What?" Malya felt suddenly much more nervous than she should have. "I didn't—" Betty lowered her magazine and frowned lopsidedly. "Who do you think you're kidding? Look, I've been thinking about what you said when we left. No, hear me out. I think you're talking a lot to us, and to your fuzzy friend there, but you're really trying to kid yourself." She nodded at Mr. Tomn. "You know what comes with him, right? And I don't just mean a shot of esper now and again or someone to eat your muffins. It comes with having that glorious machine down in the hold, too."

Malya shook her head and looked away, but Betty leaned closer to press her point.

"You keep saying you don't know what's next, but I think you do. I think you know and you just won't admit it." She sighed and softened a little. "You're not just a simple racer, princess, for all that you wish you were. You're not just royalty on the run or the biggest celebrity on the Speed Circuit for a generation, either. You're a Knight—a Relic Knight, what's more—and you've never squared with that and all the baggage that comes with it."

"Well, I didn't ask for it," Malya hissed. "There's a responsibility with being Crown Princess of Ulyxis, too, and you see how well I'm living up to that. I don't want anything I didn't choose."

"We don't get to pick most of what we get in life," Rin said laconically. "We just get to deal with it."

"When did you get so philosophical?" Malya snapped.

"When you spend as much time looking through one of these as I do, you get to reflecting on people, motivation, and life in general." Rin replied without moving. "It strips away most of the little, unimportant things. Life looks clearer through a scope."

"So you're a deep thinker now?" Betty asked with a teasing note in her voice. "I didn't think they paid you for that as a—what's the term these days? Racing Circuit Regulation Enforcement Professional?"

"That's right," Rin said indignantly. "That's exactly what I am. We just prefer being called spotters."

"You're a sniper. You shoot people."

Rin turned her head to give Betty a baleful stare. "I'm a fully accredited and bonded Racing Circuit employee tasked with preventing race interference by outside elements."

"You shoot people."

"Yes. Before they can interfere with the races and hurt or kill the racers." She waved toward Malya. "I've saved her life three times at least." She leveled a finger at Betty. "And yours twice."

"Once, for sure," Betty said quickly, raising one finger. She could not hide her smile. "That time on the Blackwood 50 doesn't count."

"Says you," Rin said, stuck her tongue out, and returned to her scope and staring.

"Look, gussy it up however you want," Betty went on, "but it doesn't change who you are or what you do. You. Shoot. People." She kept looking at Rin but turned her finger toward Malya. "And she is a Relic Knight, no matter if she's also a racer, crown princess, and just passable cook."

"Hey!"

Betty ignored the outburst. "Nothing's going to change that basic fact."

"People are a lot of things; we're complicated," Rin said. "But you're right. When you get down to it, there are some things that we are, whether we like it or not, and we have to deal with that sooner or later. That's part of what I get to see through the scope."

"If that's true, then you should have seen it for everyone down there," Malya said, miffed at the conversation and getting cut out of it. "You've nearly stared through the hull. What in all the empty stars are you looking at, anyway?"

Rin pursed her lips but did not lower the scope. "Funny you should ask. It seems like you've done a pretty good job at staying low profile. I'd guess almost nobody on this boat knows who you are."

"That's the idea," Betty said. "What's your point?"

"Well, I've noticed this chee—smooth and shiny chassis, kinda shaped like a pin-up chambermaid, awful lot of blue-white hair for a robot. She looks like a menial, but she's clearly a passenger. I've seen her near us every day for the last six days."

Mr. Tomn stepped clear from under the table, alert and wary.

"Six days?" Malya asked, sitting up straight. She had a clammy feeling in the pit of her stomach. "We've only been in space a week." She looked over at her friend and spied a porter behind Rin making a beeline for their table. "Has she recognized us?"

"I don't know," Rin said. "She's definitely seen us; made eye contact with me a couple of times, but if she knows who you are, she hasn't said or done anything about it."

"Message for you, miss," the porter said, proffering a folded piece of stout paper.

Betty was closer, so at Malya's nod, the mechanic took the paper and thanked the man. Mr. Tomn tugged on her leg, but she shooed him away.

"So, what about her?" Malya asked as the crewman started off. She shot a questioning look at Betty as she opened the message.

"Well, it happens that this is a busy place," Rin said, "and of all the times, of all the dining areas, that chee is in this one, right now, on the ground floor." She lowered the scope and looked soberly at Malya. "And of all the people here, she's staring directly at us. She's been staring at us the whole time."

Malya nearly jumped to her feet, but Betty's hissing intake of breath distracted her. She and Rin looked over at Betty who had gone pale. The letter trembled as she held it up.

"It's from Faust. He sent it just after we took off. The ship couldn't receive it until we dropped out of slip space to recharge."

"Faust?" Rin said, and her expression darkened. "Asger Faust?"

"You know any other Fausts?" Betty asked.

"He's one of the biggest crime lords on Cerci, and his star's still rising," Rin said. She kept staring at Malya. "How do you know Asger Faust?"

Malya shrugged a bit defensively. "We've brushed up against each other a couple of times. Everything on Cerci comes back to the races sooner or later, especially the organized crime."

"So why's he sending you messages, and how's he doing it when even your manager doesn't know where the empty stars you are?"

Malya swallowed past a sudden, uncomfortable lump in her throat. "I've no idea. What's he say, Betty?"

The mechanic glanced between them. She looked very pale. "He says he's sorry." She shrugged. "That's all."

"Well," Rin said with a rueful expression, "that can't be good."

Alarm klaxons blared across the ship, and all three women jumped. They glanced sheepishly at each other as the captain's voice came over the public-address system. "Ladies and gentlebeings, this is your captain. I regret to inform you that we have encountered some serious difficulties. We have pirate vessels off our port side. They have disabled our engines and are signaling for us to heave-to. I fear we must comply. Please return to your quarters immediately. I'm certain they won't—"

Static flooded the speakers and a new voice came on, feminine, confident, and sounding supremely pleased with herself. "Good day, future victims," she said. "My name is Calico Kate, and I'll very shortly be robbing each and every one of you. Have your valuables ready for us, and everything will be over quickly. Resist and, well, let's just say this is a bad corner of space to be marooned in."

The screaming erupted almost immediately. All three women

remained seated as the crowd dissolved into chaos around them.

"You think it's as simple as that sounds, just a smash-and-grab job?" Betty asked.

"Nope," Rin replied. She looked at Malya. "I have a feeling they're not just after wallets and watches."

"Yeah," Malya said. She squared her shoulders and nodded resolutely. "Even if they are, we can't take the chance. Betty, call the crew and tell them to start herding people back into the arboretum; Kate doesn't care about trees, so they should be safe there. The best place for the pirates to dock is a few sections forward of here, so they'll have to come through this food court. Rin and I can slow them down here and buy you more time."

"Copy that, boss lady," Betty said and pulled her personal comm from her pocket.

Rin grinned at the princess as she stood. "You've been thinking about this, haven't you?"

"Don't you dare tell me you haven't," Malya replied.

Rin shrugged. "Girl's got to have a hobby." She eyed the throng around them. "I'll just get my tools."

"Grab mine too," Betty called.

Rin nodded and shoved her way toward the door.

"Remember what I said about being a Knight?" Betty asked, grinning, as she took cover behind the low wall around the open space.

"Trying not to," Malya replied as Mr. Tomn jumped onto her shoulder. "All right, then. Let's show them we're not an easy mark."

She pulled esper to her, green motes of power circling her in a violent swirl. She touched the essential element of all creation, that which was both energy and matter, and bent it with her will. Just for an instant, reality moved around her. With a rush and a subsonic roar, Sedaris appeared in the space the crowd had just vacated. The people still nearby stumbled back, shocked. Though at a glance the relic resembled nothing so much as a high-performance racing hover bike with wiry arms and legs attached, the machine radiated an aura of barely restrained power and explosive speed. Malya could not stop grinning as she mounted up and slipped on her helmet and goggles. She kicked the starter. Sedaris rose gently on its anti-grav lifters, and its limbs unlocked. For the first time in over a week, she felt comfortable, controlled, and complete.

She revved the engine and shot out into the air above the food court. Two quick circuits gave her a good feel for the atrium, and years in the highly competitive Cerci racing scene showed her all the likely hiding spots for someone looking to take a potshot at her. The professional part of her took a great comfort in knowing that she'd have Rin shooting back.

The crowd had mostly vacated the floor, except for far too many who had been injured in the panic. Crew members were trying to help them where they could, and Malya swooped down to a knot of stewards around four unconscious people. She settled Sedaris beside them and flipped a switch, extending the machine's tail into a fan usually used for greater control at high altitudes and high speed.

"Put them on here," she shouted. "I'll fly them to the infirmary."

The men stared at her for a second but quickly complied.

She noticed that two of them had pistols on their belts. "You planning to resist?"

The tallest steward nodded. He had snow white touches in the dark hair at his temples and in his expertly trimmed mustache. "Yes. We've already received a reply to our distress call. There's a paladin cruiser nearby."

Malya felt her chest unknot, and she breathed deeply in relief, though the man still looked grim.

"We just don't know how long it will take."

"We're trying to get everyone we can into the arboretum. My friends and I will delay them here."

The man nodded as his people settled the last passenger on the relic. "I'll tell the captain. We'll send you some help, if we can, but if we put most of our people on the two decks above this, we should be in good shape."

She smiled at him and gunned the engine. "You've done this before, I think."

He shrugged. "Once or twice." He sketched a loose salute and shouted to his men to grab more of the injured.

As Malya rose into the air and pulled up a ship's floor plan to find the infirmary, she noticed a solitary figure standing at an overturned table. A chee woman, her chassis designed to look like she was wearing a maid's outfit, and also actually wearing a classic maid's uniform, watched her with rapt attention.

"Get to cover," Malya shouted as she flew into the hall.

The woman did not move.

She clicked on her comm. "Betty. Betty, when you get a chance, get down to the bottom deck. That chee that Rin spotted is still standing there like a yokel at a circus. Get her out before she gets killed, will you?" She shook her head and concentrated on flying.

CHAPTER 3

Tranquil Wind, food court

The screaming confused Cordelia. She had heard the announcement, first from the captain and then from the pirate, but the panic all around her made no sense. If the pirates really were just coming to take their valuables, why so much concern?

"They said they won't hurt us," she had tried to explain.

Still, the organics all ignored her and kept trying to run.

"You can get new stuff," she said, a bit plaintively. She sighed and decided that she must have missed something. Again.

Cordelia stood when someone knocked over her table and clicked on her access to the Chee Interspace Network. The familiar film of the data overlay fell across her vision. She fought to a calm space amid the pushing, shoving crowd as she searched for information on pirate attacks and Calico Kate specifically.

The data scrolled up a few seconds later. Calico Kate, pirate. Real name unknown. Self-styled "Queen" of the corsairs operating out of the Great Star Nebula. Known proclivities: Explosives. Lots of them. Often prefers to destroy captured starships instead of ransoming or selling them. Known to have no compunction about murder but Alliance Security considers her far less bloodthirsty than many of her associates. Outstanding criminal charges include piracy: 11,000+ counts; assault: 104,000+ counts; theft . . .

"Oh," Cordelia muttered as the information flowed past her. "Oh. That's not what she said." She noted the familiar woman with sky-blue and blonde hair ride into the air above her on some kind of racing bike with arms. She had several injured people on her machine, and she looked at Cordelia while speaking into a communicator. Cordelia wondered who she was talking to. Then the moving data paused on a list of Calio Kate's known violent offenses. "Kate said she wouldn't hurt us. I think she lied." She scrolled down to the common associates of Captain Kate. "Well, that makes more sense of the panic," she remarked.

"Hey," someone shouted at her.

Cordelia blinked, but she did not dismiss the data overlay. She glanced around, trying to watch the feed and the real world at the same time. The food court had mostly emptied, but a sandy-haired human woman jogged toward her. Instantly the data overlay switched to match up with her optical input. Tags appeared over the shorter woman's features, matched them to data files, and pulled up that information: Betty Jones, Pit Chief of Team Ulyxis; Racer: Princess Malya, known acquaintances—

"Hey," Betty shouted again as she got close. "Snap out of it."

Cordelia's eyes whirred as they shifted focus to Betty. She dismissed the overlay unconsciously. "So that was Princess Malya."

"What? Yeah, that was her," Betty said, her concern rapidly shifting to confusion and irritation. "You can surf for highlight vids later. Right now, you've got to get out of here."

Cordelia cocked her head to the side and finally sorted all of her data into the correct order. "Oh, right. Because of the pirates."

"And now she gets it," Betty mumbled. "Yes, because of the nasty pirates. Get to the arboretum with everyone else."

"The crew is going to resist," Cordelia said matter-of-factly. "Kate said they wouldn't hurt people, but she almost always does hurt people, so that was a lie."

"Are you . . . ?" Betty paused and frowned at the chee. "Are you okay? Were you cross-wired as a child?"

"Oh, no, I'm just a little slow sometimes," Cordelia replied in the same even tone. "But I'm useful." She reached behind her right hip and activated the release mechanism with a mental command. A metal tube attached to a square housing popped from her back into her hand, and trailed a flexible cable as she held it out for Betty to see. The tube extended with a snap. Cordelia grinned.

Betty's jaw fell open. "A vacuum? Are you kidding me?"

Cordelia's smile widened. "Wait for it."

She pressed a small button on the housing under her thumb. Her forearm opened and parts extended into the housing. The tube continued to lengthen and started to narrow slightly until it became an unmistakable gun barrel. The housing expanded and deepened, shifting into the frame and furniture of an enormous rifle.

Cordelia hefted the finished weapon, longer than she was tall, with casual ease. "See?"

Betty stared at the weapon. "What kind of maid are you?"

"The helpful kind."

Both women glanced around at the sounds of muffled explosions.

Betty shook her head and grabbed Cordelia's arm. "Well, come on, then."

Golden Vance stalked through the halls of coach-class cabins like a tornado through an orchard. All around, his crew ripped through the lodgings and tossed out anything that looked valuable with practiced efficiency. They ignored or bound those few passengers who still tried to hide, though most had fled. Vance had to admit that not dealing with the former owners of his new booty simplified things, but it still irritated him that he had no one to torture or terrify—and he viciously needed something to hit. Up ahead, he could hear shots and shouts as the crew continued to resist. He gritted his teeth and fought the urge to go up there and take out his frustrations.

His second-in-command appeared around a corner, saw his chief, and shook his head. "Pickin's 'er slim, Capt'n."

"'Course they are, Mr. Skreev," Vance snarled. "Harker brings us this fat starliner with a princess supposedly aboard, and here we are in coach. With the scraps." The crude pistons in his cybernetic arm hissed and clanked as he lashed out with his pitted metal claw to rip a hole in the bulkhead. "I'm beginning to rethink this partnership with Kate."

"Seems to be working out well for her," Skreev said darkly.

"Aye," Vance replied.

He might have said more, but a glance over Skreev's shoulder showed him Squall just a few feet away, stepping around a cowering group of battered passengers with obvious distaste. She held her jeweled staff behind her as she watched his crew work, blue-white esper drifting away from her rich auburn hair. She sneered.

He growled and shouted, "Minnow, get your worthless tail over here, and tell me if there's anything of actual value on this tub. Minnow!"

The cypher did not appear. As he looked around, Vance's cybernetic eye rested on Squall, and the ex-Doctrine witch's look of barely concealed contempt made his lip twitch.

"Why do I bother?" he muttered. "Minnow!"

"Yes, my captain. I'm here." All their eyes turned toward the voice. The mermaid cypher hovered around the injured passengers; green creation esper flowed from her hands to close up their injuries.

Vance scowled. "Front and center, little fish. Quite wasting my time. I need your sight."

The cypher floated over, dejected but trying to look brave.

Vance neither noticed nor cared. "Search this scow, stem to stern. Tell me what, if anything, has true value here."

From her silence, for a second, he thought she might try to refuse him again. But then she sighed, defeated, and her eyes clouded over.

Squall pushed in closer, studying the cypher with an almost unseemly intensity.

Minnow slowly swept her gaze along the ship, and Vance watched her expression closely. He had learned quickly that her perception could unerringly sort the true gems from the costume jewelry. She had sometimes drawn him to random things that seemed worthless but later proved invaluable, and though he knew that she tried to drive his actions and plans, he could ignore her advice and simply use her talents. Those talents now, he trusted, would keep Kate from taking the choicest loot and show her that she could not trifle with Golden Vance.

Minnow gasped suddenly, and her eyes blazed a violent orange. She floated higher, and creation esper streamed from her like sunlight. Several of the pirates stepped back, fear spreading across their faces, but Minnow quickly shook her head.

"What is it?" Vance demanded. "What did you see?"

"It—it is nothing, my captain." She tried to turn away, but whatever she saw so transfixed her that she could not help but stare.

Vance narrowed his eyes, and his voice took on a dangerous calm. "Don't lie to me, little fish."

"I—I thought it—I was wrong," Minnow continued. Her eyes blazed and her breath quickened. "It was not what I thought . . ." Her voice trailed off as her rapturous expression betrayed her.

Vance closed the distance to her in two strides and clutched her by the arm. Esper shot into him, and he staggered as if hit with a hammer. He gasped as his vision went green and white. He felt minor servos burning out and failsafes tripping in his machine arm and eye. He gritted his teeth and struggled to contain the raw energy rushing out of his cypher.

"Minnow," he shouted, "control yourself."

He felt her shudder, and the flow of esper slowed. His vision returned, slowly, though an esper-tinted haze veiled everything. He blinked and focused his power to see through the cypher's eyes. The image that had so captivated Minnow appeared instantly. The form, a woman, blazed with light—a pyre of pure esper, blinding and brilliant white.

"What is that?" he murmured under his breath.

He tried to see details within the blaze. Distantly he heard Skreev calling to him, though he could not make out the words.

"Aft. It—she—is aft. The cargo hold." Slowly, as he willed his vision to improve, he filtered out the burning aura. The image took shape in his mind, and an incredulous smile crept to his face. "You've got to be bloody kidding me. It's a maid. A robot maid."

"No, my Knight," Minnow's voice resounded with a strength

and surety Vance had never known she possessed. "It is the Source."

At the word, the connection between them ended, and Vance staggered back. His skin flushed, and heat shimmered off of his abused cybernetics. Minnow continued to glow, and esper shed from her like rain. As Vance tried to clear his head, the image of the chee still burned behind his eyes.

Squall pushed forward to the cypher. "What did you say?" she demanded. "What did you see?"

"It is the Source," Minnow repeated. "The Calamity has come."

Vance blinked his eyes clear in time to see Squall turn ghostly pale and flee.

M alya swooped around and angled Sedaris down the luxurious hallway at breakneck speed. The pirates howled and fired snap shots from their pistols as they dove to evade the relic's long blade. Only a few survived. In an instant Sedaris flew a hundred meters down the hall toward a small atrium, a confluence of corridors. Malya turned so tightly in that tiny space that she should have snapped her neck, but the esper flowing from Mr. Tomn kept her conscious, upright, and hurtling back. The rabbitlike cypher howled gleefully as they tore through the hapless attackers, and this time none of them escaped.

The relic shot out into the food court's open air and arced lazily amid scattered small arms fire as the princess surveyed the situation. Boarding parties advancing through the main passages had entered on both the port and starboard sides of the food court. They did not coordinate with each other well, and the ship's crew seemed to have bottled many of them up in the curving corridors. The sheer number of pirates cutting new holes in the *Tranquil Wind's* hull, however, threatened to overwhelm the defenses. A muffled boom rolled to her ears from the starboard side, and she recognized the sound of heavier weapons. Some captain had decided to get serious about this. Another boom and part of the bulkhead wall collapsed, opening a large hole outside of the crew's defenses. Drifting smoke and pirates spilled through the new opening.

With barely a breath, she dove at the floating form of a broadside cannon. The scent of ozone meant that the weapon had fired once already, and she hoped she had not come too late. The cannon's shield generator had just flickered to life, and a brown-and-black striped marmod stood inside the field trying to shout his companion pirates into better cover. If she had not known Calico Kate was behind the raid, the four-armed, giant raccoon-like creature would have tipped her off. She recognized the marmod as the Iron Chef by his chef's hat and double-handed frying pan. The infamous pirate turned to see her a second too late, and though he massed almost half as much as Sedaris, the relic slammed into him as if he weighted nothing. The Iron Chef careened into the far wall and fell unconscious into the rubble of a buffet. Malya turned her blades on the cannon and its defenders, and they fled or died.

Two died as they ran, and she whispered a small, thankful prayer that Rin had evidently survived. She steered wide of the stragglers to give her friend a clear shot and sliced her blade through the broadside platform. As the cannon exploded behind her, Malya rocketed down the port side corridor, scything through scattered reinforcements. Mr. Tomn's ears twitched, and he pulled on her arm, causing her to turn sharply and skid to a halt just past a bend in the hall. At the other end of the corridor, a crowd of pirates, easily the contents of an entire boarding shuttle, rushed forward. Without hesitation, Malya gunned her engine and slapped a lighted panel on the wall. Double-thick emergency bulkhead doors hissed shut inches behind her.

"That'll hold 'em," she crowed as they sped away, but Mr. Tomn pulled on her arm again. She turned, confused, and saw the ominous shape of another broadside cannon floating out of an earlier breach in the hull. It had hidden as they passed, and now its grinning skull muzzle turned toward them. "It's a race," she shouted and kicked in the overbooster.

With only inches on either side, she hurtled down the passage as the cannon's charge coils glowed brighter. The gun crew struggled to aim and maneuver but suddenly one dived for cover, and an instant later the others had followed. Malya soared over the weapon, ducking below her control bars to avoid the ceiling, and still scraped Sedaris on three sides. She howled as they ran, but when she glanced back, she saw the crew had turned the cannon after her.

"There's no way they can miss," she whispered.

Another emergency bulkhead door closed with unstoppable force around the cannon. The weapon's shield flickered and failed. The meshing metal plates sliced the platform in two as easily as cheese. She stuttered to a halt just shy of the entrance to the food court as the boom of the exploding charge coils echoed from the other side of the barrier.

She looked at Mr. Tomn. "I didn't even see a control for that door."

He shook his head, astonished.

She heard approaching footsteps and glanced around to see Rin jogging over debris, her rifle ready. "How did—" the sniper started to ask.

"Forgive me," a strong, aristocratic voice announced from her right. "I have no doubt you could have handled that cannon, but we're rather short of time, I'm afraid, so I took the liberty."

Malya's head whipped around, and Rin slipped on fallen decking as she tried to raise her weapon. Through the wreckage of an assault shuttle breach stepped a tall man dressed in scarlet, gold, and black. His high-collared cloak and pressed trousers had a vaguely military cut, though his cuffed boots and flowing brown hair were nothing like regulation. As they watched, a woman of regal bearing and ruffled clothes appeared from behind him. A rapier rested casually in her hand, and she regarded the women with an experienced fighter's dispassionate appraisal.

The man halted in the middle of the ruined corridor, set his hands on his hips, and smiled. "Introductions are in order. My name is Augustus Harker, captain of the corsair ship *Marianne*." He bowed from the waist. "At your service."

Rin and Malya exchanged shocked glances. Mr. Tomn could not stop staring at the man. Something moved in the shadow from which the man had come, and Rin had her rifle up in an instant. Malya had just enough time to glimpse the huge form moving with impossible grace through the rubble.

"Noh," Rin shouted as she sighted down the barrel.

A red and amber flash knocked the weapon aside. The shot flew into the bulkhead door, putting a proper dent in it.

The flash resolved into a large, ancient parrot that swooped through the narrow space to settle on Captain Harker's shoulder.

The pirate put up his hands. "Stay your weapons," he said with reassuring authority. "This man means you no harm, I assure you."

The women turned disbelieving eyes on the hulking, demonic form, his red skin painted in strange white patterns.

"Apologies, again, but Kenobo here is an exile from his people, and he is as much their enemy as you are."

The noh bowed deeply to them, with bent knee, his bound hair and curling beard brushing the floor.

Malya spoke in an assured tone that matched Harker's. "You keep strange company, even for a pirate. What's your interest in talking instead of attacking?"

The pirate's manners and bearing reminded her too much of a thousand state functions before she had fled Ulyxis.

Mr. Tomn climbed higher on Sedaris and stared intently at the strange crew.

"Excellent, to business," Harker said, looking straight at Malya. "I have come to enlist your aid, your highness. We have an opportunity to stop the Calamity, and I need your help."

Malya stared for a second. "You—" she sputtered. "You attacked this ship, attacked all these people, just because you wanted to get my help?"

Harker looked genuinely apologetic. "No, not precisely. I came here for you and one other. Calico Kate attacked this ship because she believes that the reigning Cerci Prime champion and Crown Princess of Ulyxis must travel in unimaginable opulence." He shrugged. "Since I needed her help, I did not correct her error."

"Wait, her and one other?" Rin asked.

"Yes," Harker replied, "most astute. Sadly, Miss Farrah, not you, I'm afraid—though you would be most helpful and very welcome. No, the other is not here, but because Kate and Vance accompanied me, and because we attacked a civilian transport with important diplomatic personages aboard—" he nodded to Malya— "he will be on our trail very soon. Which is partly the cause of our undignified haste."

"Now wait just one minute," Malya said, esper rising around her. "I'm not—"

Harker raised his hands. "Your highness, please listen. Our galaxy, our universe, is out of time. I can gain us a little more and perhaps save us all, but I cannot do it alone. I require help—your help, specifically. I know you have many questions, and I will answer all of them that I can, but we've no time. For now, on faith alone, you must believe that I know how to save this galaxy from the Darkspace Calamity, and I need you to accomplish that." He held out his hand. "Will you join me?"

Malya hesitated. She glanced at Rin, who could only stare, dumbstruck. She looked to Mr. Tomn. The lop-eared cypher studied the parrot on Harker's shoulder like he could see its atoms. The parrot stared back.

Mr. Tomn frowned. "This is unusual."

"Something is interfering," the parrot said.

Malya blinked. The parrot hadn't spoken; no sound came from its beak. Yet she would swear that the words she heard in her head originated from the avian cypher.

"We all know," Mr. Tomn said, and glanced at Kenobo.

"Something else. We've discovered what, and we have a chance to stop them."

Mr. Tomn shook his head. "There isn't time."

"There will be," the parrot replied.

"Oh," Mr. Tomn said, his demeanor shifting sharply. "Oh.

That game. And if the Source appears while we're gone?"

"Then we'll actually have the chance to do this properly."

Malya glanced from one cypher to the other. "One of you needs to explain what you two are talking about," she demanded.

Mr. Tomn slowly turned to her. "Hope," he said softly.

"This is what you were looking for here, isn't it?" she demanded.

"I—" He hesitated an instant before nodding firmly. "Yes, I think so. I think that this is our path." He shot her a rueful grin. "Remember when you said that if you could do something to help, you would? Well, this is it. I say we go."

Malya turned back at Rin, finding no more words than she had a moment before. The sniper looked frightened, something Malya could not remember ever seeing before, but Rin hefted her rifle all the same. "You're not going without me."

For no more reason than that, the princess felt infinitely better. She rounded on Harker. "We'll go. But I bring my crew."

"Of course," Harker replied. "I'd hoped as much. I have two boarding shuttles standing by."

The woman behind him produced a small datapad and tapped a few keys.

"Moffet is transferring their locations to your relic. Inform your friends and have them meet us as quickly as possible. We must be gone before Kate realizes she's been manipulated."

"When do you figure that will happen?" Malya asked.

Harker summoned a chronometer display from the datalink disguised on his left forearm. "Oh, any minute now."

CHAPTER 4

Tranquil Wind, cargo hold 7

Cordelia's rifle sliced clean through four pirates and the cargo containers behind them but missed the large man with the mechanical arm. Despite everything, he seemed to be laughing. She had just killed several of his friends, and not only did he not care, he actually seemed to enjoy the fight immensely. She triggered her thrusters, flying left behind an overturned loader as pistol bolts flashed and hissed around her. She set her rifle to quick recharge—she did not have many of those strong shots left—and engaged the Interspace Network. The image and profile of the pirate captain Golden Vance appeared on her overlay a second later. Cordelia would have swallowed nervously if she could have.

"Hey, miss helpful," Betty said from behind more cargo crates a few feet away. "You okay over there?"

Cordelia nodded. "I'm fine, yes." She jerked her thumb over her shoulder at the pirates fanning out through the cargo hold in an attempt to flank the pit crew. "That's Golden Vance. He's a very bad man."

Betty looked back, dumbfounded. "You don't say." She snapped off a shot that blew away the pirates' cover and stalled their advance.

Cordelia switched her view, dismissing the profile for a schematic of the cargo bay. She studied it for a second. "They're not trying for the arboretum," she called to Betty.

Betty shot her a confused, incredulous look. Her crew was frantically trying to uncrate a second exo-frame. Between the first salvage mecha they had put into the fight and the giant, vaguely simian shape of Betty's chee best friend Lug, the pit crew had a tight hold on the port side approach to the arboretum.

"They're coming around the wrong side." Cordelia started to point to something on her overlay, shook her head, cleared the overlay, and pointed off to her left. "That way leads to engineering."

Betty shook her head. "If they're not aiming for the arboretum, why are they attacking us at all?"

Cordelia shrugged. "I don't think that they care about the passengers, but I don't know what they really want. If we figure that out, we can beat them."

Betty rolled her eyes and fired another burst from her huge rivet gun. "One minute you're surprised that pirates are bad people. The next minute, you're running this fight like you've done it your whole life. You're a very strange chee."

Cordelia moved to a crouch as her rifle beeped. "Well, I am only about a year old."

"Oh. That explains a lot." Betty started suddenly and put a hand to her ear, speaking low. "Okay, people," she shouted a second later. "We're leaving. Get that wrecker free, and then push up the left side. We need to get to the small food court, like, yesterday."

"I can clear the way," Cordelia said, and immediately rolled clear of the loader. She heard Betty shouting something at her but could not make out the words. An instant later she saw what the mechanic had meant when all the corsairs rose from cover and charged. Cordelia flipped a conversion switch on her rifle and pulled the trigger. Fins popped up around her gun barrel, and a vortex formed an inch beyond the muzzle. All the pirates in a wide cone in front of Cordelia began to shriek as the force of the gun's suction pulled them off their feet and spun them like leaves in a sewer drain. She stepped back behind the cargo loader, her barrel just clear of the machine, as the first attackers began sailing past her at bone-shattering speeds. Some slammed into the far wall, others into the scattered debris, and no few smacked into the loader.

Vance rose and stepped purposefully into her vortex. As he flew through the air, he angled his flight directly toward Cordelia.

She ducked and heard him strike the loader, but the impact sounded wrong. Glancing out, she saw that he had locked his claw arm into the machine. Yellow-gold esper danced over his skin like sunlight. His broken nose straightened and healed. A missing tooth grew back, and the bent struts in his arm straightened out. She released the trigger, ending the vacuuming effect.

Vance gained his feet in an instant and dove across the loader. He shoved her off balance with his organic arm and wrapped the mechanical one completely around her torso. "'Ello, love. You and me've got business to discuss." He turned, using the loader as cover against the scattered shots from the pit crew, and sprinted back for the far passage. "Come on, lads," he shouted. "Time to go."

Malya waited with Harker by the last shuttle, counting the pit crew as they ran by. Smoke billowed from some of the upper decks, and the princess felt a new sense of urgency. Lug appeared from around some rubble, hauling what looked like a half dozen injured people. Despite the burden, and his almost comically small legs, he navigated the wreckage superbly—benefits of being a salvage and repair robot.

Malya shouted to him, "They ours?"

Lug nodded, and she ushered him aboard. A second later, Betty scrambled clear of the debris and jogged toward them. Her rivet gun hung loosely from her shoulder, and she looked exhausted.

"You the last?"

"Yeah, boss," Betty gasped. She sank down, hands on her knees, and just gulped air for a few seconds. "Lots of—" Coughs wracked her for a moment. "Smoke. Lots of smoke back there."

"The passengers?" asked Harker as the mechanic straightened up.

Betty shot a look at Malya, who nodded, but the pit chief still looked warily at the pirate captain. "Safe as they get, I reckon.

They're still in the arboretum. We were holding the door, but the pirates attacking us broke off just after you called." She coughed again. "Weirdest thing."

"Who lead them?" Harker asked.

Betty kept frowning at him. "The chee said his name, but I don't remember it. Bronze . . . somebody, maybe? Big guy, with a replacement arm. Ugly piece of work, too, but incredibly strong."

"Golden Vance," Harker muttered. "And that is an apt description of him."

"She was talking about the arm," Malya said, and turned to Betty. "How many did we lose?"

Betty shook her head, and her solid, calm expression cracked for a second with grief and fatigue. "Eight, including the chee. Remember the chee Rin spotted? She came with us to help. Pulled the biggest friggin' gun I've ever seen a single sentient carry out of thin air and knew how to use it. The pirate—" She glanced at Harker. "Vance, I guess. He got in close, grabbed her, and ran for it."

"That's not good," Harker said. "If Vance grabbed your friend, it's because he feels she's worth something."

Betty shrugged. "She's a robot maid. Maybe he's got vacuuming to do."

"He certainly does, but that's not the reason." Harker shook his head to dismiss the thought. "There isn't time now. Get aboard. I'm told the paladins have just arrived."

Betty put up her hands. "Wait, wait, wait. Who is this guy, and why are we running when the cavalry just showed up?"

Malya grabbed her friend's shoulder. "Long story; not now. This is Captain Harker. He's a pirate." Betty's eyes went wide and her hands went to her gun, but Malya squeezed her shoulder tighter. "We're going with him because he says he can stop the Calamity with our help."

Betty froze. "And you believe him?"

"I—" Malya stopped. Without Mr. Tomn, without the urgency of the moment, without the feel of Sedaris supporting her, all her reasons for joining Harker sounded so silly. But Mr.

Tomn had been certain, and when she thought for a second, so was Malya. Harker just might be able to stop the Calamity. "Yes," she said. "I don't know why, but I do." She shrugged. "And besides, I promised Mr. Tomn I'd try."

Betty nodded. "Good enough for me. Let's go." She trotted onto the shuttle as Malya stared after her.

"It's strange, isn't it," Harker muttered to her, "that feeling when someone you value and respect just accepts your word and follows your lead? I've commanded ships for more years than I care to count, led some of the finest men and women in the galaxy, and that feeling still gives me shivers."

"I don't—" Malya swallowed. "What if I'm wrong?"

"Then you're wrong," he said, smiling, "and a lot of people you love may get hurt or worse. But someone has to make the choice, and they clearly think there's no one better than you to do that." He clapped her on the shoulder. "Consider that they may, actually, be correct. But consider it on the shuttle."

Malya clung to the wide viewport behind the pilots' station as the shuttle pulled free of the *Tranquil Wind*. She watched as two pirate ships sparred with two enormous cruisers painted in the colors of the Order of the Shattered Sword. Around one of the paladin cruisers, the drive flares from assault shuttles flickered to life as they raced toward the stricken starliner. The corsair vessels broke off from their delaying action with the cruisers, chased by plasma beams. The Shattered Sword ships immediately turned their heaviest guns on the few pirate ships still lingering near the *Wind*. The buccaneer attack began to disintegrate before the force of the paladins' response.

The ships that had engaged the paladins moved to meet up with a large, sleek vessel that had stayed on the far side of the starliner. Malya studied the ship as their shuttle approached it. Long and black and clearly built by people with an alien design aesthetic, it moved gracefully into their path, still sheltered from her would-be rescuers. The crest on its prow matched Harker's crew.

"You're a very interesting pirate," she said to her host.

Harker smiled, but the shuttle pilot clearly heard her and laughed out loud. "Princess," she said as she angled into a bay opening like a scoop from the pirate ship's ventral section, "you ain't seen nothing yet."

"They're moving," Harker muttered with a growing frown.

She glanced out the viewport and saw that at least one of the other pirate vessels had begun to maneuver away from the starliner.

"And Kate will know we're running." He activated his communicator as the shuttle slipped into a spacious hangar. "Mr. Digby, we're aboard. Send the signal and get us into slip space immediately." He flicked the comm off and called to the whole cabin. "Brace for transition."

Less than five seconds later, the entire ship shook as the slip drives sliced open a hole in the fabric of the universe and pushed them into a tiny gap between dimensions. A 'rounding error in creation' Malya had once heard it called. Riding in an isolated reality at staggering speed, moving like a tiny soap bubble on the surface of a much larger bubble, the ships plunged into a world of shifting colors and smeared afterimages, separated from reality only by the barest film of mathematics. She felt their passage even out and let go of a breath she had not realized she was holding.

Harker turned to her, smiling through his obvious fatigue. "Welcome to the *Marianne*," he said. "Come. Let's get you and your people settled."

Malya nodded and looked around at her disheveled, stained, injured, and exhausted pit crew. "Settled would be good." She blinked. "Oh. We left all of our luggage."

Harker waved the care away. "Never fear. We can accommodate you, I believe. Provided no one objects too much to our livery." He chuckled as he led her down the exit ramp. "Besides, it means Kate won't leave empty handed. That will count for nothing, of course, but I'll try to remind her of it should we ever meet again."

Malya halted mid-stride, nearly falling from the ramp. Not until she heard those words had it occurred to her that she might never see Cerci again, that she might never race again, or hear her father's lonely undertone in his weekly messages to her. She might never see Ulyxis again, and that thought struck her more forcefully than she felt it should. What was Ulyxis to her but the planet she came from? It represented only burdens and duties and all that was stultifying and wrong with the Alliance. And yet, her heart still chilled.

Mr. Tomn bounced up in front of her. He did not smile or say anything reassuring. He simply touched her leg, looked in her eyes, and nodded.

Betty shuffled down the ramp. "What have we gotten ourselves into, boss?" the pit chief muttered, eyeing the *Marianne's* crew.

"I wish I knew, chief," Malya replied. Then squared her shoulders and started forward. "But we're in it neck-deep now."

CHAPTER 5

Lucky Chance, Mezzio system, Alliance Space

Kisa sat cross-legged in the center of her small ship, slowly swishing her tail. The tonnerian's meditations often wandered, especially when she could spend time just floating deep in real space, and she enjoyed the sensation of drifting perceptions. She felt her black feline-like cypher Scratch reclining on her lap and sharing her trance. The creature's vastly alien mind provided a comforting familiarity to Kisa. She could feel Mihos, her obsidian cat-shaped relic, curled on a pile of cushions against one of the round chamber's walls. She could hear the sound of fabric rubbing as the draperies on the walls and tapestries depicting key events in Doctrine history drifted in the ship's ventilation breeze. And she could feel the deck plates vibrate as Fiametta approached, shifting the plush maroon and gold pillows strewn across the floor. She brought her mind up enough to interact with her friend but still retain her calm trance.

Fiametta stopped at the room's airlock. Kisa could feel the other woman's unease and suspected it related to the force barrier above them; currently the only thing between them and the blackness of space. Or possibly not. She carefully probed at Fiametta's emotions and detected an imbalance different from her usual state. For all the six cycles that the human had accompanied Kisa—ostensibly as the Doctrine's official 'monitor' for its only Relic Knight but really as her willing cohort—she had grown to know Fiametta well. From her affinity for fire magic, love of adventure, seeming immunity to the aura of ill luck that Kisa unconsciously radiated, and even the strange affection for her wizard's hat; Kisa thought she had her best friend figured out.

But now, feeling the edges of the human's agitation, she found that she still had more to learn.

Perhaps she was watching the crystal array that seemed to grow from a graceful jade and onyx urn in front of Kisa. The crystals flickered and glowed softly, shifting with her thoughts as she guided the ship. Perhaps it had to do with the message.

Kisa licked her lips and cleared her throat. "What did Squall have to say?" she asked without opening her eyes.

She could hear Fiametta shift to lean against a wall and the half-smile in her friend's voice. "She says that Star Nebula Corsairs have captured the Source."

Kisa frowned and forced her eyes to remain shut. "That's strange, for her. The Source is a myth."

"I thought so too," Fiametta replied, sounding a bit more serious. "But it's not like Squall to make that sort of thing up. She's certainly never done that with me, and she wouldn't make a near-panicked call to her old friends just for a joke."

Kisa sighed. "No, that doesn't sound like her. But she's been gone for a long time now. People change."

"Not like that," Fiametta said. She moved a bit and, by the sound of it, sat on one of the cushioned stools. "Ask yourself this: isn't it a little strange that she'd tell us and not Calico Kate? She was rushed, clearly, and sounded genuinely frightened. I think she only had time to make one call. She's been an unrepentant pirate for cycles. Whatever they've found, it must be something truly powerful, or supremely dangerous, if she'd rather see us have it than Kate."

Kisa's frown deepened. Fiametta was using logic to box her into doing something she hadn't chosen to do, and probably to do it for all the right reasons. Again. Kisa gritted her teeth.

"There's more," Fiametta continued. "Squall didn't encrypt the message or wait for a secure channel; this is how I know she was rushed. It looks like Alliance Security intercepted the transmission."

Kisa groaned.

"They've already dispatched a ship and ordered that we

rendezvous with it immediately or leave Alliance space."

Kisa dropped her head and opened her eyes. The last red and orange lights faded from the crystals. "Fine." She stood abruptly, dumping Scratch with a screech, and glared at the stars overhead as though this had all, somehow, been their fault. From the corner of her eye, she could see Fiametta hiding her smile. Kisa finally shook her head and triggered the armored hull to close over the force field with a wave of her hand. "Fine," she said again and turned to Fiametta. "Did Squall say where they were?"

Fiametta shook her head as she rose and followed Kisa to the far end of the room. "No, but if the corsairs were busy grabbing something like that, I imagine we'll hear about it pretty quick."

"You'd think," Kisa muttered. She moved some pillows to uncover a secondary control interface and tapped a short sequence into the keypad. The computers unlocked, and half a dozen holographic displays blinked to life around them. She brought up images of the surrounding space. A small purple wedge appeared, clearly on an intercept course for them and closing fast. "Well, they're taking this seriously, at any rate, which means we should too." She rubbed her nose. "I'm getting a quick shower. Put out the welcome mat, would you?"

Fiametta nodded, grinning, and hurried out.

Twenty minutes later, Kisa stood at the bottom of her ship, waiting for the large airlock to finish cycling, and trying not to fidget. Fiametta waited much more calmly, arms crossed, her pointed wizard hat flopping coyly off to the side. She did not exactly appear relaxed, but she certainly seemed more accepting of the delay and forced passenger. Kisa wondered at that. Maybe it was just because this was her ship, and she liked the idea that she decided who came aboard and who didn't, but the whole situation rankled her. If the Source, whatever it was, was so important, they needed to get after it, not wait to pick up some stuffy Alliance rep with nothing better to do than get in the way. The airlock hissed and turned, and Kisa let out a long breath. Finally. Then she stared at the person who stepped through.

The first description that came to Kisa's mind was bubbly. The athletic, pink-haired woman nearly bounced into the ship. She had a pair of almost bottle-shaped pistols riding on her hips, and she smiled like she had just arrived at the best party in the galaxy. A small, three-tailed, foxlike cypher looked out from behind her legs. The woman shook Kisa's hand with what the Relic Knight could only call exuberance. "Hello, hello. You must be Kisa. I've heard an awful lot about you, and I'm super glad to finally meet you. You're a legend in the Alliance, believe it or not." Kisa, rarely at a loss for words, could only nod as the woman absolutely beamed. "I'm Candy."

"Oh," Kisa managed. "Of course you are."

Candy blinked questioningly.

"Sorry, sorry," Kisa said quickly. "It's been a strange day. I meant that there aren't many Alliance reps that, um, match your description. So you have to be Candy."

"Guilty as charged. I'm—" Candy cut off mid-breath as her eyes landed on Fiametta.

Only then did Kisa feel the waves of cold radiating from behind her. She dropped the Alliance Knight's hand and stepped back. Fiametta regarded the newcomer with a fixed expression of neutral pleasance, like someone waiting her turn in a dentist chair but determined not to flinch.

Fiametta nodded at the Alliance rep. "Candy."

The Knight nodded back. "Fiametta. You, um, look well."

"I am, thanks. You seem as enthusiastic as ever."

Kisa glanced from one woman to the other. She could almost see the air crackling between them. "So, um," she said. "You, ah, you two know each other, then."

Neither looked at Kisa, but both nodded. "Candy works for Alliance Security," Fiametta said, her voice firm and controlled. "She's one of their better agents, apparently. A roving troubleshooter."

"I do get to travel a lot," Candy allowed, her voice every bit as controlled. "One of the few perks of the job."

Kisa shook her head. "Okay. I don't . . ." She trailed off as she put some of the pieces together. "You've run into each other before, right?"

Fiametta nodded.

"Quite a bit, for a while there," Candy said.

Kisa sighed. Fiametta had a reputation for chaos and a cavalier attitude toward law, order, and other people's property. She had spent quite a lot of time in Alliance space before and after the Sundering War. Kisa had no doubt that Candy had cleaned up many of those messes.

"Okay, okay. Look." She snapped her fingers and stepped between the two women. "Hey, eyes on me." Kisa waited until she had their attention before she continued. "You two need to either get a room or get over this. Whether we like it or not, we're all stuck together on this trip. We need to get along even if we don't like each other. Is that clear?"

Candy nodded at once, and Kisa believed her. After all, the Alliance Security would have forced her to work with people she didn't like. The Doctrine had tried and failed to do that with both her and Fiametta. Kisa glared at Fiametta until she finally nodded, her expression as sour as if she had swallowed a frog.

"Good, but remember, we don't just have to play nice for this one. We need to actually work together." She fixed her eyes on Fiametta for the last part. "Can we do that?"

"Yes," Fiametta said, and Candy agreed.

"So you two need to either fight this out or work this out. I kind of don't care either way," she said, pointing out the viewport on the airlock, "but one of them will happen on the inside of that airlock and the other will happen on the outside of it. I'll let you figure out which is which."

Both women hesitated and then relaxed slightly.

"Fair enough, captain," Candy said with a shrug. "It's all in the line of duty for me, and while I don't appreciate it," she snapped the words out at Fiametta, "I understand it." She softened her expression and extended her hand.

"Huh," Fiametta replied, her eyes widening a bit in genuine surprise. "Unexpected, but I guess I can't ask for fairer than that." She shook Candy's hand and looked her square in the eyes. "Just don't think this forgives everything."

"Not a chance," Candy replied, her smiling coming back. "But to be honest, I'm happier to be working with you."

Fiametta thought for a second. "Yeah, that we can agree on."

Kisa huffed and scuffed her foot on the decking. "Rats. And here I was looking for a fight." They glanced at her, and she laughed. "Come on, miss Alliance Security. Let's get you settled."

"Cool," she said and indicated the cypher beside her. "This is Cola. He's a good time and a good hand in tight places. Also, before we go too far, I brought some luggage."

She shooed the Doctrine women back to clear a wide area on the floor. Blue-white esper swirled around them, mixed with motes glowing bright orange, pink, and green, and a huge, sleek machine materialized with a whoosh of displaced air. Even compact and clearly folded for travel, the device took up plenty of space.

"Got room for this?" Candy asked.

Kisa whistled.

Fiametta shook her head. "That's new."

Candy shrugged. "New-ish. I haven't seen you in a while, so you two haven't had the pleasure." She laid an affectionate arm on the machine. "Found this little beauty buried in the back of a noh dragon ship just taking up space. Cola lead me right to it. Seemed wrong to not take it." She rapped her knuckles on the metal. "I never leave home without it."

"Cute," Kisa said, smirking. "Welcome to the relic club. Not feline enough for my tastes, but to each her own. We'll find space somewhere."

"Okay," Candy said. "My people want me to head to the Star Nebula, but I've got the leeway to go elsewhere if needed. That work for you?"

Kisa nodded. "Good enough," she said, and grabbed a floating cargo mover.

Candy put her hands on her hips and cracked a lopsided grin. "So, anyone want to take a guess at what's so all-mighty important that they sent an accomplished Doctrine practitioner and two Relic Knights to take care of it?"

"Actually, I'm afraid to guess," Kisa said and patted the relic. "Let's stow this, get underway, and try and figure it out."

CHAPTER 6

Hydra's Will, Dragon Fleet To flagship, Elesso
system (dead world)

High Priestess Zineda stepped sinuously through the heavy smoke. The long prayer scrolls hanging from the noh priestess's shoulders, hips, and horns swirled the haze filling the room. Pungent incense laced with stronger hallucinogens drifted from the six small fire pots around the enormous warrior kneeling in the center of the round room. The clouds lost their potency almost immediately but hung in the air to dim the amber lights and obscure the ring of softly chanting priestesses.

The ornate floor tiles beneath the warrior's knees seem to writhe and move like the serpent coils they resembled. Zineda crouched beside the man and passed her clawed hand over his sweating red skin with the lightest touch. He was beautiful; possessed of the raw, brute power of noh males tempered by the discipline of the Hatriya warrior order. An embodiment of her species's ideals. His sweat dripped onto the slave-embroidered strips of rich cloth that gently draped her voluptuous form and mixed with the thin lines and splashes of blood.

"Do you see?" she whispered to the warrior.

He gasped, his tusks quivering. Zineda turned slightly and ran a finger across the chest and shoulder of the human slave behind her. The woman moaned softly at the touch, and she whimpered like a weak kitten when the high priestess's claw pierced the flesh just above the collarbone. Blood trickled down the noh's long fingers to pool on her palm. The slave mewed but only had the strength to roll her head, smearing blood across the floor.

Zineda ignored the human to whisper over the blood in her

cupped hand. She lifted it to the warrior's mouth. "Drink," she whispered. "Drink, my love, and see."

His eyes still closed, the warrior parted his lips, and she poured in a trickle of fluid. She watched him shudder as the esper-infused blood burned through him. His hand flashed out, gripped her arm, and pulled it close. His tongue slid across her skin to lap up the last of the offering, and the tonnerian-skin prayer strips that hung from her wide horns danced around her face as she shivered.

"What—" She paused to wet her dry lips. "What do you see? What does our god say?"

His grip relaxed, and she pulled free to step back and watch him. The warrior shook for a long moment more. Then his eyes snapped open, and he surged to his feet. The energy and motion proved too much, and he sagged, nearly falling before Zineda grabbed his shoulder. Other priestesses moved in to extinguish the incense pots and help guide the warrior to a side chamber. As the ship's circulation began to clear the haze, the scents of cleansing water and purifying oils drifted to them from the antechamber.

On the threshold, however, the warrior shook off the others and turned to Zineda. She felt an instant of trepidation as he took her and lifted her to meet his still distracted, vacant gaze. Only when his eyes cleared and focused on her did she see that her love, Mamaro To, Grand Warlord of Dragon Fleet To, had indeed returned to her.

"I have seen it," he said in a hoarse, harsh whisper. "The Source. It has appeared, as our god promised it would. Just as the Pale Herald said." His gaze drifted for a moment, and he swayed, but his raw strength held them both up. "Nozuki showed me where to begin our search. We will find it, claim it, and no power—not even the Herald—will stop us."

She smiled wide, her fangs bared, as the great warrior set her gently down. "And when we do," she said, guiding him into the side chamber, "all the universe shall fall before us."

———◆———

Zineda lead her entourage of six senior priestesses into the embarkation chamber. She wondered for a second at the number of Hatriya warriors arrayed across the room. It seemed too few, but she dismissed the concern—she had not had the vision, after all. She directed her cadre to their place between the warriors. The ceremonial prayer scrolls draping their bodies swirled sensuously against and across the warriors' ornate heavy armor. For all the impressive display of noh power and physicality around her, Zineda could not long keep her gaze from the towering figure of the warlord at the head of the assembly. She frowned slightly when she recognized the aged ambassador of Dragon Fleet Ki speaking to Mamaro To in a low voice. As she approached, the elder noh bowed to the warlord and high priestess before withdrawing. Her glare followed the soot-painted councilor as he departed.

"What did that crafty old raptor want here?" she asked.

Mamaro To, resplendent in his finest armor and imposing with his massive tesubo slung from his back, shrugged as he moved to the head of the column. "What we must undertake here is rather more delicate than how Dragon Fleet To is accustomed to behaving." He noticed her sharp look but shook his head. "The vision was quite clear on a few points. We must not try to command or force what happens next; the situation is too delicate. We seek assistance this time, not dominion, so I sought advice."

Zineda's frown only deepened. "I dislike this course. It clashes too much with our ways." She reached out as he turned to her and ran a clawed finger gently down his heavy jaw. "Do not mistake me. We serve the Endless Hunger as he dictates, and sometimes we must learn new ways." She shrugged, the prayer scrolls swirling enticingly around her. "But I long for blood and slaves."

Mamaro grinned. "And you shall have them, my love. The vision was also very clear on that."

They took their places and faced the rift generator. Spite, Zineda's cypher, coalesced in a puff of scented, esper-heavy smoke and settled onto her shoulder. She grinned at the impish creature and reached up to stroke her face. Spite purred but kept her gaze fixed on the rift anchor point.

Zineda watched the slaves and noh wayfinders adjust the rods and discs that made up the huge rift generator. Gifts from their hydra god, the rift generators opened tears in reality and created bridges across dimensions to let noh raiding parties, war bands, and even whole dragon ships move instantly across the stars. For a group so large, however, even the more robust portable generators were inadequate, but Zineda's own travels among her people had rarely let her see the function of one of these larger, fixed devices.

A nod from Mamaro sent the half dozen slaves scurrying to activate the arcane machinery. It thrummed and rasped and chuckled and a gauzy haze appeared shimmering in the air before them. Zineda grinned slightly and studied the vague shapes in the smear of air before them. Used carefully and with low power, the rift generators could create a sort of window onto the selected location, though it took skill from the wayfinders and care from the slaves. This limited its use for scrying but had proved invaluable for raiding; the noh had long ago learned to look before they leapt.

Zineda stared through the filmy haze as if trying to look through a piece of thick paper soaked with grease. She saw a simple room, clearly space for food preparation, and several beings within. After a second, she realized that it was on a starship of some kind. A huge, vaguely furred creature with four arms and an incongruous tall hat stood before an array of stoves and ovens, clearly preparing several dishes at once. A marmod, Zineda realized, though she had never seen a living one before. A lithe, auburn-haired woman wearing an eyepatch and the ostentatious regalia favored by corsairs paced behind the marmod and gesticulated broadly to punctuate her tantrum. Zineda sneered, and she felt Mamaro's discomfort beside her.

"So these are our allies," he muttered.

"Tools," she hissed to him as the rift began to solidify. "They are tools of convenience, nothing more."

The priestess paused, her guard going up, and looked around as the rift gained form. An instant later, with a blast of ozone and a sound like ripping flesh, a wound opened in the universe, and

Mamaro To lead the high priestess through to the pirate's ship.

Zineda immediately noticed the lack of the familiar warmth and humidity common to all noh ships. The musty, poorly scrubbed ship's air had the scent of astringents rather than blood and fear. The woman had drawn a pistol and triggered an alarm, and the marmod brandished a two-handed frying pan, but Zineda refrained from anything more than casting a cool glance at them. When Mamaro To did not draw his great weapon, the woman lowered her pistol slightly and signaled her companion to hold.

"I am Grand Warlord Mamaro To, leader of Dragon Fleet To," the warlord beside her said. "You are the pirate called Calico Kate."

Kate nodded, clearly still assessing the situation, but responded with a bravado Zineda had not expected. "That's *Captain* Calico Kate," she said steadily, her pistol still aimed squarely at Mamaro's chest. "Or Pirate Queen Kate, if you're being formal." She smiled and glanced past the warlord and high priestess to the intimidating line of monsters behind them. "I'm not seeing enough of your friends to make a good fight, so is this a social call?"

Zineda was impressed despite herself. Spite hissed but only half-heartedly

"We have come to speak." Mamaro slowly lifted his left hand and removed his mask. "Our god Nozuki, the Endless Hunger, has given me a vision. The Calamity has come to this last galaxy, and I have seen that an artifact of great power lies within our grasp. He has commanded me to seize it."

Kate looked at him like he grown another head. "Well I don't have it," she said, and then seemed to remember her confidence. "And even if I did, jumbo, what makes you think I'd just hand it over at the asking?"

"If it lay in your possession," Zineda said, barely hiding her irritation, "we would not have come to talk."

The marmod brandished the frying pan again, but Kate nodded slightly, accepting the point.

"But you do know where it lies, or more accurately, with whom," Mamaro To said. "One of your servants acquired it very recently."

A flash of realization crossed Kate's features, but she schooled her expression quickly. "Can you be more specific about this artifact? We've picked up a lot of things just of late."

"The vision was not clear," the warlord said, "but it is not a thing. It is a person of great power—a woman."

Kate ground her teeth and swore too softly for Zineda to hear. "Harker. That scheming, back-stabbing, stuck-up—" She spit. "It has to be Harker."

Mamaro frowned. "Captain Augustus Harker?" the warlord asked.

"Aye, that's the bastard," Kate agreed, clearly still distracted. "What's more, I know what—or who—your artifact is."

Zineda managed to keep her face composed, but Mamaro To gaped.

Kate nodded, apparently angry enough at this Harker to gloat. "We hit a starliner less than a week ago—at Harker's suggestion, of course. He said that Princess Malya was aboard, and then he scarpered off just before the paladins turned up. No princess anywhere to be found," she sneered. "Now where did she run off to, do you suppose?"

"She fled with Captain Harker," Mamaro muttered, lost in thought.

"What I can't figure is why," Kate went on. "Kidnapping and ransom's not his style. If the vids are to be believed, the princess is no stranger to keeping low company but only of her choosing. He must need her for something."

"Or he wishes to keep her from something," Mamaro To growled.

Something about the story struck Zineda as wrong, yet she could find no fault with the thinking as far as it went. They could not be certain, of course, but Kate would know her captain better.

Spite nuzzled up to whisper in her ear. "We have met Captain Harker before. He dogged our ships in the galaxy we called Korrketi."

Zineda's eyes narrowed, and she glanced at her cypher. "So he has tracked us, studied us."

Spite nodded. Zineda moved toward Mamaro To, but the warlord spoke before she could say anything.

"You will tell us where to find Captain Harker, and we shall take this princess in our god's name."

Kate's eyes snapped back to the huge noh. She scowled. "No chance, big red. Harker's my man, and any of his plunder is mine to claim, not yours." She pursed her lips. "And I'm not sure where he is, more's the pity. He's got several bolt holes and out-of-the-way ports that he favors, but I've no notion of which he's chosen." She smirked. "If I did, I'd already be tanning his hide for new boots, make no mistake. But I'd still not turn his plunder over to you just because you asked so nicely."

Mamaro To rumbled, the muscles of his massive arms rippling like a coming storm, but Zineda quickly put her hand around the warlord's wrist and stepped forward.

"But you would be wise to reconsider that," she said with casual ease.

Kate turned her contemptuous gaze on the high priestess, and it took all of Zineda's self control to let the affront pass and keep her voice calm.

"We have mutual interests, you see. We seek this artifact, nothing more, which is only of value to our god. You would claim your due portion, or more, of your rebellious subordinate's treasure."

Kate nodded reluctantly, and Zineda spread her hands as if the solution was obvious.

"Then we both want to find Captain Harker and claim our separate prizes. We both stand to gain from cooperating."

Kate wagged a finger. "No, no, pretty lady, it's not that simple. Whatever that sweet princess may be to you, she's worth a lot to me in ransom. She's the Crown Princess of Ulyxis, the last Forum World and, thus, capital of the United Planetary Alliance. Her father will pay a fortune to get her back." She laughed. "For all I know, her father paid Harker to bring her home."

Zineda shrugged to show that this objection meant nothing.

"You misunderstand me, Captain. You see, I do not wish to chase Harker. We could search the galaxy and never find him. But we may bring him, and her, to us." She smiled a predator's grin at Kate's confused look. "We can draw them out. You've said that she is most likely not a prisoner."

Kate nodded after a heartbeat.

"And as a Knight, she has a tendency to find trouble. So, we create trouble for her to find."

The pirate chewed on that thought for a moment. "Aye, there's something in that. As I think on it, they did head off in the direction of Ulyxis; not a straight course, mind you, but nearby."

"Perhaps he is trying to conceal her in a place of safety," Mamaro To said.

Zineda grinned. "Then Nozuki smiles on us, for we have found our way. We will attack Ulyxis. We will sack her home world. If she is there, we will find her. If she is not, then she will know that her people and her family will fill our slave pens, and its treasures will overflow your holds. No Knight of her reputation could stay away from such a fight. You get your ransom and more. We get our prize."

The glimmer of greed that flashed in Kate's eyes gratified and revolted Zineda in equal measure. "That's a sweet, tempting offer, I admit, but I don't have the men or ships to sack a whole world, let alone—"

"Your men are ill-suited to such large scale ground warfare," Mamaro To cut in. "Mine are not. Likewise, your crews and ships are skilled at naval engagements and boarding actions, yes?"

Kate nodded, intrigued.

"There again my priestess is wise, for our skills complement each other perfectly." He put his hand up to forestall Kate's objections. "You require time to assemble your captains, of course. We need time to gather our strength as well. We will also undertake raids near this Ulyxis to draw off its defenders. Even Alliance Security cannot be everywhere at once. How long do you require to prepare?"

Zineda could see Kate's reservations falling away before her warlord's simple assurances and the lure of all that plunder. "Two weeks, standard, to get everything ready and make the trip." She nodded firmly. "We can meet you in orbit over Ulyxis in two weeks."

Mamaro To nodded back, equally firm. "Then we shall be there in two of your Alliance standard weeks. Do not fail in this, Captain Calico Kate, and you shall have treasures beyond your dreams." He turned and strode back through the rift.

"Just make sure you get your ugly carcasses there on time," Kate replied, holstering her pistol.

Zineda nodded to the pirate queen and followed her warlord. The rift wavered and gratefully closed behind her. She took a few breaths to gratefully soak in the familiar sounds and scents of her home. Then she turned to her warlord.

"There is something hidden here," she said.

He paused in his instructions to his Hatriya to look questioningly at her.

"I have an instinct for deception, else I should not have long survived in Nozuki's temple. The pirate was holding something back, or there is something that she did not know."

Mamaro To considered for a few seconds. Then he dismissed his Hatriya and strode over to the high priestess. "Perhaps," he said in a low voice. "But I think it matters little. Your plan is a good one. Whatever misdirections the pirate might try or misinformation she might possess will wilt in the heat of raw battle. We shall draw out our prize and claim it regardless of any deception."

"And then," she said, touching his chin, "the great work can truly begin." One of her priestesses cleared her throat a few steps away. Zineda's eyes narrowed, and she growled as she stepped closer. "Speak."

"High lady." The young woman kept her eyes firmly on the floor. "We have visitors to see you both. Kasaro To is here. So is the Herald, and she brought another. They await you in the conclave chamber."

Zineda started. "Another? Of the Herald's own kind?"

The priestess nodded. "Another pale one, female, and clearly subordinate. The Anointed One, however, has brought many of the Kyojin with him."

"Of course he has." Zineda rolled her eyes. "Send them our greetings, and say that we shall receive them shortly. Bring refreshments and make note of all that they consume."

The priestess could not help smiling slightly, though she still did not look Zineda in the eye. "We offered them simple fare, as a courtesy, and slipped an extra dose of sedatives into the berserkers' soup. The Kyojin will be lucky if they can stay awake."

Zineda shared the grin. "Well done. Go and see that they are comfortable and watched."

The priestess nodded and scurried away.

Zineda returned to Mamaro To, her jaw firmly set, and shook her head at his curious look. "The slaver has come with his entourage. To talk, it seems."

The warlord's expression remained neutral, but his grip tightened on the vambrace in his hand as he removed his armor.

"There is more. He has brought the Herald and one other of her kind."

Mamaro To looked genuinely shocked. "Another?" He paused, considering, and moved mechanically to let the slaves remove the rest of his armor. "I suppose there must be others. I had simply never considered it." He shook his head, his words mirroring Zineda's thoughts exactly. "We have dealt with the Herald alone for so long that I never gave it enough thought." He frowned as he shrugged on his more formal robes that covered the angles of his body but left his powerful arms and deeply muscled, scarred chest exposed. "I wonder what this portends."

"Opportunity," Zineda replied. She waved away the slaves that came to take her limited vestments. "Come. Let us see what opportunity they have brought us."

CHAPTER 7

Black Spot pirate ship, unnamed berth, Star Nebula

Vance sat in his wide cabin flanked by his bosun, Johnny Patchwork, on one side and Mr. Skreev on the other. Before them sat a small gray-haired mechanic who twitched nervously and adjusted his small glasses every few seconds with grease-stained fingers.

"I'm telling you, capt'n, I can't make up nor down of it." The mechanic shrugged for the fifth time in two minutes. "She's a chee, like any other I've seen. She weren't built as one, that's the truth; more like as an automated maid, like she looks. Somehow, her neural net expanded and she, just, woke up, I guess." He shrugged again, and Vance had to restrain himself from ripping the man's arms off. "She don't seem special in any way. I'm sorry."

Golden Vance sighed heavily and finished his grog. "Not your fault. I knew this would be a knotty puzzle, but we had to start somewhere."

He nodded toward the door, and the mechanic gratefully fled with several near-bows and a continuous stream of mumbled apologies. When the door shut, Vance swore and slammed his mechanical fist onto the table. Johnny Patchwork, a lumbering chee composed of parts as mismatched as his captain's, placed a fresh mug of grog beside the new dent in the tabletop.

"What in the rotting stars am I supposed to do with a super-powerful artifact," Vance complained to no one, "when she don't seem to be anything more than a mechanical maid?"

Mr. Skreev scratched at the stubble on his deeply scarred jaw. "Well, you could ransom her, I guess."

"To who?" he demanded. "Who would believe in her worth?"

He turned an accusing metal finger on his cypher, who floated dejectedly in a far corner piled with discarded clothing. "You told me she was valuable, you stinking faithless fish."

"A treasure beyond price," Minnow said, again. She had the same firm tone she had used on the *Tranquil Wind,* though her heart clearly was not in it.

"Anything beyond price is no good to me," Vance shouted, "when the price is all that matters." He cursed colorfully and downed his grog. "The bloody crick of it is, I can see it," he said, leaning across the table toward Mr. Skreev.

The bosun poured more grog.

"With her sight, I could see it. Esper poured out of that maid like an endless fountain. She shone like a star. But we've poked and prodded her every which way and learned nothing. She is something special, no doubt. But that does us not a bit of good if we don't know why." He sat back, putting his feet on the table with a bang, and swirled his drink as he contemplated the stars. "Someone knows. Someone somewhere knows what she is."

"Probably Harker knows," the bosun said. The words weren't directed at Vance, but the captain glared up at the misshapen chee all the same.

"Let that idiot nobleman rot in whatever hole he's found. I only want to see that cowardly, double-crossing pretty boy again if I'm putting a blade through his back, and for nothing else."

The crewmen all muttered dark agreements as their captain drank to that glorious day.

"You know who might know something," Mr. Skreev said, speculatively, after a silent moment, "is Squall. She high-tailed it out of the starliner almost as fast as Harker did after Minnow called that maid the Source."

Vance cursed again. "She's a spy. A bloody nursemaid sent by Kate to keep me in line, and the less I see of her, the better." He paused suddenly, sitting up, and a cagey look dropped over his heavy features. "Wait. Where is she? Before the raid, that meddlesome fire-hair hadn't been more than a dozen paces from me. I've not seen so much as a glimpse of her in the six days since."

The bosun automatically glanced around the cabin. The chee had his uses, but he also had a number of obvious shortcomings.

Vance sighed. "Mr. Skreev has a good point. If anyone aboard is likely to know something of this Source, it's Squall. And now I think of it, I don't like not knowing where she's at." He turned a malevolent look on Skreev. "Find the witch, keep her contained, and call me."

Skreev nodded, malice glittering in his dark eyes, and strode out.

"We'll turn some profit from this yet," Vance said as the bosun refilled his mug. "Just you wait and see."

A signal whistle blew through the cabin. Vance sighed and cursed again as he hit the blinking light on his chair's worn arm to silence the sound. "What is it?"

"Message coming in, capt'n," the comm man on duty said over the link. "It's from Kate."

"Of course it is," Vance muttered. "Put her through, then." Golden Vance rose and walked to the center of the cabin as the cobbled-together holodisplay creaked and sparked out of the ceiling. The display flickered and blinked but steadied as Calico Kate's viciously beautiful features came into focus. "Your highness-ness."

Kate's smile never wavered, but her voice had a knife's sharp edge. "Mind your manners, Vance. This is business. We've a chance of a huge haul, but it comes at great risk. Are you game for some serious cutthroatery?"

Vance laughed, short and harsh. "When am I not?"

"Well good, but be sure. We're raiding a planet."

Vance's eyebrows shot up.

Kate nodded. "It gets worse. We're raiding Ulyxis."

"But—" he stammered, "but that's—"

"Impossible. Aye, it would be, save that we've some rather disposable allies. We can expect to see a large part of Dragon Fleet To there alongside us, doing most of the heavy lifting on the ground."

"The—The noh?" Golden Vance found himself actually

speechless. "What in all the empty stars is this, Kate?"

"It's a better deal than we might have got," she replied. Her face fell just a bit but enough for Vance to realize that this was more than just a 'good opportunity.' "We're to handle things in space while they hit the surface. Once we've got orbit secured, we follow up behind 'em and grab everything that's not nailed down. When we've got what we can get, we run for it."

"And they'll just let us go?"

Kate shrugged. "They're not after loot. I don't even think they're after slaves this time. The warlord's hot for some sort of holy relic or some-such." She frowned and glanced aside, as if she had heard something, but turned back quickly. "It's nothing to do with us. They've given up their share of whatever we take."

"That's a bit too generous, if you ask me," Vance said, also frowning. Now that he listened, he thought he could hear something too—an echo somewhere.

"Well I didn't, and I don't care. They get our help topside, and we get their booty dirtside." She glanced around again, irritated.

"And if they change their minds, or think we've left too early?"

"Let 'em come," Kate said with vicious defiance, and Vance wondered if that was to convince him or her. He definitely heard an echo from her transmission that time, though. "What is that?"

Vance glanced over at the bosun. The chee had started fiddling with the comms console almost as soon as the transmission began. He shook his head. "Not sure, capt'n, but I think there's another terminal open somewhere."

Golden Vance clenched his mechanical fist hard enough to strain the servos and hissed, "Find it. Trace it back. Two-gets-you-ten it's the witch." He glanced at Kate, but she appeared not to have heard them. He took a breath to keep his voice even. "Some sort of double up on the receivers. Like they're registering the signal twice."

"You're overdue to fix that bucket, Vance," Kate said with a studied smugness. "And soon you'll be able to in style. Be over Ulyxis with all your people in two weeks."

"One last thing, oh Pirate Queen," he said, sneering. "Will

the good Captain Harker be present for this?"

"No," Kate replied a touch too quickly. "I've sent word out, but Harker's got too much to answer for. That suit you?"

"Wonderfully well," Vance replied with transparently false courtesy.

Kate cut the transmission before he could.

He rounded on the bosun. "Well?"

"Almost. It's somewhere in the lower decks."

Vance gritted his teeth. "I know where." He slammed his hand down onto his chair arm and opened a comm line directly to Mr. Skreev. "Emergency control room, by engineering. She might still be there." He grabbed his weapons as he bolted for the door.

Racing down half a dozen decks, he shoved and shouted his men out of the way until he burst into the grimy, cramped, and musty access ways just forward of engineering. About twenty yards ahead of him, several burly crewmembers stood tense near a small bulkhead door, clearly added well after the ship was built. A bolt of esperic lightning arced from the doorway and blasted a man clean off his feet. The air smelled of ozone and tasted of blood.

Mr. Skreev stood sheltered behind the entrance to the access way. "You're only making it worse for yourself," he shouted at Squall. He nodded to his captain as Vance approached from the opposite direction. "Once we get a few chee and some of the bigger hands down here, you'll be in for it. Give up now, and we'll go easy."

Squall said nothing, and for a second, Vance thought they might actually have to blast her out. Then she darted clear of the door, her staff leveled at Skreev. Golden red esper danced around her like St. Elmo's Fire. Vance launched toward her and summoned his own power around him.

Squall felt it an instant too late. Her lightning bolt went wide, skittering along the walls and conduits like water on a hot pan. She tried to turn, but Vance barreled into her, and the staff went flying. He pinned her under his knees, until he could get his flesh hand over her mouth and his mechanical hand on her throat.

Once she was immobilized, he hauled her up, her feet dangling well above the deck plating, and panted into her face.

"Well, my lovely," he said, still a bit breathless. "I wondered when it would come to this. And who have you been talking to, then? Does dear Calico Kate know about our prize? I dare say if not, then she will soon. Well, no matter, truly. She won't care now, not with a whole planet to plunder. And if she ever does, she's welcome to try and take it." He leaned in and watched the fear and revulsion deepen in Squall's eyes. "Fact is, I rather hope she does try. We're long overdue to clear the air, she and I. Meantime, little witch, we've got plans for you." He turned to the crewmen. "Get the injured up to sick bay, and clear a path to the hold. Prep the suppression cage right next to the chee. This one's going to watch her precious Source squirm until she tells us what the chee is and how to get paid for her."

He laughed as he dragged the struggling pirate out, her muffled screams lost in the narrow, echoing passage.

CHAPTER 8

Lucky Chance, slip space

Kisa barely noticed Candy's presence in the round room anymore. She had started coming in while Kisa meditated, and as far as either the Knight or Fiametta could tell, Candy just lay there looking at the stars. Even Scratch had accepted her quickly, and he and Candy tended to curl up on some of the cushions and conspire. The Alliance Knight was not, in herself, disturbing. Her presence was just a constant reminder of how Not Right the situation had become, even if she did not actively disrupt matters. Indeed, aside from the occasional little verbal barb between her and Fiametta, Candy fit in like she had been with them for years. Even the tiffs had lost their venom and verve. It was almost like the two continued to snipe at each other as a game.

But despite the familiarity, Kisa still could not concentrate especially well, and the message alert chime that Fiametta had hurried off to answer a few minutes before had not helped. Kisa sighed and opened her eyes. She felt a little surge of reassuring esper and saw Scratch lean in to rub against her knee. She scratched him on the head.

Fiametta came back into the room at a jog. Candy sat up slowly, but Kisa stood in an instant. The expression on Fiametta's face chilled her.

"What is it?"

"That was Squall, again," Fiametta said, a little breathless. "We have to change course."

"What happened? What's wrong?" Kisa demanded.

Fiametta had gone white. "Vance. Golden Vance has the Source. And he's heading for Ulyxis."

"What?" Candy and Kisa asked together.

"I don't know the details, but Squall was listening in on a transmission between Calico Kate and Golden Vance. Kate has apparently made some kind of devil's bargain with the noh. She's calling all her captains. They're going to raid Ulyxis!"

"Corsairs and the noh?" Candy asked and frowned, considering. "That—that could work. When?"

"I think with the noh, yes," Fiametta said, still shaken but steadying. "That's what it sounded like. And in about two weeks."

"Not good. Not good," Kisa muttered and dashed to the hidden console. "Did they say anything about the Source?"

"No. I don't think so." Kisa glanced back at her friend as the computer unlocked. Fiametta looked stricken. "Squall didn't have much time. And her transmission cut off mid-sentence. They found her, Kisa. Vance found her."

This time, Kisa felt a chill from her stomach to the tips of her fingers and toes. She knew Golden Vance's reputation.

"Sweet stars and divines," Candy muttered; then she looked at Fiametta. "I've run into Squall a number of times. I know this doesn't help much, but if anyone can handle herself in that mob of cutthroats, Squall can. She's small but mighty."

"I know," Fiametta said, her voice shrinking. "I know. But it's Vance. And he—He knows how to deal with the Doctrine."

Kisa shook her head as the computer flashed up the answers to her queries. "I can't believe they'd hit Ulyxis, even with the noh. I can't believe even Kate would cut a deal with the noh."

"I can't believe the noh made a deal with anyone," Candy replied, thoughtful. "That's not their style. Kate may not have had a choice."

"Well," Kisa said, studying the numbers. "If we change course now and burn most of our fuel, we can just make it in time."

Fiametta hissed, and Kisa turned around, her hands raised, but Candy cut her off.

"Listen, drop me at the nearest system. Set me on dirt, and I'll find an Alliance ship to take me to Ulyxis. I'll go myself." Fiametta turned her drawn expression toward Kisa.

Kisa shook her head. "No can do," she said. She put her hands up to stop Fiametta's protests. "Listen, I know. Squall's been your friend for a long time. She risked a lot to get this message out, but she didn't call for help. Did she?"

Fiametta hesitated and then shook her head slowly.

"No, she didn't. She risked life and limb to let us know that Ulyxis needs help. To tell us where the Source will be. I don't have any idea what the Source is, exactly, but Squall has given us a chance to grab it. So that's what we're going to do."

After a long few seconds, Fiametta nodded and then hung her head. "I know," she said so quietly Kisa almost did not hear. "And I know that the Source has to come first." Her head came back up and fire literally burned in her eyes. "But Vance will be there, and so will Squall, if she's alive. One way or the other, he and I are going to have words."

"That's my girl," Kisa said, grinning, and laid in the new course.

Candy appeared beside her, examining the console. "I need to get word out about this on the priority channels."

Kisa indicated another section of the panel, and Candy bent over it to input the Alliance code words. When she had finished her transmission, she stood back and grabbed a discrete rail while the *Lucky Chance* transitioned from slip space.

"Ulyxis. Wow," she muttered as Kisa adjusted the ship's heading to the new course. "Why, I wonder."

Fiametta grabbed the same rail and shook her head. She looked better, if not exactly good. "I'm not sure. Squall said something about the noh raiding the surface while the pirates fought in space. Said the noh were after something specific, an artifact she thought."

"Makes sense," Candy said, thoughtful. "That plays to their strengths and seems like a solid motivation for the noh. I wonder what it is."

"I've got a sinking suspicion that I know." Kisa punched the slip drive button. The ship shuddered as it broke through the dimensional barrier. "Let's just hope we get there before they figure it out."

CHAPTER 9

Marianne, slip space

Malya set her fork down and glanced around the long table. The usual crowd of dinner companions made the usual varying quality of conversation, but she ignored most of the voices. Rin continued to look remarkably comfortable in the long dresses that the crew had provided and that she oddly insisted on wearing to dinner. She chatted animatedly—about guns, by the sound of it—with Harker's first mate Constanza Digby. Mr. Tomn sat on the sideboard with Caesar perched next to him, sharing something that looked like custard. Betty still looked as nervous and withdrawn as ever, surrounded by the *Marianne's* officers and senior crew, and kept trying to huddle into Lug. The huge chee looked perfectly at ease, though it had taken a few days to get there. He traded jokes with several of the engineering crewmen, displaying an easy grace Malya had never seen in him.

Only Harker himself seemed different, now that she thought about it. The princess regarded the pirate, seated opposite her at the far end of the table. He glanced up from his plate when he felt her gaze and returned her look silently. She had also chosen to wear a dress tonight, though she could not have said why when she picked it out. Now, rather than feeling self-conscious, she remembered all those agonizing family and formal dinners growing up, and drew confidence from knowing just what image she presented and how to best use it.

"Captain Harker," she said, projecting so that her voice cut through every other conversation. She paused for three breaths as all other voices stilled. "You have been exceptionally generous and accommodating. Do not for a moment believe that we don't appreciate everything you've done. But we have been in slip space for six days, and we have not yet received the explanations you promised us on the *Tranquil Wind*. I think that we are due at least some of them now." She noted that several of the crew members looked a little concerned, though she could not tell whether this related to the nature of her question or the way she asked it.

Harker regarded her for a heartbeat or two, set down his wine, cleared his throat, and stood. "You are perfectly right, of course, your highness. I apologize for what must seem a selfish delay. It might be some excuse to say that matters have proceeded far more quickly than I had anticipated, and this has occupied my attention, especially given the difficulty of communications in slip space." He gestured to the party. "But tonight is a surprisingly appropriate time to discuss this. And since we seem to have reached that point in the evening in any event, I'll ask the companions of the princess to follow me. Mr. Digby, you have the ship."

The statuesque brunette stood to attention, somehow managing to make her floor-length, asymmetric dinner dress seem military. She nodded and snapped a few quick commands. The officers and crew around the table acknowledged and trotted off.

"Moffet," Harker said, "if you would care to join us, I would be most grateful."

The duelist smiled up at him from her seat beside his. "It's nothing I don't know," she said with the aloof sadness that characterized most of her conversation. "But I suppose you'll want me to embellish some of it, won't you?"

"Illuminate, my friend," Harker said with a wry smile. "I've never needed help embellishing."

Moffet actually laughed, a clear and rich sound that Malya knew for a certain fact that she had never heard before. "Too true, captain." She stood and gestured toward the room's rear door. "Lead on."

Crewmen appeared as the group strolled out, already clearing the table, and Malya marveled again at their efficiency. She knew that the space would be a briefing and chart room again within minutes. The sight of the next room, however, drove away such distractions. Malya had never been in this room before. The ceiling became barrel-vaulted, rose by several feet, and the walls stretched back to the proportions of a fine house instead of a corsair starship. Antique lamps in an oddly alien style hung high on the walls and spread warm light across the thick wooden floor planks. Armored glass windows two decks tall marched down the length of the hull on her left to display the smearing, shifting colors of slip space. The far end of the room lay in thick shadow, and Malya noticed Mr. Tomn peering intently into the darkness.

All of the Cerci crew marveled as they milled around at the front of the cabin. His cabin, Malya realized. She inspected the heavy desk, its surface a mixture of organized piles and scattered papers or datapads. She noted the simple but deep bunk built into the wall near the door; through a trick of the architecture, it both lay out of the way and had a clear view of the room and the windows. She felt suddenly intrusive, as if she had invaded the captain's private space rather than been invited.

Harker, of course, displayed no discomfort. He spread his hands to indicate the room. "Welcome, all. The *Marianne*, as you've no doubt guessed, was not built in this galaxy, and though I've modified her rather extensively, I did keep a number of the more distinctive sections intact. And now, to business."

He turned and waved his hand. A baroque apparatus of what looked like brass globes and gold rings and blunt arms wrought in a strange wood descended from the ceiling. It whirred and chuckled and several of the globes began to spin. A strikingly crisp holoprojection of the Last Galaxy appeared around them, thought the color balance seemed just subtly off. Malya found herself squinting at it slightly.

"This, as I'm sure you recognize, is all that remains of the universe." Harker pointed, and a spot in the middle circumferences of one spiral arm glowed. "That is Ulyxis, the last forum world of the United Planetary Alliance, just for reference." He pointed to a small, blinking speck moving slowly across the arm on a course that would bring it quite close to the forum world. "And we are approximately here."

The pirate captain waved them toward the comfortable furniture scattered around the softly lit space. "A little background first. I've traveled extensively; far more than most beings now living. I have sailed the stars for decades, and I've spent a great deal of that time in other galaxies chasing, fighting, and studying the Calamity." The comm on his forearm beeped and he touched a button there. "In that time, I've accumulated a great deal of information. But that's proven of singularly little help."

"So what makes you think this time is any different?" Malya asked. She perched on the arm of a tall chair and crossed her arms.

"This time, I finally have the pieces I need," Harker said. "Allow me to explain." He paused as the cabin's door chime rang, and he pressed a button on his chair. The portal slid open, and the monstrous noh strode in.

Lug stood a little straighter and stepped slightly in front of Betty. "As long as you're explaining things," Lug rumbled, "let's start with him."

The noh raised one eyebrow at the chee and then bowed.

"I've asked Kenobo to join us because of his unique insight into his people and their role in this tragedy," Harker said, his tone firm. "We've sailed together for," he hesitated and glanced at Kenobo. "I honestly don't know how many cycles it's been."

The monk shrugged and replied in a surprisingly soft voice. "Nor I, captain. I've lost count." He had a strange accent, sharp on the hard consonants, that made Malya's jaw tighten slightly. He turned to regard the group. "You have nothing to fear from me, though I doubt you believe that. Most don't."

"The noh illustrate an uncomfortable fact about the Calamity. Consider how long their dragon fleets have plagued us," Harker said. "We have records of noh raids that go back over ten thousand cycles, nearly to the founding of the Alliance, and I've seen descriptions of their attacks that are older still. But what do we really know about them? We mostly know them as reavers, slayers, and slavers. We know they are divided into separate dragon fleets of different names. Some even know that they worship a hydra god. But how many, do you suppose, know that his name is Nozuki? How many know that each of the dragon fleets bears the name of one of his heads, and that each represents an aspect of his personality or psyche?" He gestured to the huge monk. "Dragon Fleet To is the best known, for they represent Nozuki's bravery, making them among his vanguard. We've fought them for millennia, but we know almost nothing about how they live, what they believe, or what they want. So it is with the Calamity."

"Sometimes knowing that they're pouring out of rifts to kill you is enough," Malya said flatly.

"When you find yourself staring at the business end of one of their blades, certainly," Moffet replied laconically. "But has that limited understanding helped us to defeat them? Has it stopped the raids, or even slowed them down?" She looked at the princess's withering stare without flinching. "No. They're an opponent like any other, however, and studying them is the key to defeating them."

Malya shrugged, conceding the point. "So which fleet is he exiled from?"

"I am not exiled from my fleet," Kenobo replied, solemnly but without rebuke. "My fleet is exiled from my people."

"You're—Wait, what?"

Kenobo actually chuckled, though he seemed surprised and quickly schooled his features. "Yes. As Captain Harker has said, our hydra god's different heads embody different parts of him, and our separate dragon fleets are each dedicated to one of these aspects. My fleet is Go, named for Gomandi, the head of wisdom." He bowed from the shoulders.

"Not a trait I think of when I think of the noh," Rin said with a chill in her voice that nearly made Malya shiver.

"Indeed," Kenobo said. He seemed unfazed by her tone. "There's good reason for that. Ages ago, Nozuki offered my people a chance to reave, slave, and slay across the universe in his name, and he would exalt us above all others. We accepted, and he remade us into this form. Down to our cells, we are his creatures, but we retain our intelligence and," he paused, "curiosity. Even as we stripped our world to build the dragon fleets, questions were asked that had only uncomfortable answers. We set off on our holy mission with some of us already uneasy in our minds. After millennia of faithful service, too many of us had reservations that could no longer be ignored."

He sighed, and his eyes unfocused. He hesitated, twice, clearly biting off words at the last second. "Rather than answer those questions, our god chose to attack. In his own realm, Nozuki's eight other heads ripped Gomandi from its neck and burned the stump with hellfire. The fleets drove us out, killing many. Most of the monks of my order served as advisors and spiritual guides among the other fleets. Less than a dozen of us escaped."

His gaze returned slowly to Rin, who had gone pale. "Ever since, we have wandered the galaxies seeking the truth behind Nozuki's words. For not all he told us was false. Not all his promises were lies."

He spoke a word in a language none of them knew, and the hologram whirled. Red starbursts began to appear, first along the fringes of the galaxy and then slowly deeper, like fingers of bloody frost spreading over a window.

"He told us, for instance, that the rift generators that move our warriors and ships between dimensions would aid us in our task. Beyond their obvious use, however, it is clear now that they weaken something in the fabric of this universe. When we come to a galaxy, noh raids follow predictable patterns, outside to in, and along certain routes scouted and mapped by the Sarva, our scouts. My fleet first determined the signs that they follow, however, though we knew not what they meant."

"But you do now?" Malya asked, her throat dry.

"In a way," Kenobo said. His huge clawed hand traced one of the loose lines of starbursts. "We do not know what trail these routes follow, but we do know that the flows of esper in a galaxy change markedly behind them. The dragon fleets alter a galaxy's esper, and the crystals grow thick in their wake."

Betty frowned at the pattern of starbursts. "They look like they point somewhere, don't they?"

"I also thought so, at first," Harker said, leaning forward, "but I have realized that, rather, they point from somewhere. In every case I can find, the noh raids herald the beginning of the end. Though it may take centuries or longer for a galaxy to die, the noh are the first sign. And they are not alone. As best I can find, the Calamity—for lack of a better way to personify the problem—enters a galaxy at a point somewhere along its edge. Somewhere the noh raids passed early on, where the crystals have grown thickest."

"You believe you've found that point here," Malya said.

Harker nodded.

"And you believe you can get there and stop it?"

He nodded again.

She shrugged, ignoring the sinking feeling in her stomach and Mr. Tomn's intense gaze on her. "They why do you need me?"

Harker raised one eyebrow. "You can't be serious. Do you really have to ask?"

"Yes I do," she said, heat rising to her face. She jabbed her finger at Mr. Tomn. "Because if you say it's about him, we're leaving." She gritted her teeth. "Because if it is, then what you need is a Knight, any Knight. Not. Me," she hissed.

Harker's eyes slowly narrowed and his jaw set. From the corner of her eye, Malya noticed Moffet's surprise at his expression and saw her take a step back.

"Crown Princess," the captain said, "grow up." He stood slowly, as Malya blinked in surprise, and his voice rose with him. "I have seen the Calamity eat the universe, eradicate uncountable trillions of lives, and nothing anyone has tried can even slow it down." He got at least some of his control back as he inhaled, and he ceased shouting. "I have personally witnessed the end of three separate galaxies, and each of them went down swinging. It made no damn difference." He pointed to Caesar and Mr. Tomn. "Of course it's about them. We, and only we, are the people in what remains of the universe who have even a prayer of succeeding. Just because you don't want the responsibility that comes with a cypher doesn't mean you can escape it.

"And no, it can't be just any Knight." His tone had turned sarcastic but that vanished almost instantly, and for the first time, Malya could hear and see just how drained Harker was. Decades of vain struggles, of living on hope alone, had sapped nearly all the strength from him, but even here, at the very last, he refused to collapse or give up. She could not even guess what the effort must cost him.

"I tried that." He sank back into his chair. "The cyphers are the sign. They mark us as different, as destined, and believe me when I say I understand that burden. You," he said without accusation, "are famous for your willfulness. You refused everything you had—which was literally everything anyone could want—in favor of only that which you chose to earn." He sketched a salute. "Kudos to you, princess, but you've never understood that we don't get to choose our lives. We only get to choose what we do with them. You are a Relic Knight, and a responsibility comes with that." He held out his arm, and Caesar glided gently to him. "It isn't all power and glory. We all have to pay for it at some point."

"I earned all I've got," she said almost before she realized it.

"I know," he replied quietly. "So did I. But these," he indicated the cyphers, "aren't rewards. The Peers have a saying, 'The work does not end with praise; praise heralds more work.' The esper doesn't choose you because you helped widows and orphans."

Kenobo cleared his throat, and Harker nodded.

"Yes, yes, the esper doesn't technically 'choose' anyone. But your cypher and your relic aren't the fruits of long labor. They're the tools of still greater work to come. You are uniquely suited to do something momentous in this last, dark chapter of history. You can either run from that," and now he fixed his gaze on her eyes, "or you can embrace it."

She blinked again and glanced away. "Once more, and this—" She put her hands up to prevent questions. "This doesn't mean what you think it does, but I really need to know. Why me?"

He stared for a few long heartbeats. "At first, I didn't think it needed to be you. The, um, signs, if you will, that I saw were so general that I thought they could apply to almost any Knight, as you've said." He stroked Caesar's feathers. "That's why I've failed twice before to halt the Calamity. I need at least two other Knights, and apparently I need specific characteristics in each of them." He leaned back, thinking. "'Fast enough to outrun life and death, strong enough to accept sacrifice, and pure enough to care nothing for glory.' I think that's how it goes." He smiled at her. "It's a poor translation of what's rather good poetry in the original language, but that fits you, I think."

Malya quirked an eyebrow. "If you say so, but that really could be anyone." She glanced at her friends, but all of them looked on with speculative, approving expressions.

"No, that's her," Rin said, "whether she knows it or not. But what about the other one? You said there was another."

"Yes," Harker said dryly. "Also surprisingly specific. That line talks about strength of character and leadership and a spirit so strong that only it could break itself. It's much less effective poetry, honestly, but as best I can tell it fits only one Knight that I've ever heard of." His forearm comm beeped again, and he regarded the display for a few seconds before tapping it. He glanced back up but at Malya instead of Rin. "Sebastian Cross, First of his Order."

The princess laughed, just once, harshly. Harker waited, watching placidly.

"Wait, really?"

Harker nodded, and she laughed again.

"You've got to be kidding me."

Harker shook his head.

"The Sebastian Cross. Paladin of the Six Peers. First Paladin of the Shattered Sword."

Harker nodded.

"The literal poster boy for the galaxy-spanning organization of militarized do-gooders?"

"I see you've heard of him."

"That's why you attacked us," Betty said. Everyone looked at her, and she shrank back, but Lug gave her an encouraging push. "I mean, it makes sense. You needed the princess, and maybe you could have asked, but when else would you have been able to get close or even have a hope of convincing her?"

Harker agreed and waved for her to continue.

"And what better way to get the paladins' attention than to kidnap the Crown Princess of Ulyxis and reigning Cerci Prime champion?" She grinned at the sheer audacity of it. "I mean, who else but Cross is going to come after you?"

"Who indeed?" Harker said, smiling himself.

"You slimy, conniving . . ." Malya said, though even she could not muster much anger.

Harker shrugged.

"There's a flaw in that plan, though. Whenever Lord Cross figures out where we are, he's going to come in guns blazing. You won't have time to convince him that this is all an elaborate scheme to try and save the world."

"Very true, your highness," Harker replied, letting Caesar hop up onto the back of his chair. "That's why you're going to convince him."

Malya finally sat, stunned, in the chair beside her. "What?"

Harker shook his head as he stood. "I'm so very sorry, your highness. I had hoped to spend more time on this, to show you the evidence I've gathered, to introduce the arguments more slowly. I expected to have at least another week, but events—as I said— have proceeded faster than anticipated." He spoke an alien word and the hologram shifted again. Their location expanded and a projected flight plan appeared as a ghostly trail extending to the galaxy's edge with three highlighted points along the way. "We had carefully left rumors and vague hints of our intents, destination, and likely path, all intended for Cross to figure out how to find us. He had to think that we were sincere in our abduction, or he would suspect a trap."

"He figured it out early, didn't he?" Malya asked. She glanced at Rin, but the sniper had returned to staring at the dark end of the room.

"He did," Harker replied ruefully. "I'll have to remember that about him. In any case, we have detected drag buoys near our course, likely placed by the paladins." The first highlighted point glowed more brightly. "I had expected that he would not reach us until we had passed one of these points. But . . ." He shrugged and turned to Malya, his expression earnest and appealing. "I know I've had no time to actually convince you, so I must again ask you to go on faith. I know you and Cross are the Knights I need. I have details of how the Calamity will reach this galaxy that will give us a chance to stop it. What's more, I now know where it will appear."

"But I don't," she said. "I know we have to do something, yes. I have to—" She looked away for a second before she could go on. "I'm not arguing that. But I don't know what you're planning. I don't have any idea if it will work. Without more to go on, how can I believe it, let alone convince Sebastian?"

"Because Captain Harker believes it, and he will go with or without you," said a clear, sibilant voice from the shadows.

Everyone turned as another line of lamps kindled and quickly gained the strength to dispel the shadows. The woman who approached through the growing light wore a richly embroidered silk cloak and hood and a few bits of carefully arranged equipment. Water mixed with amber esper swirled and flowed through the sculpted armor across her chest and the attached apparatus at her throat. It cast an eerie, mottled glow across her face. A long wooden staff, twisted and gnarled like coral, tapped the decking beside her bare feet.

"He has fought and run for cycles upon cycles," she continued. "But he knows that this is the time to stand. Likely he will fail, if you do not go." She stopped several paces from them. An amphibious cypher with huge, frog-like red eyes peeked out from behind her cloak. "But he will go, nevertheless. Because he believes." She cocked her head. The lamplight shimmered strangely off of her pale blue-green skin. "Now you must."

Harker looked genuinely embarrassed. "Forgive me. Some of my friends and crew have unusual needs, and I do my best to accommodate them. Soliel values her privacy."

"And I have long and gratefully valued your consideration, my captain," she said with clear appreciation. Frost-white esper motes floated around her head. "But there is no longer time for reticence."

Rin spoke Malya's thoughts. "And just who are you?"

The strange woman cocked her head slightly, regarding the sniper as if she could see through the human's skin to the sub-atomic things that made her real. "I'm the witch."

Harker cleared his throat. "Lady Soliel has been many things in her life; scholar, archeologist, navigator, soldier, and that's just since I've known her. Currently she is my councilor. Her connection to the esper is, um . . ." He struggled for a word. "Shifted. Warped is perhaps better. She sees esper and the world differently."

"And with the correct aid, what I see tells me that Captain Harker can succeed," Soliel finished.

"I—" Malya hesitated, licking her lips. "I'd like—I want to believe he can. But it sounds like we've only got one shot at this." She glanced at her crew. "And before I put anyone else on the line here, I need to know more. Just one thing," she said to Harker, almost pleading. "Give me one good reason to believe that we can actually do it."

Harker pursed his lips, considering, but Soliel answered for him. "Because, highness, he has nearly succeeded twice before."

Everyone's heads swiveled first to her and then to Harker. Even Moffet looked surprised.

"And this time, he will have you."

Malya nodded. "Well. That will do."

She sighed deeply and saw Mr. Tomn looking at her. He had a smile like she had not seen since she decided to leave Ulyxis. She found herself smiling back.

"Okay. Now we just need to convince the paladin. Don't know what I'm going to say to him."

Harker's comm beeped again, and he glanced at it. "Well, you'll figure it out, I expect."

A warning chime echoed through the ship, and Mr. Digby's voice followed it. "Attention all hands. Attention all hands. Brace for real-space transition in ten seconds. Transition in ten seconds."

Malya shot a glare at Harker. "Now? Are you serious?"

"I'm afraid so, highness," he replied, gripping the arms of his chair. "I did say the paladin was cleverer than I thought."

The *Marianne* shook and actually lurched as she shifted fully back into reality; likely part of the force from the drag buoys, Malya thought. The holographic display immediately blinked and reappeared with a real-time image of the space immediately around the vessel. Malya watched as the three other corsair ships emerged from slip space around them, represented by golden wedges with ID and telemetry information above them. She noted nearly a dozen sickly green wedges arrayed before them, all positioned to block the easiest run paths to slip space. The largest wedge maneuvered toward them. Without thinking, Malya glanced out of the armored glass to see a true stellar behemoth turning its port broadside on them.

"That," Moffet said into the silence, "is a Valorous-class battlecruiser. There's supposed to be only three of them in service and six more in the yards." She turned to Harker with a look of genuine surprise and, almost, satisfaction. "We couldn't have pissed them off that much, could we?"

Harker pushed to his feet and moved to the windows. "I wouldn't have thought so. At least they're taking this seriously." His comm beeped again, and he smiled as he glanced at it. "Yes, Mr. Digby. Put him through."

The holodisplay flickered again and resolved into the upper torso and crossed arms of a serious-looking human man. He wore the paladin's dusky brown shipboard uniform though the hologram's strange color tinted it a dull gray, along with his— probably—brown hair. His eyes came through as piercing hazel, and his voice lost nothing of its authority or power in transmission.

"Attention Captain Harker, this is the Shattered Sword ship *Inexorable Justice*. In the name of the Six Peers and by the authority of the United Planetary Alliance, you are placed under arrest and ordered to heave to. Lock your weapons, power down your engines, and stand by to be boarded."

Harker rolled his eyes but only slightly. "If I had a half-credit for every time I heard that," he muttered. "Well your highness, you're on."

"What? Me?"

Harker arched an eyebrow, and Malya cursed.

"Fine. Where do I stand?"

He pointed to a spot on the floor and she shifted over. Almost immediately, the holographic paladin blinked and readjusted his gaze.

"Ah, hello," Malya said. She swore she could hear a slight echo in her voice and wondered where the pickups were hidden. "Hello. Um, this is, I mean—" She cleared her throat, squared her shoulders, and imagined one of the many dignitaries that her father disliked and she loathed on the other end of the transmitters. "I am Malya Ulyxani, Crown Princess of Ulyxis, three-time Cerci Prime champion, and Relic Knight." She could not have said why she included all of that, but she had, so she soldiered on. "I presume that you are Sebastian Cross, First of the Order of the Shattered Sword."

A slight pause followed as the hologram pursed its lips, and the transmission delay could not account for all of the time.

"I am paladin Cross," the man finally said, "and, I must admit, I'm slightly confused. We were told you had been abducted by pirates from the starliner *Tranquil Wind*. I can't say I expected to find you answering communications from a corsair vessel or quite so," he lifted a hand toward her, "formally dressed."

"Yes, well." She glanced at Harker, who shrugged. "It's been an interesting week. I'm sure you're anxious to blast the *Marianne* and the rest out of the stars, but I'd appreciate it if you held off on that."

"I'm sure you'd like to leave the ship first," Cross said dryly. "And I can assure you and the good Captain Harker that I'm much more interested in prisoners than I am casualties. If he and his crews surrender, I'll see that they—"

"That—" Malya paused, almost as surprised by her interruption as the paladin. "That isn't what I meant. Captain Harker did not, exactly, kidnap me."

Cross evidently refused to be surprised or put off by anything. He simply crossed his arms again and waited.

"I—I came along willingly." She gestured toward Harker. "He approached me in the middle of the battle—saved my life, actually—and told me he had a way to stop the Calamity from destroying this galaxy."

"He did," Cross said in a flat, even tone.

Malya nodded. "Yeah. And then, when we talked it over, he said that he had figured out where that was going to happen and how—well, sort of—and about when, I guess."

"I see," Cross said.

Malya licked her lips. "Yeah." She paused and glanced at Harker again. "It does sound kind of silly when I say it out loud."

"Did he explain how the Calamity would come or how he would stop it?"

She looked up at the image of Sebastian Cross and noticed that a small head had peeked over his shoulder. A second later, an armored cypher—its face almost completely obscured by a knightly helmet—rose beside the paladin and regarded them intently over the link.

"Well, no," she admitted. "We hadn't had a chance to get to that yet."

Cross nodded slowly and sighed. "Very well. Your highness, I applaud your bravery and desire to aid the galaxy, but I fear that you're simply too trusting. We and other specialists have long studied the Calamity, and we've found no way to—"

Harker snarled, tapped his comm, and stepped to another spot on the floor. "You smug, self-important fool. You think because you and your Doctrine friends don't know something then no one does. You think—"

"Shut it, both of you," Malya shouted. She could already see where this was going.

"Your highness," Cross said, in a measured tone that made her teeth grind, "Captain Harker is a liar and a murderer and not to be trusted. If he claims—"

Malya put her hand up, and the paladin fell silent with a look of mild surprise.

Harker shrugged again. "He's not wrong. I am a pirate."

"I know that. I also know," and she turned back to Cross, "that he's the only one of the Knights here—and there's at least three of us—actually trying to stop the Calamity."

"Highness, if he had a way to stop it, don't you think he'd have attempted it already?"

"My lord paladin," Malya shot back in the same patronizing tone, "what do you think he's doing now?"

"Her highness is correct," Harker said quickly, his hands raised and his voice conciliatory. "I have information that might let us succeed where all others have failed, but I cannot do it alone. Please, let us talk, and I will show you everything."

Cross frowned, clearly fighting with himself. "I should arrest you all—"

"Oh, grow up," Malya said. The echo of Harker's words to her rang in her ears, but she refused to let it stop her. "What you should do is what you know is right, not what you're supposed to do."

Cross's jaw set firm and hard. "What makes you think this is right? You said he never offered proof, so why do you believe him?"

"I—" She took a deep breath. "Proof, no; he hasn't offered proof. But he's got a lot of evidence. And it's pretty compelling, even if I don't understand all of it." She pointed to the cypher on Cross's shoulder. "Sometimes, you go where the esper leads. If there's even the slightest chance that he can succeed, it would be wrong not to help." She fixed the paladin with a hard stare. "The least you can do is hear him out."

The cypher leaned over and whispered into Cross's ear.

He nodded. "Agreed. Come aboard, and bring all the evidence you have. I'll send a shuttle."

"Lord paladin," Captain Harker said, "you're more than welcome—"

"You will come aboard my ship on my shuttle," Cross said with an air of finality. "Your highness will please accompany the good captain, along with any companions you have with you."

Just in case this doesn't work out. "Okay, okay. It's a deal." She motioned to Harker, who cut the transmission. "I know it's not everything you wanted, but you got your meeting."

He nodded, more to himself than her, but met her eyes before replying. "I did, yes. And a bit more, I think." They both looked up to see the flash of a shuttle launching from the *Inexorable Justice's* port hangar bay. "Well, best get ready for company."

CHAPTER 10

Hydra's Will, Dragon Fleet To

Atroop of guards followed as the high priestess and grand warlord entered, moving to take up positions along the walls. The conclave chamber lay on the great dragon ship's uppermost deck, half its area exposed to the blackness of space. Under that dark dome, the cushioned reclining seats favored by the noh surrounded an open space. Here would slaves light fires, set up meeting tables, or dance or bleed out their lives for their masters' amusement.

The chamber stood largely empty now, the lights along its curving walls darkened, and only the thin starlight fell across the waiting figures at the far end. Zineda waved her hand, and red-green esper lamps along the roofed portion of the room glowed softly. The three figures turned to regard them. Zineda could see the outlines of great noh warriors kneeling in a semicircle behind the towering figure of Kasaro To. Huge even by the standards of her species, the Noh Empire's sole Relic Knight, the Anointed of Nozuki, glanced at them. He hesitated for a few impertinent heartbeats before he turned to face them. He carried no weapons, but he needed none. Azi, his cypher, leapt from his perch on the wall and clambered up the Knight's rippling torso to his shoulder. Spite flexed her claws, and Zineda cooed to her.

Mamaro To stopped a dozen paces from his guests and inclined his head, the bare minimum respect required. "Forgive the delay, Anointed Knight. We were engaged on critical matters."

Kasaro To rolled his eyes and sneered. The expression allowed the low light to glint off the decorative rings on his tusks. "Save your platitudes and empty pleasantries. I care nothing for what you say or what you were really doing." His eyes drifted briefly over Zineda before fixing back on the warlord, making clear exactly what he thought had occupied them. "I have come on the direction of our god, and no matters are more critical."

"And you have brought guests," Zineda said, injecting smoothness into her voice with some effort. She bowed from the shoulders at the aliens. "Welcome, Amelial, Herald of the Void. To what do we owe the honor?"

The Herald fixed her gaze on the high priestess, and a cold wave washed over Zineda. She suppressed a shiver. It angered Zineda to admit how much the strange alien's species unnerved her. Amelial's smooth, ghost-pale features closely resembled the human slaves', but her face's sharp angles and frigid perfection set her clearly apart as something strange even to the noh. She wore the same supple body suit and smooth armor that Zineda remembered, both backlit by subtle streams of flowing green-black esper. The almost skeletal frames rising from her back held only the shadowed outlines of the dark violet esper wings that they usually projected; the lamps' light tinged their edges with a sickly red. Beside Amelial stood a slim figure with shadows draped around her like gauze. Zineda could just see the esper-traced bodysuit, curving armor, and a hint of flowing robes.

"A critical time approaches," the Herald said. Though she spoke softly, her words carried to every corner of the vast chamber. "We must act together to ensure that all transpires correctly."

"Amelial requires our warriors," Kasaro To said peremptorily. "Events are beginning to move quickly. You must fulfill our agreements. Give your ships to her direction, and destroy her enemies—and ours. This is as it must be. Nozuki has shown me this."

"Really." Mamaro To did not speak the word as a question. "Fascinating. Our god continues to show you great favor. Tell me, did he send you a vision, perhaps speak directly through a priestess, or did you find a written note on your pillow one night?"

Kasaro To snarled. "I am the chosen of the Hydra God. I am the manifested will of the Endless Hunger. I am his anointed champion, warlord. Never forget that."

"All true," Zineda cut in, her voice sharp, "but you are not a priestess. You do not commune with him. He touches your mind, yes, but he gives us clarity and direction. You are his instrument," she jabbed a finger at him, "but we are his voice."

"He does not tell you everything," Kasaro To growled, a bit more restrained than Zineda had expected. She sensed an opening.

"Nor you, it seems. He grants visions to those who require them." She ran her claws delicately over Mamaro To's arm. "He has had such a vision."

Kasaro To's eyes narrowed. "Has he?"

"Yes," she snapped. "Through the rituals, all correct and ordered." She cocked her head in question and injected razor-edged silk into her tone. "Do you doubt the word of your high priestess?"

In her thoughts, she dared him to challenge her, to impugn her office and reputation. She resisted the urge to goad him. If he pushed her, she would question him on the exact details of Nozuki's direction to him, pull apart his words to reveal only his own desires and nothing divine. Then they would see whom the Hydra God truly favored.

"Pray, share this vision, if you can."

Zineda waved Kasaro To's comment away as if it had no more importance than dust. "Such visions, as you know, are between Nozuki and his chosen. When you need to know, you shall." She spread her arms with her palms out, as if revealing everything. "All that matters for the moment is that it is important to He Who Hungers, and therefore cannot be ignored."

Kasaro To ground his teeth. "The Endless Hunger has directed our dragon fleet to fulfill our obligations." He jabbed a finger at Mamaro To. "You are the Supreme Warlord of Dragon Fleet To; therefore you must fulfill these duties." He gestured to Amelial. "She requires soldiers. Send them."

"I am supreme warlord," Mamaro To replied, unruffled. "Tell me, Herald, for what do you require us?"

Amelial glanced from one of the hulking warriors to the other, as though she might actually be able to see their conflict sparking in the air between them. "Our enemies—yours and mine—gather to thwart my master. This must not be. They shall attack us at a place far from here. We require your warriors and your ships, so we must leave immediately." She shook her head at the warlord's unspoken question. "Your rift generators cannot carry you to this place directly. That is damaging to us. We must wait and destroy them when they arrive."

Both Kasaro To and Mamaro To bristled at Amelial's calm orders and preemptory manner, though the warlord hid it better.

"Very well," Mamaro To said. "For your aid in this galaxy and others, we shall do as you ask."

A flash of satisfaction crossed Kasaro To's face, but he hid it quickly.

"I am supreme warlord, as you have rightly pointed out, Anointed One, and the warriors of Dragon Fleet To are mine to command." He raised a hand to the Relic Knight. "By that authority, I command you, Kasaro To, to take your Kyojin warriors and those dragon ships already under your banner and go to the aid of our allies, the Herald of the Void and her people." He paused for a second. "If you feel your power is sufficient to the task."

Kasaro To went livid. He sputtered for a second before his restraint snapped and he roared. "You arrogant dog! You cannot command me. I am the Chosen of Nozuki, and I follow no will but his."

"And he has directed that we do this, as you said," Mamaro To replied in a voice thick with anger and self-control. "I suggest you obey him, if you think you can."

Blue-violet light flashed from Amelial like a dying star. It washed the room in the colors of night, and all voices fell silent. "Enough of this." She rounded on Kasaro To. "Your warlord has spoken. Whether you like his words or not means nothing. All that matters is that I obtain warriors who can actually defeat our enemies. Captain Harker has expanded his own strength and recruits more allies; we think that he is rallying other Knights to join him."

Zineda started at the name but kept her eyes fixed on the Herald.

"If we are correct, Harker could bring several Knights, likely at least one a Relic Knight, and the considerable power of his fleet to bear against us. Perhaps even some of the paladins." She waved a hand at Mamaro To without looking at him. "Your warlord has hinted that your strength may not be enough. Even if he said these things only as a goad, I must know the truth. Can you and your vaunted Kyojin berserkers defeat such a force?"

Kasaro To glared at Amelial with enough hate to ignite stone, but she never flinched. Blood red esper rose around the noh like a gathering storm. "Of course," he finally said in a voice hoarse with rage. "My Kyojin live only to sate our god's hunger. His touch on their minds has granted them a divine madness, made them perfect incarnations of his appetite." He nodded toward Mamaro To. "This dog may fear to use them, but I do not. They are pure servants of Nozuki's will." He glanced at the warlord. "And I am that will." His fanged maw broke into a cruel grin. "Never doubt me, Amelial."

"Very well," she said and turned to the other noh. "Do not think me unobservant or foolish. I can taste the esper around you both. What does the name Captain Harker mean to you?"

Mamaro To spoke slowly. "He has fought us before, in more than one galaxy. He has studied us. He—" The warlord broke off, clearly contemplating. "He was part of my vision."

Both Amelial and Kasaro To stared at him. Zineda put her hand on his arm. "My lord, after so much today, perhaps now is not the time—"

Mamaro To fixed his gaze on the Herald. "My vision is of an artifact, one Nozuki wishes us to acquire. One we believe Captain Harker has."

Amelial's eyes narrowed and her voice took on a power and feeling it had lacked, though her face remained fixed and porcelain. "What kind of artifact?"

"We know little beyond the hints and metaphors of the vision,"

Zineda answered smoothly before her warlord could speak. "We suspect that Captain Harker has seized it, but he has vanished. Perhaps if you could reveal his whereabouts, Lady Amelial, we could strike at him now before he can mass his strength against you."

The alien's gaze remained suspicious as she spoke. "Lady Zineda, if we knew the captain's location, we would already have directed you thus. Alas, Captain Harker has long opposed us, and he knows our ways. Something hides him from our sight. But of this artifact—"

"Whether Harker has indeed taken it, or if the vision was only meant to show that he would oppose us," Zineda went on quickly, "is unclear. If he has it, he has taken it into hiding. We shall seek it, as our god commands, but of it we know only that it is powerful."

"A font," Mamaro To said, almost too quietly. "A fountain of esper."

A gasp drew their attention to the shadows. The creature behind Amelial moved forward. "The signs were right," she said, her pleasing voice animated and eager. "They echoed through the void like thunder. The Source has appeared."

Amelial nodded. "Then the Calamity has come. All the more reason for haste. Warlord, you must pursue this artifact."

"Our god has so commanded," Mamaro To replied in icy tones. "That is all the instruction I need."

Amelial gestured to the other woman. "Fine; I care not for your reasons. Your search will likely distract Harker and certainly reduce his power if you succeed. You seek the Source, and Tahariel shall aid you."

The other alien woman drifted forward, the low light glinting from her curving armor plates. Though almost human, the warrior wore an esper-traced bodysuit and plates of armor tinged with darkness. A great circle that whirred and clicked with channeled esper rose behind her head, matching those that topped her bejeweled staff and supported her armored boots. The blackness that pulsed in the center of each circle swallowed light and esper, and was clearly holding the creature aloft. Her scant robes drifted in a breeze none of the others felt. A small automaton cherub cypher flitted around her on circular wings that gave it the same lift as its mistress.

"She is my favorite hound," the Herald said, "the finest huntress among our void witches. She also has great experience in this galaxy already."

Tahariel inclined her head to the noh.

Amelial looked at the younger woman. "You know my will. Do not fail."

Tahariel bowed more deeply but remained silent.

Mamaro To nodded, clearly considering their options. "I will assign you to Marikan To. She is the satra—the leader—of our Sarva scouts. She is also a Knight and among the most gifted huntresses our people have ever known."

Amelial glanced from Tahariel to Mamaro, but her expression betrayed nothing. "Excellent. I am pleased you take this matter so seriously. Now we must go. Even if Harker himself cannot threaten me, he may send his allies and minions. They must be slain." She turned to Kasaro To. "Come, Anointed One. Show us the strength of your devotion and arms."

The Relic Knight growled. "Do not taunt me. You are not untouchable." He glared at Mamaro To and Zineda one last time. "And neither are you."

Then he stalked from the room. The berserkers rose silently and shuffled after him, their drug-induced quiescence obvious from their unsteady movements. Amelial followed last.

When they had gone, the noh turned silent, hard stares at the strange woman called Tahariel, who remained under the dim stars. "So," she said pleasantly. "Where shall we begin?"

CHAPTER 11

Inexorable Justice, unknown region, wildspace

The *Inexorable Justice* proved as impressive on the inside as it had on the outside. The size and efficiency of the hangar impressed Malya, as did the determination and intensity of the green-haired paladin who guided them through the ship. The confidence and strength she radiated perfectly matched both the impressive power of the ship and Malya's mental picture of the Shattered Sword. The decorations and embellishments she saw nearly everywhere surprised her, however. She had expected only spartan austerity from the Peers and certainly from an Order so overtly combat-focused as the Shattered Sword. Yet tiny details continually caught her eye, such as the gentle suggestion of wings embossed on walls edging the starfighter bays, the jagged sword motif on the bulkhead doors, and the sculpted settings for the lights in public spaces.

As they disembarked from the shuttle, they made quite a sight, the little troupe of pirates, racers, and oddities. Kenobo had raised more than a few hackles and pulse rifles, though discipline and the monk's carefully peaceful manner kept things from getting out of hand.

"My people have been killing paladins for thousands of cycles," the noh muttered as he eyed the soldiers. "And, well, I am a pirate." He shrugged. "I can hardly blame them."

A terse word from Sebastian Cross had defused the situation and granted the giant safe passage if no actual trust. He never raised his voice, and did not even sound stern. A calm, quiet, "Stand down," that seemed to fill the whole bay was enough. Malya had seen the paladins fight dozens of times and met some of their most celebrated heroes, but she understood instantly how Sebastian Cross could rise so quickly to command one of their Orders.

And now, she realized as she surveyed the briefing room, she had to convince him to chase a faint hope on the word of a pirate. A sinking feeling dragged at her while Cross introduced his aides, Purifier Second Isabeau Durand, the green-haired woman, and another young woman Malya recognized from ten thousand holovids as Jeanne Romee, Paragon and standard-bearer of the Shattered Sword. Cold tendrils radiated out from her stomach and sucked the strength from her limbs as Harker recounted to the stern and silent paladin what he had already told her. When Kenobo illustrated again the movement of the noh fleets and explained the correlation with the esper crystals' growth, Cross's eyes lit up, and he leaned forward.

"We had seen no connection to the crystal growth," he said, "no discernible pattern."

"Nor did we, Lord Cross, for an extremely long time," Kenobo replied. "Indeed, not until my fleet could safely trail our brethren did we even suspect a connection, and even now, at the very end, we cannot be absolutely certain of its nature."

"But we are certain of the connection," Harker cut in. "The data I collected from other galaxies allowed us to check them against known dragon fleet movements." He pointed to the pulsing dot in space deep among the thickest and oldest part of the noh's depredations. "And in this galaxy, as in the others, the invasions trace back to one area. In that area are certain confluences of gravity, galactic rotation, near stellar bodies, esperic flows, and other factors." He zoomed in the hologram above the table until a large, pitted asteroid dominated the view. "And this is it. Origin Point." He glanced around the table and seemed vaguely disappointed when no one reacted to the name.

"This thing?" Isabeau asked. She arched an eyebrow and tapped on the meeting room table as she frowned. "What makes you certain?"

"Aside from all the evidence he just cited?" Rin asked, but the paladin ignored her.

"A fair question," Harker allowed, "considering the number of other asteroids, small planetary bodies, and random debris in the area. Yet, given the gravity fields there, I'm positive this is it because it shouldn't be here." He pulled the hologram further back, and whirls and loops appeared over the debris field to represent the effects of physics. "This data is almost two months old but has remained unchanged, as best we can tell. All the bodies around this rock move as we expect, arranged in logical patterns. But this asteroid does not move. It sits, perfectly balanced, in the midst of forces that should send it spinning with the rest." He held out his hands toward the image and settled back. "There it is, in defiance of science and esper. The Origin Point."

"Is that really what you're calling it?" Jeanne inquired. Her short, blond hair carelessly framed her round face and set off her soft blue undress uniform with the Paragon discipline insignia on the shoulder. Her lionlike cypher Gallant sat in her lap, carefully watching them all but purring nevertheless as she stroked his neck.

"Well, that's what it is—the origin of the Calamity in this galaxy." Harker sniffed. "What else would you call it?"

"Calamity Junction?" Jeanne offered, her smile a little too wide.

"Enough," Cross said without heat. "Much as I appreciate the attempt at levity, Paragon Romee, we should stay focused. However interesting the evidence for this Origin Point, I still don't see how this is the origin of anything. We don't even know what the Calamity is, exactly."

"Not exactly, no," Harker conceded, "but we do know in broad terms that it is the end of a galaxy, and we know that it is not identical across galaxies. Some gradually succumbed to their fate and others vanished practically between eye-blinks. But those that I observed displayed a clear pattern: the noh raids, the proliferation of esper crystals, and then attacks."

"Attacks? From what?"

Harker frowned and slumped slightly. "I don't know, not for

certain. I've fought them. They are beautiful and deadly, but I don't know what they are. All I know for certain is that they are not native to any of these galaxies. They arrive in a galaxy, their way prepared by the shifting esper flows, and they kill everything before them." He paused, considering. "No, that isn't correct—or rather, it isn't complete. They don't just kill, they erase everything in their path. There is literally nothing left behind except the empty void. Not even heat." He looked at Cross, and once again Malya was struck by the pale fatigue that pulled at the pirate. "They aren't simply the death of a galaxy. They are angels of annihilation, embodied oblivion. And they are coming."

"And you think you can stop them." Cross did not phrase it as question.

"I believe that I can," Harker said. "I don't know, but I think so."

He explained the alien poetry, the supposed prophecy that seemed so tenuously to describe Malya and Sebastian Cross, but the paladin simply accepted it. Malya supposed that in Cross's profession he saw and heard a great deal that was every bit as strange. Especially being a Relic Knight. She felt a rueful kinship in that.

"So," Isabeau mused, "why not just atomize this Origin Point with plasma beams?"

"In every case that we know of," Harker said, "the Calamity is marked by three events. The raids of the noh dragon fleets we have already discussed. The rampant spread of esper crystals is the second. However useful we find these things, and the Doctrine certainly make great use of them, they invariably signal the end of a world or galaxy."

Malya nodded, recalling an exhibition race on Galator IV very early in her career. The multi-hued, six-sided crystals had sprouted from nearly every surface. She had practically seen them growing. Workmen had carefully cleared streets and doorways early in the day, but the clusters had returned by the next dawn. The formerly thriving agricultural planet had shifted its economy entirely to crystal harvesting by that time. Two cycles later, nothing could live on it. Less than a cycle after that, Galator IV and its galaxy had vanished. She shuddered at a deep chill and tried to pay attention to Harker again.

"The third is the appearance of a being called the Herald, one of the invading creatures. The Herald's duty appears to be to prepare a galaxy for invasion somehow. It took me far, far too many cycles to identify the Herald for this galaxy, for she has operated in a way I have never seen described. She is called Amelial, and she has somehow managed to coordinate at least four of the dragon fleets in this galaxy, including Dragon Fleet To."

All of the paladins sat up at this assertion and glanced at Kenobo, who nodded. "My peoples' spies among the other fleets have confirmed the existence of this demon with the angelic face. It's how we learned her name." He gritted his massive teeth. "She holds a sway over my cousins that I've not seen any outside creature wield in our eons-long history."

"So, wait," Betty said, putting up her hand. "Wait, wait, wait. Are you saying you want us to fight the Noh Empire? Because if so, I'm just going to jump out an airlock right now and spare myself the waiting."

"No," Harker said, smiling sadly. "Nothing quite so romantic or hopeless. But it's the reason I haven't simply blasted Origin Point to atoms, as the good paladin here so succinctly puts it. Without that asteroid, they will simply make another, and it may take more time than we have to locate it. This way, we know exactly where they will be. If the Herald has revealed herself, then they will be here soon." He looked around the table. "I propose that we go to Origin Point and destroy whatever device they will use to enter our galaxy."

"They won't just show up from slip space with a battle fleet?" Jeanne asked, scratching her cypher under his chin.

"No. They don't travel between galaxies as we do. I don't know exactly what they will do, but there is always a triggering event of some sort connected to the Herald. They open some kind of breach in reality. We must simply prevent that."

"Oh," Jeanne said, smirking. "As easy as that, then?"

"Not at all," Harker replied. "I believe we can expect significant resistance. The reason that my data on the asteroid is two months old is because I dispatched a small ship to inspect the site, and that was the last time they reported. I suspect that hostile forces are there already."

"But that also leaves us no time to gather more troops," Sebastian said. "Are you proposing we take on the noh and whatever force these creatures can muster with just the paladins here and your pirates?"

"Each of my captains and most of their crews have lost lives and loved ones to the Calamity," Harker said with icy calm. "I have recruited them from across nearly a dozen galaxies. All of them know that, whatever else we may do in the meanwhile, when the time comes, I will throw them against the forces of oblivion. Each of them sails with me for the chance at that fight, for the chance at revenge." He sat back and crossed his arms. "They are more than reliable, Lord Cross, I assure you."

Cross nodded, adding that to the scales in his mind, and turned to Malya. "And you, your highness. Are you committed to this?"

Malya started to speak and stopped. She chewed her lip and collected her thoughts. "Everyone keeps asking me if I believe in this or if I'm confident in success. I'll level with all of you, I'm not." She pointed to Captain Harker. "He believes it, and he makes a great argument. And that belief is enough to convince me that this is the right move. I just—" She cut off as realization dawned on her. "I just don't know what good I'm going to be. I don't know what I'm doing here, no matter what the poem says." She tossed up her hands. "Gods of our fathers, I can't tell you how much I wish I was racing right now. That I understand." She scrubbed at her face for a few seconds. "But you don't enter every race because you want to. Sometimes you do it because you have to. And there's no guarantee, no matter how good you are, that you'll win. That's—" She paused, remembering a little tonnerian girl. "That's why you run the race. So, yeah. I don't have any idea what I can do or why I'm here, but I guess that if Harker believes

I need to be, that's good enough." She gestured to her friends. "I won't speak for anyone else, but this is right. I'm in."

Mr. Tomn landed on her shoulder, grinning.

"I'll speak for the pit team," Betty said after a glance at Lug. "We're in too. Where the princess goes, we go. Simple as that."

"Likewise," Rin added. "Heh, after that buildup, you couldn't keep me away."

"Very well," Sebastian Cross said, setting his palms on the table and standing. "We will go to Origin Point. As you said, your highness, if there's even the slightest chance that Captain Harker is correct, we must help." And then he smiled and shrugged. "Besides, I can always arrest him later."

Malya let out her breath. "Okay." Then she leveled a finger at both Harker and Cross. "But the very first thing we do is stop calling me 'your highness'."

CHAPTER 12

Pullish marketplace, Alexian, Ulyxis sector, Alliance
space

Marikan To straightened up very slowly, just peeking her head above the rubble that surrounded her. Movement caught her eye, and she froze. A message crept into her mind—not a voice or even words, but simply an impression of nervousness, fear, and a desire to escape. She rose a bit more and saw troops in worn Alliance Security uniforms scurrying through cover. Perhaps a dozen humans and though frightened, they held their rifles with purpose and their positions with determination. She sank back, chewing lightly on her lip. To her left, the strange alien Tahariel also drifted back down into cover. She did not actually touch the ground, but she had an unnerving stillness to her all the same.

"Too many for a quick kill," she whispered to Marikan To. "Too many and too ready. Perhaps if you distract them, and I come in from the side."

Marikan considered this for a second and then cocked her head to listen. Both of them had developed this habit over their hunts together as a way to show the other that they had connected with their cyphers. Lakmi, her avian cypher, gave her an impression of the whole ruined hall from her position in the remains of the rafters. Her compatriots in the dragon fleet had laid waste to this block three days before and moved on to not draw attention to her hunt. She still could not fathom why the Alliance troopers had remained to contest the wrecked building, but the noh's continuing raids had them on edge. She could use that.

"No need, I think," she whispered. "We'll let them do the

work."

She selected an esper-charged arrow from her hip quiver and sent instructions to Lakmi. The cypher called, long and eerily in her rough, too-deep voice, and dove toward the Alliance position.

"Be ready to put on a show," she said.

She began feeding esper to Lakmi. She could hear and smell the result. An echoing, roaring sound rose from the shadowed edges of the space, following Lakmi's path like a horde of monsters. The dim light around them wavered and flickered, and illusionary horrors dashed ever closer among the rocks. The troopers shouted and rushed around.

"Now," she hissed to Tahariel and they rose from cover.

Marikan To took a second to aim and sent her missile arcing over the lead Alliance troopers. It exploded when it struck the debris just behind them, sending sparks and a concussion wave and unnerving streams of esper out in a flash. Tahariel also attacked, sending half a dozen bolts of yellow-black esper into the enemy ranks, killing one and striking at least two others, who shrieked as the energy corrupted and putrefied their flesh in seconds. The other troopers panicked and fell back with their wounded. Marikan To and Tahariel dropped back to cover, grinning at each other like children. They waited until both of their cyphers had declared the Alliance soldiers well and truly gone.

"I admit I was hoping to kill more of them," Tahariel said as they moved forward. She glanced at the dead with only superficial interest.

"Too many, as you said, and we don't want the wrong sort of attention. Let them think that here there be monsters." Marikan picked her way over the unstable landscape that her companion simply floated above. "It gives us the time we need."

"And I can't say it wasn't fun," Tahariel said, her grin returning. "The door is . . ." She scanned the partially collapsed wall at the back of the cover the troopers had used. "Here."

Her staff moved in a compact, jagged pattern, and esperic tendrils pulled away the intervening debris. They regarded the partly crumpled metal door. Marikan To thought it resembled all the other nondescript doors they had seen in this abandoned building.

"I don't . . ." She hesitated, still searching for the right word and falling back, again, on the inadequate nearest approximate sense. ". . . smell anything. Not that I know what this artifact would smell like."

Tahariel glanced at her, eyes glinting a bit, and the grin playing around her lips. "Have you tried just looking?"

"Don't start that again," Marikan grumbled. "I can't do it on command."

"That's because you've never been properly taught. You have outstanding senses; it's another shame of your people that you've never been trained to use them."

Marikan To bristled, tired of this particular thread of discussion. "I'm good at this, and you know it. You've said it."

"Oh yes." Tahariel sent her wispy tendrils out again to rip the door free. "You're gifted—a natural hunter with tremendous talent. But there's so much more you could be doing. You could make so much greater use of the esper."

Marikan To sniffed, unable to argue with the assertion. "We prefer to make use of our physical talents rather than rely too much on outside power."

"And wise to do so, generally," Tahariel agreed. She smiled companionably. "But when you can use the esper, why not make the most of it?" She stepped into the empty doorway and gestured to the darkness below with her staff. "For instance, you could tell me now if what we seek is in there." She finally got a look at Marikan's expression and softened her tone. "You have it in you. You've just never had to do it."

"And you know how, yes? You'd deign to teach me?"

Tahariel frowned and put her hand up in a conciliatory fashion. "I meant no offense, then or now, and no, I've not the talent or skill to see esper flows." She smiled again. "But you do. You've never been taught to, and that's no one's fault. I can't teach you, but you might be able to learn anyway. Take a deep breath."

Marikan To fumed a few seconds longer and then did as told.

She closed her eyes, cleared her mind, and then looked again. Her perception did change. The landscape around her seemed haloed, as if a hidden lamp lay behind it all. Sparks broke off of the sharp edges of the rubble and darted around, fractured bits of fire that streaked her vision but did not illuminate it. She smelled smoke—scorched stone and burnt wood—but not the sharp, crisp scent she often detected on the dragon ships when near to large esper sources. Her eyes hurt. She closed them again and thought she heard a low hum, like the sound she associated with many of the Alliance's machines.

She shook her head. "Nothing. I don't see anything."

Tahariel finally frowned. "Well, either you're not seeing the Source or it's really not there." She brightened slightly and started into the dark opening. "Let's find out."

They descended the ruined staircase past two blocked landings to the reinforced basement storage area at the bottom. Marikan To sighed as she surveyed the overturned and damaged sea of, well, stored items around them. "This is all worthless to us."

"Agreed," Tahariel said. "I feel nothing."

They both glanced at their cyphers. The mechanical cherub floating behind Tahariel scanned the room with glowing, pulsing eyes and shook his head. Lakmi simply perched on the twisted stair railing and preened her coarse feathers.

"This was the most likely place on this world," Marikan said, distracted as she felt the space around them. "And there's esper here, but it's deeper. Likely welling up from the soil. If we have to work to feel it, then it's not the artifact."

Tahariel nodded. "Not even close." She sighed, her mood only slightly dampened, and started back up the stairs. "Right then. We're done here, I suppose. Come on. I'm hungry."

Once they had enough open space, Marikan activated her portable rift generator. The comforting warm, humid air of the dragon fleet wafted out of the wet tear in reality, and she stepped through gratefully. Tahariel followed an instant later. Marikan took a deep breath and stretched in the cavernous space of the *Hydra's Will's* largest rift embarkation chamber. Her eyes traced the graceful arch of the walls and drifting banners hung from the roof. She turned and took a careful look behind them before closing the rift. She nodded to the leader of the Hatriya guards and tossed her rift generator to one of the slaves. The man fumbled the catch and dropped the device. The nearest guard cuffed him across the back as he reached down to retrieve it and sent him sprawling. Marikan To turned away toward the door, her mind already onto the next task, and saw Tahariel's expression of distaste. She looked a question at her companion and led them toward the door.

"If your bow slipped and spoiled your shot, would you break it over your knee?" she asked.

Marikan frowned incredulously. "Of course not." She glanced behind them as they stepped into the ship's corridor and then back at Tahariel. "Do you mean the clumsy slave?"

"Seems a waste. If you value them enough to capture them, train them, and feed them, why would you not treat them well?"

Marikan To shrugged, baffled. "They're slaves."

Tahariel sighed, letting the whole thing go. "Well, it's disappointing that we found nothing, but at least we have checked every possible location in this sector. I believe we've covered all the ground we can."

"We have, yes," Marikan To agreed. She felt suddenly quite tired. "Nothing for it now but to go to Ulyxis and draw the princess out of hiding." She took a deep breath, bracing for what came next. "But first, though, I'd better report." Marikan found that the prospect of presenting yet another failed hunt to her warlord did not bother her as much as the possibility of having the high priestess present to hear it.

"If you feel the need," Tahariel said distantly. "I'll come along, if you don't mind."

Markian To shrugged, but she felt a certain relief that she did not want to admit to. Something in the woman's manner and outlook tugged at Marikan's mind. She found it both reassuring and unsettling, but with the atmosphere she feared to find among her superiors, she decided that she liked the idea of having a distraction in the room.

They found the control deck of the *Hydra's Will* darkened and largely deserted. The minimum crew needed to monitor ship's functions moved relentlessly from station to station, and a solitary figure sat draped across the command throne. High Priestess Zineda sat forward as the hunters approached. Marikan To kept her expression clear of the confusion and sudden trepidation she felt. The high priestess would not have dared such an arrogant display as her casual occupation of the throne were the warlord present or even awake. She had to be absolutely confident that Mamaro To would never find her thus. Marikan could imagine several circumstances that would occupy him sufficiently, but the act still rankled.

"The brave hunters return," Zineda said lazily. "And empty handed, again."

Marikan To knelt and bowed her head. "Alas so, my Lady Zineda," she said, letting her voice ring through the deck. "We have followed now all the trails in this sector to no avail. We await your wishes."

Zineda sat back and waved her hand. "We expected nothing more. I do not doubt your efforts or skill, but if the artifact could be so easily discovered, Nozuki would not have tasked his mightiest servants with its retrieval."

"Of course," Tahariel said with a tart note in her voice. "Still, better to be thorough."

"Indeed," Zineda replied, paying her little attention. "We have entered the edges of the Ulyxis system, and our brethren and allies gather. Soon we will approach the world by stealth. We are less than a day away. Warlord Mamaro To is preparing for the coming battle. We will require your skills in the attack."

Marikan To bowed again and felt a thrill run through her at the thought of a straightforward fight. "I serve with devotion and joy, Lady Zineda. I request only a chance to refresh and rest."

"Naturally. Go and sleep. Prepare. You have served us well, and we shall not forget it." She had stopped regarding the women altogether.

Marikan To nodded and rose. She turned and strode from

the room. Not until she stepped through the door did she realize that she had not been formally released; the dismissal had been so clear. She sighed as Tahariel joined her.

The alien put a hand on her shoulder. "That went well enough." She licked her lips and looked thoughtfully at Marikan To's expression. "Didn't it?"

The noh frowned slightly and started off slowly down the hall. "Enough. I should have waited for her to actually dismiss us."

"She'd forgotten about us before you even stood."

"Yes," Marikan To said, and immediately felt guilty. She shook it off. "Let's get that food."

"And then I should return to Lady Amelial," Tahariel said. She sounded a bit sad. "Though, if the Source is going to show up here, perhaps I should stay."

"I thought you didn't like us," Marikan To said too quickly. She glanced away from Tahariel's questioning expression. "Well, you do spend a lot time complaining."

Tahariel laughed. Marikan To realized that, for all the smiles and apparent good humor, she had never heard her companion laugh.

"I do, don't I? Well, there's a lot to complain about, as I see it. But by comparison, this," she spread her arms, "is so much better than being cooped up at home." She shrugged. "And there, I don't get to complain much at all."

Then Marikan To laughed. Not much, and not hard, but it lifted her immediately.

"So maybe I'll get to stay a little longer. And I can't say I wouldn't welcome a chance for a simple bloodletting. I'll report in and see what my mistress desires."

"We live to serve," Marikan agreed, though the notion bothered her a bit.

CHAPTER 13

Hydra's Will, Ulyxis system, Alliance space

It took Marikan To a few minutes to fully realize that she had awoken and perhaps another ten minutes of staring at the inlaid ceiling to admit that she would not go back to sleep. She pushed aside the thin blanket and rolled to sit beside her pallet. As leader of her sisterhood, she could have taken one of the private chambers around the edge of the long hall reserved for the Sarva of Dragon Fleet To. Indeed, she reflected with a tinge of longing, several remained unclaimed even now. She had many reasons for merely claiming a cleared platform among her sisters in the main chamber, and she generally did not regret it. The closer connection and camaraderie with her fellow hunters had proven too useful, both in the field and in the—sometimes deadlier—politics of her people. She yawned.

Lakmi shifted, turned a bleary eye on her, and tucked her head back again. Marikan To scratched the cypher under her neck feathers, and after an obstinate minute, she began to make a low, happy sound in her throat. Marikan smiled at her companion, the source of so much joy and trouble.

"If only you'd told the priestesses that Nozuki was sending you to me," she muttered to the owl-like creature, "they might not dislike me so."

Lakmi raised her head and looked at Marikan with one eye. "They didn't need to know."

Marikan chuckled, but the sound died in her throat as a faint, tantalizing scent caught her nose.

Marikan sniffed and looked around. The scent passed again, there and gone like distant blood on a shifting wind. It must have been what had drawn her awake. While her missions in pursuit of the artifact had not been too taxing physically, they had drained her mentally and emotionally, and she needed sleep before battle. Still, something kept her mind from rest. Now that she sought for it, she found that the air had a tang to it beyond the usual comforting smells of her home. A slippery and pungent flavor ran under the normal scents. She dressed automatically and picked her way silently from the hall.

Though they maintained a day and night cycle, a dragon ship never truly slept. The priestesses, warriors, slaves, and slave masters who saw Marikan To prowling the corridors gave her a wide berth and asked no questions. Though she had spent many of the years since acquiring Lakmi detached to Kasaro To's command, she had grown up on the *Hydra's Will* and could still walk its corridors blindfolded. Yet now, she twisted and wound her way through the halls and passages like a nervous animal. The elusive scent seemed always just ahead of her, and at times, she thought she could hear something like gentle water.

"Has someone snuck aboard?" she whispered to Lakmi.

The bird said nothing. She flitted from one perch to another along Marikan's path, always watching her Knight with a keen interest.

Finally, when they had circuitously reached the ship's port side and still seemed no nearer to their goal, Marikan sighed and slipped into a prayer chamber. She was a level above those that the priestesses reserved for their own use, and the cell-like prayer chambers lined the outer hull of this area. Their armored glass windows revealed the full spread of space, the millions of stars in the galaxy and the absolute blackness of the nothing beyond. Marikan knelt on the room's firm cushion and stared out. She still felt drawn, but she could not say where.

"It smells like a trail, doesn't it?" Lakmi asked quietly. "You act like you've got the scent of blood in your nose."

"I feel like I do," Marikan admitted. "But it's not that. This is—Sweeter? Sharper? I'm not sure. More like mint than salt."

Lakmi slid the sharp edges of her beak across each other. The sound made many people wince, but Marikan To had learned to ignore it.

"Well, if this was a trail," Lakmi asked, "what would you do?"

"I'd look for signs, for clues, but there's nothing here." Marikan To drove her fist into the padded wall beside her and sighed. "I didn't realize how much this bothered me."

"This isn't what's bothering you," Lakmi said, her voice low and firm. "Admit that."

Marikan huffed and said nothing, but she did nod after a moment.

"That's a start," Lakmi allowed. "So if you want a distraction, you need to embrace that. Do what you feel you must, not what you think you should. What do your instincts tell you?"

Marikan eyed the bird askance for a few seconds. "That what we're after is out there."

Lakmi nodded. "All right. If you're sure, let's take another look."

Marikan To stood and approached the window. The vast sweep of stars shed glittering light across the massed ranks of dragon ships. She could see the familiar shapes of Dragon Fleet To arrayed around them. Mamaro To had called in nearly every ship not assigned to the Anointed One Kasaro To for this raid. To her surprise, she recognized more than a dozen ships from Dragon Fleet Rah. Most of the pirate captains had arrived as well, and the ragged vessels kept a wise and respectful distance. To her right, the glare from Ulyxis's sun painted the pirate craft in garish shadows. She could see the light growing brighter. By her estimate, they had perhaps two hours before they reached the planet's near-space defenses. The battle would be fierce and fast, the only way the noh knew how to fight. The anticipation of battle grew in her as she surveyed their forces, but the stirring sight did not reveal her prey, and she snarled in quiet frustration.

"Now, now," Lakmi chided. "Down girl. Calm conquers. Deep breath and take a closer look."

The cypher's eyes burst into light, and fire-red esper shone out in a torrent. Across their connection, Marikan felt that power pour into her, felt her body lift and her mind open. She turned her eyes back to the blackness, but they did not reveal anything new to her. Instead, she smelled it. She inhaled sharply, shocked, and cried out.

Lakmi broke the flow of power. "What?" she asked. "What did you see?"

"Nothing," Marikan To said when she had caught her breath. "But I recognized the scent. I knew it when you fed me your strength." She regarded the anxious cypher with wide eyes. "Esper. I smelled esper. I tasted it. I heard it flowing like an unseen stream."

"What kind of esper?" Lakmi asked as Marikan To gathered her things.

"Every kind. That's why I couldn't identify it. It smelled like every kind of esper, and it's coming from out there. I smelled it coming through space and into this ship."

Lakmi squawked and launched into the air. "That is the Source."

"The what?"

"The Source of all things," Lakmi replied, as if she were speaking to a great gathering. "The gateway of esper from here to beyond and back again. It is the key that opens the way and sets the shape of what will come." Ribbons of destruction and essence esper rippled out of the cypher and haloed her in the dark room.

Marikan To set a gentle hand on her cypher's ruffled head feathers and stroked them back into place with her claws. Lakmi blinked and settled onto her Knight's forearm, the esper fading behind her.

"Shhh," Marikan said. "Calm conquers, remember? I'm sorry, little one, but I don't have any idea what you're talking about."

"I—" Lakmi paused to collect her thoughts. "The Source is, well, the point of all this, of everything. It's the goal and reason for the Knights, the cyphers, even the Calamity as far as mortals are concerned. It is the reason cyphers appear, the thing that all Knights fight for, and the ultimate prize at the end of time."

"Not to build it up too much," Marikan said with a grin.

"Sorry," Lakmi replied, quiet. "There's no reason you would

know. Cyphers know all this instinctively; we manifest with the knowledge." She shrugged as best an avian could. "But in any case, the Source is the object of all our searches. Though something has interfered with this process of late."

"What does this Source look like?" Marikan asked as she pushed to her feet.

Lakmi flapped gently into the air. "I do not know; it is protean. But we need to find it, wherever it is, and get to it. Now."

"Then keep up," Marikan To called, already sprinting out the door.

Though empty of slaves or the skilled noh wayfinders, the cavernous rift embarkation chamber still held a portentous weight. Marikan To slowed a bit as she entered, keenly conscious of her rushed and nebulous plans. She went to the wall sconces that housed the various types of rift generators and selected a portable model. She took it to the center of the staging space and began to adjust its settings.

She closed her eyes, remembered the mixed scents, as she manipulated the spatial controls. Long centuries of scouting ahead of the dragon fleets made her intimately familiar with such devices, but she would freely admit that she lacked the wayfinders' instinct for locating just the right place for a rift. Still, as she moved the proposed opening, and the device's probing fields weakened reality, the smell of esper grew stronger. When it weakened, she adjusted the device again until the scent filled her senses.

"This is it," she muttered. Her eyebrows rose when she noted the device's rendering of her destination. "A pirate ship? Why would it be on—" She shook her head. She could figure that part out later.

The jagged disk in her hands began to vibrate as she set its activation sequence. It purred, as if pleased, and the air in front of her tore apart with a sound like ripping flesh and breaking bone. Beyond, she saw the dark, grimy interior of a starship. Rift generator in hand, she stepped through into a cool, greasy atmosphere.

She stood in a service corridor. Conduits and ductwork ran

along the ceiling and walls. She smelled coolant and lubricant and sweat and hot metal. Under all that, though, she could smell the esper. She searched for a moment, and it seemed like it flowed away behind her. She crept carefully after it, her bow ready, and paused at each intersection. Three times crewmen in untidy coveralls and stained red-on-black uniforms passed by, and she drew shadows around her with esper to go unnoticed.

When she found a ladder with a sealable bulkhead at the top, she climbed up carefully through three decks. She moved more cautiously as the areas around her grew busier, but she could smell the esper more strongly now. She slipped off the ladder and ducked unseen behind a stack of supply boxes in what clearly served as the ship's kitchen, among other things. She watched the sparse crew bustle around, a mix of species and all rough and ready types. She had fought corsairs before and knew them as tough, if often ill-disciplined, fighters. The half dozen she spotted looked equally adept with ladles as with swords and pistols.

Near the far end of the kitchens, the trail lead to a heavy, sealed bulkhead door that she had to grease with esper to keep from creaking as she opened it. A quick glance through the doorway revealed a massive open space beyond. She slipped in and closed the door. Erected against the far wall were seven large enclosures made from shaped metal bars. They curled and twisted in the rough forms of cages, all large enough to hold a fully armored Hatriya warrior. Only two held prisoners, however, neither all that large.

On the left, a small woman in torn and stained clothing sat against the bars. Marikan To noticed the chains attached to her left wrist and right ankle had a strange, glossy shine. Small motes of esper rose from them. The whole thing smelled wrong, like muted esper but corrupted and rotting, and Lakmi bristled her feathers at the sight. In the next cage sat another woman, dressed incongruously like the domestic servants Marikan had seen throughout this galaxy. She was a machine, however, one of the strange, sentient robots the noh had encountered in greater and greater numbers recently. Both women seemed to be asleep, though Marikan wondered if that term quite applied to the robot. Chee, she remembered. They called themselves chee.

She took a deep breath and nearly choked. The scent of esper wafting from the chee almost overwhelmed her. She slunk closer and inspected the cages' locks. She thought she could force the gate, but she doubted that its pitted, clumsy lock was the only thing keeping it secured. And it likely had alarms. She crouched by the cage, indecisive, and finally retreated back to the sheltered space by the bulkhead door. She pulled out the rift generator and called up the return preset. The humid, fragrant air of the dragon ship tickled at her nose. It did not comfort her for some reason, but she darted through without examining the emotion.

Several rift acolytes had arrived, beginning to prepare for the massive rifts needed for the assault, and they looked at her strangely when she tumbled out of the air. She ignored the confused priestesses and abandoned the rift generator on the floor of the embarkation room as she raced toward the control deck. The *Hydra's Will* had awakened in her absence, and warriors of every discipline had started to assemble. She darted and pushed through corridors and twining side passages and did not slow until the paired Hatriya at the control deck's armored doors challenged her. A barked order from within stopped them.

"Let her approach," the warlord's voice boomed out.

Marikan To still nodded respectfully to the guards as she hurried past.

Mamaro To and Lady Zineda both stood on the command dais, though Marikan To could not help but notice the high priestess's discreet distance from the throne. "My satra of Sarva," Mamaro To said in a pleased tone. His attention clearly stayed mostly on the data flowing across the huge displays in the air above him. "What do you require? Are your sisters ready?"

Marikan To hesitated, caught off guard by the question. She dropped to her knee and lowered her head. "Forgive me, my warlord, but I have not overseen their preparations. My guthrra are reliable and know their duty." She winced slightly at the automatic choice of words, given her own recent breach of duty, and pushed on. "I have been pursuing a—a trail."

"What?" Zineda perked up, turning her gaze fully on Marikan To. "You were to be resting and preparing for this battle. What could have pulled you so strongly to draw you from your duty?"

There's that word again, Marikan thought. "I do ask, again, for forgiveness, but—"

"Peace, my lady," Mamaro To said, giving them both a calm look. "To be independent and follow her instincts is the place of the Sarva, and the finest of them become satra for that reason. She has done her duty in training her subordinates well, so her guthrra are more than capable of preparing her sisters for this attack. If Marikan To felt compelled to follow a trail, then she should do so." He smiled. "That is also her duty."

Zineda nodded, though she still looked unhappy. Marikan To could not blame her.

"But now she is here, and eager for a fight, if I read her right. I must go oversee the Hatriya vanguard. Make your report to High Priestess Zineda and then join your sisters. Together, we shall bleed this world until we find what we seek." He strode from the dais and the control deck, calling for his armor.

Marikan To looked to Lady Zineda.

The high priestess turned back to the huntress, clearly a bit distracted. "Please, satra. Tell me what you have learned."

The younger noh took three breaths. "My lady, I found . . . something. I don't know what, exactly." She hesitated only an instant, wondering why she had not named the Source, but she had to push on. "I sme—I followed an esper trail. I don't know another way to describe it, but I knew it was esper and it lay like blood from wounded prey." She kept her eyes focused on the platform at Zineda's feet, but she could tell that the high priestess had leaned forward. "It led me to a, ah . . . ." She shook her head and drove on. "A person, a chee. One of their living machines. She was locked in a cell on one of the pirate ships, but I could almost see it." She raised her gaze and paused at the intent expression on Zineda's face. "The esper came out of her like water from a spring. It flowed forth in limitless amounts. I—" She shook her head. "I have never seen or heard of anything like it before today. Perhaps it was the artifact we have sought, but I don't think so. It was still a being, not an object."

"There are stories," Zineda said, at least partly to herself. The high priestess licked her lips. "Stories of those who could see or sense the esper. Perhaps . . ." She trailed off and refocused on the huntress. "Tell me where. Show me where you found it." She rose, confident and imperious. "Point me to that place, and I will see what you have found. You may, perhaps, have saved us much trouble." She shrugged and smiled without much kindness. "Or brought us a great deal more. We shall see."

Greater trepidation than she cared to admit churned Marikan To's stomach as she led her high priestess to the embarkation chamber.

CHAPTER 14

Marianne, unknown point, real space

Malya tapped her foot on the floorboards. She stopped with some effort when she noticed, but that nearly drove her back to pacing. She settled for tapping her foot. Finally she shot a glance at Harker, sitting quietly at his table with stylus in hand, and groaned. He did not look up.

"How can you just sit there? What's taking Cross so long? Why did he want us to drop into real space anyway? I'm sure the drives could use the charge, but we were fine, weren't we? Aren't we on a schedule?" She threw her hands up at his calm silence. "How can you just sit there?"

"Patience," he said, raising his left hand. He made a few quicker notes and then sat back, turning his chair to look at her. "I don't know what the lord paladin requires, but he's aware of our urgency. If he felt it important enough to interrupt the journey, then I believe him. We'll just have to wait and see."

She eyed him balefully. "You're awfully calm for someone rushing to save the world."

He raised one eyebrow. "You're awfully anxious for someone who doesn't quite believe she should be here."

She stuck her tongue out at him. "Oh, ha, ha. You're just lucky I decided to tag along."

"I am," he replied, serious, and turned back to the table.

Malya sighed and tried to think of something else to say—she had stopped nervously tapping as they talked—but the door chime interrupted her.

"Enter," Harker called.

Sebastian Cross strode into Harker's cabin, and Malya found

her nervousness evaporating in favor of good old-fashioned worry. The paladin had a worn, tight look to his features. He carried a small device in his hand, and the Paragon Jeanne trailed behind. She looked almost as upset as Cross. A few steps behind them came Rin, Betty, and Lug.

"Forgive me, Captain," Cross said as Harker stood and frowned at the procession. "This matter concerns her high—" He cleared his throat. "Excuse me, the princess and her companions, so I took the liberty of bringing them along."

Harker nodded and motioned for Cross to continue.

The paladin stepped to the table and set the device on a clear spot. "This portable projector contains all the current encryption keys for Alliance Security and the Peers' highest priority messages. We received this message on our slip-comms less than an hour ago, but I could only share it with you on this device." He glanced at Malya, whose heart chilled with the look. "And it's the sort of thing that needs to be delivered in person."

Harker dimmed the lights as the projector flickered into life. The face of a woman with bobbed pink hair and bright eyes formed before them. She had laugh lines around her mouth and eyes, but her face remained serious as she spoke.

"This message is to all Alliance Security and affiliated agencies. I have received credible intelligence of an omega code event, repeat omega code event. At least one noh dragon fleet has made some sort of bargain with Calico Kate to lead an unknown but likely substantial number of corsairs in a joint attack on Ulyxis within two standard weeks. I repeat, credible intelligence points to a joint pirate and noh attack on Ulyxis within two standard weeks. I have not corroborated this intel, but the source is rated beta green at least. Please take all possible precautions. I am proceeding to Ulyxis now."

Cross reached over and shut off the projector. "The rest is repeats and authentication codes," he said, almost apologetically. "It's boring—" He cut off as he looked at Malya.

The princess stared at the empty air where the message had played. She felt disconnected, almost floating. Vaguely, she heard

Harker and Betty cursing. The captain said something about unbelievable boldness, but it barely registered. Someone took her arm, and Malya looked around to see Rin's face very close to her own. Rin said something.

Malya blinked and shook her head. "What?"

"Are you okay?" the sniper repeated. "I think the answer is clearly no. How about you sit—"

Malya shook her hand off. "No." She turned to see the room staring at her. "No! Don't do that. Don't look at me like I might shatter. What are you expecting?"

Cross glanced at the other paladin, and Jeanne stepped toward Malya. "We expect you to scream," she said, her voice firm but warm. "We expect you to shout or cry. We expect any number of perfectly human reactions from you when you discover that your home world and family are very likely the targets of the most rapacious and terrifying slavers and murderers in the galaxy." She shrugged. "Frankly, your current calm is a bit more unnerving."

"I'm really not all that calm, if it makes you feel any better," Malya said. Her arms started to shake. She took a deep breath and turned to Sebastian Cross. "Do you know what is being done?"

The paladin studied her for three breaths before nodding very slightly to himself. "The Six Peers are responding even now, of course. A series of noh raids by three different dragon fleets over the last week has put us on alert and stretched us a bit thin in the sectors around Ulyxis, but it now seems clear that these were intended as diversions. Unfortunately, it means that we must race to consolidate our strength. The Order of Praetor's Hundred should be on-planet any day now, and others soon after. We can but hope that it is enough."

"It's not," Harker said grimly.

Jeanne shot him a poisonous look, but Cross nodded.

"True enough, Captain. I know that Alliance Security has already deployed their strength on Ulyxis, called up their reserves, and is negotiating a contract with Black Diamond." He sighed. "Not ideal, but we all know they are capable soldiers, and for whatever reason, it seems that both Sophia Drake and their Relic

Knight One Shot are available." He shrugged. "Not cheap, but quite effective."

Malya nodded, the information washing over her. She tried to think but kept coming up blank.

"You want to go," Harker said. He looked at her with genuine empathy. "You might make it. From here, straining the slip engines, you might make it."

"I believe it can be done," Cross said, glancing from the princess to the pirate and back. "I have already ordered the *Inexorable Justice* to plot a course. They will likely not arrive before the battle begins, but they will hopefully tip the scales. I will send Navarre Hauer, First of our Paragons. He's already near Ulyxis, having chased the raids around the sector. He is legendary—"

"I know his name," Malya said, realizing only after she had spoken that, in fact, she did. "I'm sorry, Lord Cross. That was rude." She took two deep breaths.

The paladin shrugged. "Understandable. They await only my command to depart."

"You're not going?"

"No. I have given my word to see through this chance to stop the Calamity, and I will. Only the *Justice* and her complement will go to Ulyxis."

Malya nodded, her mind finally sorting through everything. "And you want to know if I will go with them." She had not asked a question, but both Cross and Harker said yes. She drew in a long breath and let it out slowly. "No. Tell them to go now."

Rin and Betty exchanged glances. "Boss," Betty said gently, "we understand. I think everybody does. If you want to go—" She faltered and stopped as Malya turned to her.

"Thanks, chief. Really. But I also promised Captain Harker that I'd go to Origin Point if there was any chance of stopping the Calamity. I think there is, so I'm going. Ulyxis is only one world in this galaxy. There's not much that I—" She stopped, thought, and then chuckled. "Okay, that's not really true. There might be a lot that one more Relic Knight could do on Ulyxis, but it's only one world. I've got a chance to stop the Calamity from eating the whole rest of the universe. I've got to go with that choice." She nodded slowly to the room. "And that planet really hasn't been home for a long time."

"Your family is still there," Harker pointed out.

"And Lord Cross here will make sure that Lord Hauer keeps an eye on them," she said. "As if he needs to be told to take care of the planetary ruling family."

Now Sebastian Cross chuckled.

Malya smiled. "I'm with you, captain."

"A moment, then," Cross said, and opened a comm channel. "Captain Molay, First Paragon, you are ordered to proceed to Ulyxis with all speed."

"Understood," a man's voice replied. "We will update you when we learn the situation."

"Thank you, Lord Hauer," Sebastian said. He paused. "Take care. Something is out of joint here. This looks like a suicide mission, and yet Black Diamond is willing to risk both Drake and One Shot. Send Aspirant Rehfeld to liaise with them, and have her keep her eyes open. Nothing about this situation smells right."

"I completely agree, my lord. At least the fight will be straightforward."

Cross shook his head, smiling. "We can only hope. Strength through honor, Navarre."

"Glory through service, Sebastian," Navarre replied, and the link cut off. Out the armored window, they saw the massive battle cruiser's engines glow as it accelerated, rapidly reaching the impossible speed where it wobbled, bled into multi-spectrum light, and then vanished.

A silence settled over the room. Malya sat and kept staring out at the stars.

"It makes no sense," she heard Jeanne mutter. The woman seemed not to realize that she had spoken, because she looked embarrassed when everyone turned to her. "I mean the attack. Why would the noh drive so deep into Alliance territory? Why would the corsairs assist them? What do any of them have to gain from it?"

"I don't know," Malya said. "From what we just talked about, I don't think anyone knows. Maybe Kenobo could shed some light on it, but I doubt it. In the end, it doesn't matter. Ulyxis will stand or fall with the forces we send. But that fight doesn't matter if we don't succeed."

After a moment, Jeanne nodded.

Malya looked to the others to find them agreeing. "All right then. Let's get on with it."

CHAPTER 15

Hydra's Will, entering Ulyxis orbit

Once the wayfinder assured her he had fixed the proper location, Zineda dismissed Marikan To to join her sisters. Zineda kept her displeasure disguised; those working in the embarkation room had no business knowing her opinion of the Sarva Knight. And in all fairness, she had to admit that she could find no fault with Marikan To's performance or service. This fact did not, in any way, lessen the high priestess's displeasure. If this discovery proved as important as she suspected it would, however, that displeasure might ebb slightly.

The first waves had already departed for the orbital stations around Ulyxis, ravaging the defenders to let the pirates deal more effectively with the Alliance's ships. She could hear the warnings, alerts, and preparations of a dragon ship at war echoing through the *Hydra's Will.* The deck occasionally vibrated from the vicious deep space combat gaining fury around them. Most of the wayfinders and rift acolytes had moved to the holding pens in the ship's bowels to transport the beastmasters and their charges, and Zineda appreciated the emptiness of this space. The air before her rippled and wavered as if from an intense heat and split slowly along a thin seam. It reminded her of the wound that opened when she drew a single claw across soft flesh. She could feel and smell the other ship's atmosphere washing over her like blood.

She inspected the darkened space. As Marikan To had described, she saw the cages and felt the esper around them, or rather the lack of it. Something clearly dampened the movement of energy in the cages, and Zineda found it a wonder that the tracker had sensed the esper at all. "Keep the rift open," she told the wayfinder, "and summon some of my priestesses to join me." She stepped through the portal as the man bowed in reply.

The air felt cool and smelled of cleaning chemicals and fear. An alarm rang in the distance. A yellow light flashed somewhere off to her right, bathing the cages and prisoners in intermittent strobes. Two pirates in worn and patched red uniforms rushed around the corner directly in front of her, their pistols unready. Their surprise cost them their lives. Spite hissed and leapt toward the one on the left, while Zineda lashed out at the other. Her claws sank through the man's neck as if punching through dough. He pawed at the wound while he sank down, unable to scream as his life flowed out over his fingers. She stepped quickly to the other who was still batting at her cypher, and ripped his throat out. She lifted her fingers and twined her tongue around them to catch all the blood that she could. It taught her much about the men she had killed, but she savored it purely for the jolt it gave her.

She strode to the cages. Spite bounded ahead to the prisoner on the left, but Zineda only had eyes for the chee. The robot lay inert, with only a little light flickering in her vacant eyes.

Spite had begun clawing on the other prisoner's legs, and she awoke as the high priestess approached. The short, redheaded woman kicked at the cypher, but when she saw the noh, her eyes went wide, and she began to shake.

"No," she said without strength.

She tried to stand and rush forward at the same time, but her limbs could not support her. She fell, and then twisted as the shackles on her wrist and ankle pulled her up short. She cried out, low and weak, and Zineda saw the marks of clumsy torture across her back, shoulders, and arms. Her captors had beaten and probably lashed her.

"Get away from her," the woman hissed. "Or by all the doctrines of esper, I'll—"

Zineda glanced at the prisoner and smiled. The hungry expression brought the feeble flow of threats to a choking end.

"No," Zineda said. "I don't have an interest in you, little witch, but if you prove bothersome, I might change my mind."

She set her hand gently on the lock of the chee's cage. Raw destruction esper flowed from her, and the lock blackened as after decades of corrosion. The bars on the door bent and drooped like wilting vines. She flexed her fingers, took a firm hold on the ruined metal, and wrenched the gate free. She stepped across the threshold just as the far bulkhead door hissed open. A crowd of corsairs raced in, heavy weapons raised, led by a furious man with a mechanical arm.

"You'll step back from that chee, if you know what's good for you," he bellowed. He leveled his sword in her direction as he closed on Zineda. "She's my prize, and I'll say what happens to her."

"Your prize," Zineda said carefully. Her mind raced, abandoning the idea of attacking almost at once. They could too easily drive her away and then move the chee. She licked at her blood-flecked lips. "You took her?"

"Aye," the man said. "I'm Captain Golden Vance. The *Black Spot* is my ship, and that chee is my prize. Now. Step. Back."

Zineda glanced at the faintly shimmering rift as she moved slowly away from the cage. She could make it if she needed to, but this opportunity was simply too good to abandon yet. "You took her, but you've done nothing with her save this."

Vance frowned but said nothing.

"Yes, there's little more you could do, I expect." She thought of Calico Kate. "There's no profit in that."

"It's nothing to you," he said.

"But what if it could be?" Zineda said quickly. A fish-tailed cypher rose over the captain's shoulder but looked at nothing save for the chee. "If you could have profited from her, you would have already. And what good is a prize that brings no profit?" Zineda spread her arms slowly and held Vance's skeptical gaze. "Perhaps we can both profit from her."

He squinted doubtfully, but the point of his sword lowered. "How?"

"I wish to study her." She saw his defenses start to return and hurried on. "I believe she is an artifact our god desires." She cast doubtful eyes on the recumbent robot. "But I can't see why. I cannot do anything with her until I understand her."

"She's of value to you, then," Vance said. He made no effort to disguise his calculation, so she let her interest show. "I'll not loan her out. If you want her, you buy, and I won't sell cheap." He sneered, though she could see more bravado than actual contempt in the expression—a negotiation tactic. "Your people aren't famous for their wealth, least ways in any form I can use."

She shrugged, showing that the price mattered little to her. "I can give you your life," she tried.

He laughed and lowered the sword completely. "No, you can't, since you're not likely to leave here with your own. But even if you could, that's not enough. There's no good being alive and poor."

She smiled. She had his measure now. "A man who knows what he wants. Good. My people will give you more than your lives." She grinned, showing all her teeth. "We'll give you a fleet."

Vance frowned, suspicious but intrigued, all banter gone from his face. "What do you mean?"

"You're a subordinate to Kate, yes?" His growl told her all she needed to know. "And not happy about it. Good. That speaks to your ambition. Give me the chee, and I will see that you serve no master but that ambition."

"You have no fleet to give. I won't take dragon ships."

"Of course not. We will give you this fleet. In exchange for the chee, we will help you destroy Kate and take her place as king."

The man growled again, and for a moment, she thought she had misjudged him. Then his eyes flashed with the same light as Kate's had. "And how would you go about this?"

"We'll wait until this raid ends, so you gain all your plunder. When you return to the Star Nebula, we will strike at her weakened captains and slay those that will not serve you." The plan lacked nuance and detail but sounded plausible enough, and Vance nodded to her.

"Right, then. I reckon there's a bargain in that. But it's not done." He pointed to the chee. "She stays here, in that cage, until we're back in the nebula and Kate's dead."

"If I can't study her, there's no bargain. I will stay here to do it, but I must begin."

Captain Vance tapped his sword point on the deck plates three times before nodding. "Agreed," he said, "but I kill Kate."

The high priestess shrugged. Vance extended his flesh hand. Zineda took it gingerly and shook.

CHAPTER 16

Black Spot, secondary cargo bay

Zineda sat in the cage next to the remains of the chee. Long slave-hair ropes suspended the robot's frame from the highest bars and strung together her largest pieces in a grotesque parody of her actual form. The high priestess had wasted no time in bringing over her assistants and slowly, gently vivisecting the semiconscious machine. She had kept the chee strung in this loose semblance of her shape to aid understanding, but it had availed her little.

"She certainly feels pain," Zineda said to Spite.

Her venomous cypher hissed happily as she dug out another component from the creation's deformed chest piece and handed over the bundle of twisted wires. The robot moaned slightly, though her eyes never did more than flicker open. Zineda felt a distinct disappointment in that.

"Normally I like them more responsive," she muttered. "Give me your sight," the high priestess commanded, and Spite's eyes went brilliant red with esper.

Zineda examined the metal and stamped carbon composites in her hands, but they gave off only the faintest shimmer. They looked as if they had been dipped in esper, rivulets of it running off and the thin layer of energy still coating the parts. She turned her gaze from one piece to another, all carefully arranged on the floor around her. Everything held only the faintest glimmer of esper, but when she looked back at the robot's nearly hollow shell, the blinding glow returned. She cut the connection to her cypher and let her vision return to normal.

"I don't understand it," she said again. Spite frowned. "I don't see it, but it is there. Where is this opening? What is the origin of the energy flow?"

"Perhaps it is not a part but the whole, mistress," Spite replied in her hissing voice. "What does it matter? She is the Source, and that is enough."

"Is it?" Zineda snapped. The two priestesses closest to the cage jumped at her tone. "She is this great artifact, but what good is that? If I do not know how she functions, then I do not know how to use her. And if we cannot use her, what value is she?"

"That will become clear," Spite said in a soothing tone. "In time, she will be the most valuable slave we have ever taken."

"In time. In time." Zineda nearly spit. "Patience is not something I have in great store just now. I have too much need of leverage." She tapped her claws against the deck plates.

Distantly, through the esper, she could hear Mamaro To calling for her, to ask her council, she supposed.

"Perhaps it is time to bring allies in. Our enemies will arrive soon enough."

Spite nodded.

Zineda regarded her cypher. "Go. Answer my warlord's call and conduct my message to him."

Spite sneered and glanced at the chee. "The Heretic is engaged near the mercenary Relic Knight called One Shot. He can be of little help to us, less even than usual."

Zineda's hand flew like a serpent striking. She caught Spite across the face, the trailing tips of her claws drawing pale blood when they sliced the creature's cheeks. Spite hissed as she recovered, baring her fangs and extending her claws.

"Come at me, little imp," Zineda said through clenched teeth. "I need to hurt something, and you will do if I find nothing else. I have told you before not to speak thus of the Grand Warlord, and I will brook no violation of that."

"He feuds with Nozuki's chosen. He opposes the Anointed One. That is heresy."

"That is the way of our people, as you well know," Zineda said, her frustration dimmed by the outburst. "The conflict makes us stronger, which is as Nozuki desires."

Spite hissed again but relaxed. The thin cuts on the cypher's cheek had already closed. "He would also desire that we take our prize and go," Spite said firmly. "We must take the Source and join the Anointed One and the Herald."

"In good time," Zineda replied smugly. "I will share this prize with whom I choose and when I choose. For now, the warlord is of greater aid to us. Find him and act as my mouthpiece."

The cypher glared at her but vanished in a puff of esper. Zineda called one of the priestesses to her and instructed the young woman to fetch carrying gear from the *Hydra's Will* to transport the chee. She studied the parts around her for a few more moments until she felt the call from Spite. Through the cypher's eyes, she saw her lover's face from a strange angle, looking up his arm. She tasted blood and knew that Spite had bitten him to use the blood as fuel for the connection. She could also see Mamaro To's rising rage and quickly moved to push her mind through her cypher. She could hear him growling with his anger.

"Peace, my warlord," she said, and her own voice came from Spite's small mouth. "I have good news. I have found the artifact we sought. It was concealed among the corsairs all along."

Mamaro To rage grew. "They betrayed us?"

"Not yet," Zineda replied, trying to sound amused. "This was unknowing. I have traded with the captain called Golden Vance. We shall acquire the artifact once this raid ends and we have assisted him in deposing of Calico Kate."

Explosions echoed from behind Mamaro To, but he did not flinch. "Can we not just seize it?"

"We may have to," she replied. "It will not be long before other Knights discover our prize. The warrior called One Shot, who now opposes you, will soon learn that it is here through her cypher and likely find it. I suspect Kate will discover it even sooner, and others likely will too. You must prevent One Shot from leaving the surface. The pirates will want to flee before long; they are looting even now, and their courage will not last long after their holds are full. Keep the Knight in place only until then, my love."

Mamaro To looked skeptical but determined. "She shall not leave the planet. But can you use the artifact? What will it do for us?"

"I do not yet know, but I do not need to. That Nozuki commands it is enough, and He shall reveal its use in His time. And then, we shall be the most exalted of his servants." She mirrored his broad smile and shook at his triumphant roar.

CHAPTER 17

Lucky Chance, slip space, entering Ulyxis orbit

Kisa could see Fiametta glancing uneasily at her. Again. She rolled her eyes but tried to keep her frustration out of her voice. "I can hear you thinking, Fia. Just say it."

Fiametta cleared her throat. "Fine. Are you sure about this?" The bright spectrum smear of slip space reflected on Fiametta's doubtful expression.

Kisa quirked an eyebrow. "Am I sure? No, of course not." She settled back in the pilot chair's deep cushions.

She tapped a secondary monitor to bring the real-space projections of Ulyxis near-space and high orbit onto the main screen. From behind them both, Candy and Cola leaned forward for a better view. Scratch crawled onto Kisa's shoulder. Though only a rendering based on what little data the sensors could gather in slip space, it looked bad. Debris from numerous planetary defense installations filled the edges of the image, while pirate vessels of every description and dragon ships from at least three fleets dominated the center.

"But have you got a better idea?" Kisa asked.

"Not that doesn't begin with getting out of here," Fiametta said.

Kisa saw motion from the corner of her eye, and glanced back to find Candy, Cola, and Scratch all nodding.

Candy shrugged. "She's only saying what we're all thinking. We're still going in."

"Then I don't want to hear another word unless it's a suggestion for a better way in." Kisa glared at Scratch. "Traitor."

The feline cypher only settled down and started cleaning his paws.

Kisa sighed. "Actually, Candy, you can tell us what your message from Alliance Security said."

"Not much useful, I don't think," Candy replied. She made a concerted effort to keep up her usual bubbly good humor, though she wasn't succeeding very well. "Intelligence thinks the Source is some kind of weapon. They're not sure of that, but given what little we know, it's a reasonable guess."

"Pfft," Fiametta snorted. "Of course you'd think it was a weapon."

Candy let the comment pass. Kisa and Fiametta shared a glance that meant that they both knew from the silence just how seriously Candy took the situation.

"We can't afford not to think of it as a weapon," Candy went on. "Even if it only exists to bring flowers and puppies into the world, until we know that for sure, we have to assume that the noh and corsairs are planning to detonate it, or whatever, on Ulyxis. Nothing else makes sense of all the data."

Fiametta humphed, and Candy sighed.

"All the Alliance knows about the Source comes from the few scattered mentions in the Doctrine histories we retained after the Sundering War. And those references are kind of the definition of vague," Candy said pointedly.

Fiametta rolled her eyes, crossed her arms, but agreed. "Yeah, that's true. I've been scouring every reference I can find, without access to the actual Library on Catermane, and they all agree that the Source is some staggeringly powerful esper generator." She shrugged. "Beyond that, who knows? It's connected to the Calamity, though. Somehow."

"Well, whatever it is, if anything big is going to go down on Ulyxis, I need to stop it." Candy sat back. "There's not much of the Alliance left, and I cannot let any more of it go without a fight."

"Well, strap in, ladies," Kisa said, closing her own restraints, "'cause the ride is about to get rough. Real-space transition in six seconds."

Kisa was already spinning the *Lucky Chance* as they punched back into reality. She cut sharply to starboard and dove below the planet's ecliptic plane as she engaged the ship's cloaking. Waves of night-black esper rippled over the vessel, concealing it from electronic, mechanical, or organic detection. The esper signature would show up, she knew, but it would be imprecise, useless for targeting solutions, and time consuming to get a fix on. It came down to speed now.

She edged the ship back into the thick of the chaotic melee. She slipped around wreckage and ducked under dragon ships like a cat stalking in high grass. Kisa's tail looped back and forth behind her chair, and Scratch purred directions in her ear. She glanced around once, when they broke briefly into a clear space, and saw both cyphers swaying in synch, almost like they were sniffing out the Source. Their eyes blazed with cool white esper. A moment later, they both leapt onto the control panel in front of Kisa and pointed in the same direction. "There," Scratch said in his rolling voice. "There, my pet."

Kisa dove the ship under a roiling furball of two pirate ships and the dying remains of an Alliance corvette determined to take its attackers down with it. There, just beyond, she saw a tall, ugly Galleon-class starship, or what had once been one. Years of hard service, inadequate maintenance, and piecemeal repairs had resulted in a vessel that more resembled a patchwork whale than the darting shark the designers had claimed inspired them. It had a predatory look nevertheless, and Kisa saw in a moment how too many captains would underestimate that ship to their cost.

"Hold on," she said, and brought her craft around to circle the pirate ship and look for a way in.

"There," Scratch said and pointed. "There. Starboard bay six. That is closest to our prey, pet."

"Bad news, hairball," Fiametta said. "That's a maintenance bay. No way this ship fits in there."

Scratch hissed but without any venom in it.

Cola turned back to Candy. "We can fit," he said, his voice firm, though a little high pitched for Kisa's taste. "We can get there."

"Excellent," Scratch said. "The Source is hurt, badly—well beyond my pet's ability to repair."

Everyone looked at Cola, who nodded.

Scratch huffed at not being trusted. "You must secure the Source. Keep it stable until we can heal or repair it. We will dock in the hangar and meet you."

"How?" Candy asked. "I can cut my way in, but they're sure to have the exterior doors on lockdown."

"I can take care of that," Fiametta said and started working the panel to her right. "I can give you a disposable one-shot spike. Plug it in on any network jack and we'll have a backdoor to their system. I can open the hangar with that."

Candy looked at Kisa, who shrugged.

"It's not a terrible idea, and I don't have a better one," Kisa admitted. "Suit up. We'll pop the cargo door open for you as we pass. Signal when you're ready. Don't take too long."

"You either," Candy said. She caught the datastick that Fiametta tossed at her and dashed from the bridge, Cola a bounce behind.

In the silence that filled the space, Kisa looked carefully at Fiametta. Her friend sat rigid, staring out the viewport, as if her glare could burn holes in the *Black Spot*.

Kisa set her jaw and turned back to flying. "I'm sure she's there," she said quietly. "We'll get her."

Fiametta licked her lips, clearly thinking unpleasant things. "I doubt it. That place is going to be a mess and even worse once we get in there." She rubbed her face. "I—I don't think we'll get to her, if she's still alive."

Kisa felt sick, but her mind kept working over the problem as she circled close to the maintenance bay. She said nothing for a while and just concentrated on flying in the tight melee. Her mind kept working at the problem, though, like a cat with a toy.

"I didn't think Squall was on Vance's crew," she finally said, focusing on a detail that kept nagging at her. "What's she doing on his ship?"

"I've no idea," Fiametta replied quietly. "Since she left us, she's sailed with Kate almost exclusively." Her brow furrowed, and she glanced at Kisa. The detail had clearly caught on her mind too. "Why?"

"Well, I can't imagine her volunteering to join Vance's crew. I think people are condemned to do that. So she had to be there for a reason, probably connected to pirate politics, for lack of a better word." She shrugged. "At least, that's the way I'd bet."

A light went off on the console. Fiametta tapped it. Candy's voice crackled over the small speaker, indicating that she was prepped and ready by the bay doors.

Kisa glanced around at the arrangement of vessels surrounding them and calculated the best odds. She fed the engines power and pushed the *Chance* into a tight turn. She popped open the cargo doors and swung the ship side-on, as if skidding toward the pirate vessel. A feathering burst from the maneuvering thrusters slowed them sharply, and the momentum flung Candy and her relic clear of the cargo bay. Kisa could feel the esper shifting around them as she slammed the throttle forward, the probabilities of different outcomes changing every second. The *Chance* lurched and accelerated, and she had to spin and flip around to avoid three collisions in rapid succession. She prayed softly that she had not used up all her luck on that.

As she circled the ship back around toward the far docking bay, she noticed Fiametta watching her closely. "What?"

"You're plotting something. What is it?"

Kisa smiled and relaxed her touch on the control yoke. "Open a comm channel to Kate and find out."

"Kate? Why do you want to talk to her?"

Kisa just smiled and nodded at the communications controls.

Fiametta looked both amused and confused as she touched the comm switches. She started by spinning through the local frequencies—all predictably crammed with battle chatter—until she found the group that the pirates were using. Violet-gold esper crackled from the Doctrine mage's fingertips as she adjusted the controls, and a second later, the speaker crackled with an open connection. A confused and irritated pirate comms operator demanded to know who they were and what they wanted.

Fiametta grinned, and more esper flashed from her fingers. "Boring conversation anyway," she said as the frequency shifted again, riding an electromagnetic trail from the starship down an otherwise secure link. Static crackled briefly before another connection opened with the sounds of battle in the background. A grainy holoimage appeared, and from the corner of her eye, Kisa saw Kate's skeletal cypher Skully toss what looked like a round, black bomb with a lit fuse toward a group of paladins. She sighed.

Fiametta cut the visual feed to preserve the signal and cranked up the gain. A second later, Calico Kate's unmistakable brogue came through loud, clear, and annoyed. "This better be good. I'm a might bit busy just now."

"Hello, Kate," Kisa said cheerfully. "Just wanted to check in."

"Who is—" The confusion drained from Kate's voice almost immediately. "Kisa. I might have known. Last I saw you was on Embry station. How'd you survive the fire?"

Kisa winced but managed to keep it out of her voice. "Trade secret."

"And your bloody luck. You should be dead."

"Hah! Neither you nor the Guild are that lucky. Don't you want to know how we found this channel?"

"No. I just want you to get off the line."

"Not yet," Kisa replied with mock sweetness. "I've got news that you'll want to hear. See, I happen to know that you're in this mess because the noh are looking for something, some kind of artifact."

"How in the dead stars do you—"

"And I know," Kisa interrupted, "that you're not stupid enough to trust them." She distinctly heard Kate snort at that. "So what would you say if I told you that the artifact they're after is actually the Source?"

"The what?"

Kisa rolled her eyes. "The Source. It's connected to the Calamity, somehow, and it's a staggeringly powerful esper generator."

The explosions in the background dimmed as Kate took cover. "Now that last part I'm interested in. What of it?"

"Well, you're not stupid enough to trust the noh, but Vance might be. What would you say if I told you that he's got the Source on his ship right now?"

"I'd say, if so, why hasn't he done anything with it?"

"Who says he hasn't?" Kisa replied. "Think about it. Maybe he's just dumb enough to think he can make the noh a better offer than you can. So. What would you say to that?"

"I'd ask why you're telling me this."

"Because he's also got Squall." A sudden, ominous silence radiated from the speaker. Kisa and Fiametta exchanged glances.

"And how might you know that, kitty cat?" Kate asked with deadly calm.

Kisa closed her eyes and rolled the dice. "Sweetie, you know it too. I'm going to guess that you put her on his ship to keep an eye on him. When was the last time she checked in?"

The silence on the other end of the line dragged out for too many heartbeats before they heard Kate swear. "That sadistic, self-serving bloody bastard. He's selling us out—selling me out. Once again," she said to Kisa, all the banter gone, "why tell me this?"

"Because the Source is bigger than us, all of us. If the Source is here, then the Calamity has finally reached the Last Galaxy. You know what that means. I'm outside the *Black Spot* right now, and I'm going in after the Source. Vance or the noh will do terrible things with it, and while I know you don't care about that, I know you do care about Squall. And Vance and the noh will do—and likely have done—terrible things to her." And you can't afford to let his treachery stand, Kisa mentally added. She let the spoken and unspoken thoughts hang between them.

"Don't think, darling, that I'm fooled," Kate said, the banter back along with a great deal of venom. "But I do appreciate the message. Do us both a service, hmm? Stay out of my way. I'd hate to have to kill you while still owing you a favor." The comm line went dead.

Kisa turned to Fiametta and grinned. "Well?"

Fiametta shook her head but could not help smiling. "You're playing longer odds than usual. Let's hope it works."

"Oh, it'll work. I just hope it works out well," Kisa replied, steering them into the docking bay. "That's the real gamble."

Candy flew out of the *Lucky Chance's* hold like Kisa had launched her from a slingshot. Candy smiled tightly, recalling the last time she had been in a slingshot. She fired her relic's jets and spun toward the *Black Spot's* maintenance bay. Star and sunlight raced across her visor. Soundless explosions bathed everything in the lurid colors of igniting oxygen. The pressure suit and air supply would hold for a few minutes, but she fully intended to be outside for only a few seconds.

Her relic unfolded as she flew, its dart-like prow pointed at the pirate ship and the oddly back-canted legs tucked up and ready to land. She extended the machine's gangly arms to aid in maneuvering, and the relic's long, slightly curved blade flew out into its hand. Esper glittered along the weapon's edge. Candy adjusted her flight just enough to strike the seams around the maintenance bay's sealed doors. An opening appeared, peeling open like a flower as air rushed out. She reversed with a flip that would have broken bones in an atmosphere and slipped in just before the emergency bulkheads slammed shut.

The bay was relatively small and cluttered with loaders, lifters, and other labor machinery in various states of disrepair. Candy gratefully pulled her helmet off as she soared over the mess. She spotted the main access and hovered next to it long enough to jam the datastick into a corroded port beside the door. It lit up and hummed happily.

Candy pulled back, got some altitude, and fired a blast of esper from the relic's shoulder-mounted cannon to punch through the interior door. Pulling the machine's limbs in close, she dove into the corridor. Much of the crew had gone for boarding parties, but the *Black Spot* did not lack for defenders. Small knots of pirates came to challenge her in disjointed groups. She struck them as fast as she could, to keep them off balance, but she still did not see anything like the Source.

"Cola," she shouted over her shoulder. "I need you to find this thing." She spun the relic as it bowled into four corsairs and sliced them apart.

The foxlike cypher laughed gleefully, clinging to the back of the relic. His usual soda bottle was wide open, drenching the walls and decking in sticky sweet syrup. "One second," he replied, giggling. He leapt off and snatched up something from one of the fallen pirates. Candy pulled up, confused, and instinctively caught the thing he tossed at her. "Here," he said, and climbed back aboard.

It took Candy a second to realize that he'd taken a communicator. She stuck its interface end into a port just past her control yoke and immediately heard the internal ship's communication. An unexpected attack had pulled most of the remaining crew off to the upper decks. Sounds like someone that they had not expected to fight, she thought, frowning. If she didn't know better, she would think that they were being boarded by other pirates.

Then her own comm beeped. A quick look showed a short message from Kisa indicating that they were almost in and something about a distraction.

Candy grinned but did not have time to think too much. Help was coming, and that would have to be enough. She turned back to find Cola stock-still and staring with eyes gone glowing white. He raised his hand and pointed to the right, still staring straight ahead. "There. That way. In the secondary hold."

"I need better directions than that," she said.

He pointed down the hall to their left. She sped off that way, twisting around two more tight turns before flying into a larger corridor that ended in a reinforced double-door.

"That'll do," she shouted and fired her weapons.

The doors buckled but held.

"Hang on!" she shouted. She felt Cola tuck into the small of her back. Candy ducked her head and turned to lead with her relic's shoulder. The impact rattled her teeth and scrambled her brain for a second, but it sent the bulkhead doors flying.

One of the doors scythed through a pair of noh women with drawn daggers. Beyond them, Candy saw maybe half a dozen cages set up along the back wall with only two occupied. One prisoner was a small, auburn-haired woman who clutched at the bars in clear pain and frustration. That would be Squall. A glowing creature, violet and white with a fish's tail, hovered near the small woman and fed her esper.

Candy looked to the next nearest cell and saw a horrific sight. A chee hung suspended and literally eviscerated from the cage's twisting bars. Her parts lay spread out across the floor below her, all coated in lubricants and sealing oil. Still more vital fluids dripped slowly from the robot's limp frame. Any organic creature would have died long since, unless kept unnaturally alive, but the chee managed to feebly rotate her head and some life flickered in her eyes. She moaned softly, as if trying to be heard.

The chee did not command Candy's full attention, however, because a nightmare rose to move between her and the prisoner. Tall by any standard, the noh woman who fixed burning, baleful eyes on Candy wore little more than a few strips of cloth and a dozen long prayer scrolls draped from her shoulders, hips, and horns. Oil and coolant coated her hands, arms, and powerful legs. The noh woman stopped and regarded the Alliance Knight with a seething hatred. Red destruction esper roiled around her form like an aura, and tendrils of crimson energy writhed along the ground at her feet.

"The Source is mine, girl," the noh said in thickly accented Standard. "As is your life."

CHAPTER 18

Blade of Israbad, Shattered Sword corvette, Origin
Point

Malya clutched the rail around the raised command dais on the assault corvette's spartan bridge. The princess had been vaguely disappointed at the far less adorned or embellished interior of the *Blade* compared to the few other paladin ships she had boarded during this trip, but she supposed that reflected the captain's nature. Captain Corvan, a white-haired human with the easy stance and air of a lifelong spacer, stood calm and stern on the dais behind Malya as his boxy, stout ship maneuvered sharply through the debris field. His gaze shifted smoothly between the screens on his console, the holographic display above their heads, and the wide view ports surrounding them.

"Entering real space as far out as we did has proven useful, despite this mess," he said, somewhat grudgingly.

"Well, Captain Harker has been here before, and none of the rest of us can say that. Seemed wise to heed his advice." She worked hard not to clutch the safety rail and turned a smile on him that she hoped was wide and pleased but she suspected actually looked nervous.

Corvan smiled back with only half of his mouth. "True, though it still rankles a bit to rely on a pirate for so much of this."

"Strange days indeed," said Sebastian Cross as he joined Malya just below the dais. Beside him, the holographic head of Captain Harker flickered and came into focus.

Malya turned from him to the overhead display as one of the larger asteroids glowed and acquire a number of computer tags.

"Well, ladies and gentlemen," Harker said, his voice crackly with interference, "there it is. Not much to look at, but like all great dramas, the Calamity begins very small. Frankly, I was expecting more defenders. Our scanners show only two vessels."

"As do ours," Cross said, referring to the data pad in his hand. "Large ones, though. Dragon ships."

Malya glanced at one of the secondary displays above them as it dissolved into an enlarged sensor composite of the enemy ships. They loomed over the asteroid like great storm clouds.

"They're—oh." Harker's brow furrowed. "We have confirmed that one of them is the *Wrath of Wyrms*."

Malya frowned at the red wedges that appeared on the larger display and back at the enlarged composites. "Why do I know that name?"

"Because it's the personal ship of Kasaro To, the Noh Empire's only known Relic Knight," Sebastian Cross said. He looked concerned for the first time since leaving slip space. "Now we know why the defense is so thin. We had thought that the entirety of Dragon Fleet To was at Ulyxis, and they must have had no more strength to spare. But if Kasaro To is here, then the Point's defenders have a great deal of strength already."

"More than I expected them to have, since I doubt they anticipated an attack by two Relic Knights," Harker said, and he frowned too. "Even so, if the accounts of the Herald are accurate, she would not leave this to chance. We should—"

Pings and chimes sounded out on three sides of the bridge behind the corsair. "Unknown contact, 101 by 087." "Cloaked contacts, several, bearing in from 299 by 304." "Esper flares, four, all 180 by 184. They're almost on top of us!"

"Ambush," Harker said with an unnerving calm. "Actions stations. Evasive maneuvers, red blossom pattern. Paladins, follow our lead and keep a distance of at least 300 kilometers. Get me firing solutions on those cloaked contacts. All commands are to protect the paladin ships and deliver them to Origin Point." He looked over at Cross. "Your ships are not well-suited to this sort of fight, Lord Cross. We will clear the way and join you when we can."

"No, that means you'll—" Cross paused, considering. He showed no pride at Harker's assumption of command or dispute with the tactical decisions, simply concerned for lives that he felt responsible for. He finally set his jaw and nodded. "Thank you, captain. Divines protect you."

Harker nodded, his features grave, and cut the link.

Cross turned to Captain Corvan. "We have our course. Send to all commands: use the pirate craft as shields for as long as possible, and make best speed to Origin Point."

Corvan nodded and began relaying orders.

Malya made her way forward until she had nearly pressed against the armored glass viewport. The debris field flashed past her, but in the darkness between the asteroids, she saw black shapes racing in front of the distant stars. Drive flares and bolts of black energy wreathed in jagged arcs of violet esper flashed across her view. Off to her left, just out of sight, something exploded silently, and a violently expanding ball of gas and flame threw brilliant orange light across razor-edged fighter craft. They suggested nothing so much as daggers.

"What are they?" she muttered.

Mr. Tomn hopped to the lip of the viewport and stared out with her. "They are murder," he said so quietly that only she could hear. "They are the armies of oblivion, and they've come to kill the universe."

She looked at him, shocked less by his words than by the serious, nearly terrified tone of his voice.

He looked at her. "They are what is wrong, what has been interfering."

"Then we shall stop them," Sebastian Cross said quietly.

Malya jumped, and even Mr. Tomn looked surprised as he turned to the paladin. Cross's cypher stood on the deck in front of him and nodded his armored head.

"I have read Harker's accounts of these creatures that aid the noh," Sebastian continued. His voice rose so it reached the entire bridge.

"I have read Captain Harker's reports on the creatures that

aid our enemies; they are beautiful, terrible, and utterly devoid of compassion. They fight and maim and kill for no other reason than the act of destruction itself. Life is nothing to them, and so they do the Calamity's work. They are the darkness of the empty sky. They are the end of all we know."

He had opened a comm channel at some point; she could hear a vague echo of his voice in her earpiece.

"But we have always stood against the encroaching night, and we have never gone quietly. We have never bent our knee to raiders, to reavers, to tyrants or terrors, and we shall not bend before these bitter angels. They come to kill our galaxy? Let them try. We are the guardians on the walls of the world, and we have never yet fallen. We are the spear in the storm."

She felt the corvette accelerating as if moved by his words.

"We are the life-sworn of the Second of the Six Peers," Cross nearly shouted. "We are the Shattered Sword, and we will not be denied! Strength through honor."

Across the bridge and over the comms, Malya heard what sounded like every paladin in the sector shout back to their First, "Glory through service."

"You sure know how to work a crowd," Malya said quietly after Cross closed the comm channel.

"We're all still mortal, and that means that we all need a boost sometimes," the paladin replied. They all took hold of the bulkhead around the viewport as the ship swerved and slipped to avoid asteroids and incoming fire.

"My lord," Captain Corvan said firmly above the low roar of a ship in combat. "We've received a signal from the pirates. It appears to be landing coordinates for the asteroid." He frowned. "I'm concerned, as scans show the location to be in treacherous terrain."

"What does the message say, exactly?" Cross asked.

Corvan looked dubious. "It simply lists the coordinates and says, 'Compliments of the witch.' Nothing more."

"Then that is our destination, Captain. If Soliel says it, I believe it. Coordinate with the other ships for landing sites at that location."

Corvan hesitated only a second before nodding and opening a secure channel.

Cross glanced back at Malya. "Princess, we should get to our assault shuttles. I don't expect the ride in to be smooth, but it will be short."

She nodded and followed.

Kasaro To stalked the rugged plains of the asteroid. Though enormous for what it was, the rock should not have held even so thin an atmosphere as it had, and he wondered again at the time and energy that the Herald's people had expended to drag this piece of debris into place and prepare it for use. That led, once more, to wondering why; what did they hope to achieve here? He ground his teeth, thinking again of the Herald's deflections, condescension, and outright arrogance. He slammed his foot down and pulverized several esper crystals. The multihued crystals grew thickly over much of the asteroid's surface, some as tall as ancient trees, and bathed everything in rainbow-tinted reflections. He ground the crystals further underfoot, feeling somewhat better for it, and stalked toward the plateau and the Herald.

She stood on the promontory and stared at the black sky. She did not acknowledge his unsubtle approach or flinch when he slammed his tetsubo into the ground behind her. Indeed, she waited six whole heartbeats before glancing over her shoulder at him. He met her gaze and waited. If she wanted to play games, then he would play too. She finally turned to fully face him with a strange look in her eyes, as if acknowledging he had scored a point. "What is it that you wish, Kasaro To?"

"Your women tell me that the central chamber is prepared," he said, doing nothing to disguise his displeasure. "They have begun expanding the other caverns. My warriors are ready and waiting impatiently. We have readied the ground around your refuge, should any of our enemies actually appear."

She quirked an eyebrow at his words and tone, and he wanted to strike the faint smirk from her porcelain features. "Excellent. I assume you have more to say about your inaction to this point."

He rumbled but kept it low. "None of my objections have changed, because nothing else has changed. We are reavers and slayers, not sentries. We should not be wasted here nursemaiding your witches."

"Then rejoice, Anointed of Nozuki," she replied, as patronizing as ever. "Our enemies approach at speed. I imagine it will be novel to have them come to you, but your people have proven adaptable and unflappable."

Kasaro To snarled. "Do not toy with me, Amelial. I've no patience for it. You have treated us like dogs long enough. We are not your pawns or your lackeys. We do not serve at your pleasure; I least of all. We are allies. We cooperate. If our enemies truly are come, then we will slay them all, but we will not do it for you. We will do it because we are pleased to do it." He leaned in slightly. "And you will thank us for it."

Her smirk widened just slightly. "Of course, Kasaro To. You fight at your pleasure and we are grateful. We will show that gratitude, as one would show favor to a most faithful hound."

Kasaro To quirked an eyebrow. His free hand struck like lightning, closing around the Herald's throat with the force of an iron vice. He lifted her effortlessly as he rose to his full height and brought her eyes level with his. She looked so small, he reflected. Void esper raced around her instinctively and pulled his immense white mane around his head and past the curving blades rising from the back of his armor. He brought her within inches of his long tusks. He could see deep red esper coursing beneath the skin of his arm and rising around him like bloody snowflakes. For just an instant, he saw doubt in her eyes—she wondered if she had pushed him too far. Not quite, he thought, but nearly.

"Never forget, little Herald, that all hounds have teeth, and even the most faithful can be kicked once too often."

"Release me," she said with the faintest rasp. He sensed the effort she was putting into sounding unperturbed and tightened his grip.

"Of course," he replied. "When I choose to, and because I choose to. Now answer me truly: do you see our enemies approach?"

"I do," she said, her voice weakening. "And in force. The pirate Harker approaches, but he brings with him paladins. I sense great strength among them, likely at least one other Relic Knight. Their order has held your vaunted warriors in check for millennia. Do you feel equal to this fight?"

Kasaro To laughed and tightened his grip. "I cannot count the paladins I have slain. I will add this Knight's head to my relic if he proves a worthy foe. But worthy or not, I will rend his body and drink his blood."

"Release me." Her voice sounded faint, and her face had grown paler.

He tossed Amelial aside like an unwanted rag. "I will prepare my warriors. I assume that you have already engaged them with spacecraft that you have kept concealed nearby."

He could see her surprise, though she hid it well.

His smiled widened. "Good; my ships are ill-suited to such combat, but they shall attack those who slip past your nets. We will feast on any who manage to reach the surface. Have no fear for your safety, Amelial. The pirates and paladins will not reach your hole."

She rose, and only his long association let him see the effort she expended to remain calm and sound strong. "See that they do not. We must be undisturbed for our work to succeed. The time is nearly come. And remember this, chosen of your god," she nearly spat. "You believe yourself the embodied will of Nozuki. Perhaps you really are. But I have witnessed the death of gods as mighty as yours, and I will again. We all have a part in this drama. Do not forget yours."

He did not look back as he strode away, merely waving his hand dismissively. Her words were all howl and no fang. Battle lay before him—he could smell it now. That was all that mattered. There would be time to deal with the Herald and her people afterward. He smiled at the idle thought of Amelial in one of his slave pens. He almost laughed as he called to a nearby priestess and demanded a rift to the *Wrath of Wyrms*. He had berserkers to prepare.

CHAPTER 19

Outside the *Black Spot,* Ulyxis orbital space

Kisa focused on keeping the *Chance* stable by the bay doors. Fighter craft and plasma beams whipped by around them, and she feared she would grind her teeth to nubs. So when the panel in front of Fiametta glowed, blinked, and started scrolling data, Kisa nearly jumped out of the pilot's couch. "What? What happened?"

"She's in," Fiametta replied, running her hand over the controls. "And the spike is in place." She glanced at her friend. "Deep breaths, oh great Relic Knight."

"Well, there's a lot going on," Kisa mumbled. Scratch looked smug.

"Okay, let me open the—"

Orange lights flashed urgently across the top of three control panels as a warning tone sounded around them.

Kisa tapped an icon. "Slip shadow. Something coming out of slip space very near to us." She blinked. "Something really, really big."

"I—" Fiametta swallowed. "I see it."

"What? No, you shouldn't be able to see . . ."

Kisa trailed off as she followed her friend's extended arm to a huge swath of space nearly over the planet's north pole. The scattered stars wavered and went blurry, as if seen through a heat shimmer. It looked like an actual shadow had fallen over a section of the sky.

"That's . . . That's—"

An instant later, a staggeringly huge battlecruiser ripped its way into reality above Ulyxis.

"Holy Mother of Night!" Kisa shouted and scrambled to keep

the *Chance* steady. "What is that thing?"

"It's flying Shattered Sword colors," Fiametta managed after a few seconds. She alternated between trying to read the data in front of her and gaping at the battlecruiser. "So I think it officially qualifies as the cavalry."

The ship hauled up away from the planet's powerful gravity well and twisted on its long axis. Ready starfighters launched from bays near its bow and stern. Its path took it across the midsection and stern of a massive dragon ship that looked almost proportional by comparison. In an impressive display of spacemanship and coordination, the battlecruiser's starboard cannons fired a rolling broadside that raked the noh ship at close range. The paladins' heavy guns punched through the ancient craft like bricks through paper. Secondary explosions rippled through the reaver vessel, and large sections of the superstructure ripped away. The dragon ship shuddered, listed, and began a slow and uncontrolled fall toward the planet below.

"They've been in real space for all of ten seconds," Kisa muttered. She shook her head. "Call them." She looked over at Fiametta and slapped her shoulder to get her attention. "Call them. Now. Tell them that we're here and to leave the *Black Spot* alone. They could blow us out of the sky by accident. Say it's a hostage rescue or whatever you think will work." She shrugged as Fiametta opened a channel. "It kind of is, after all."

She maneuvered in close and triggered the spike. The hangar bay yawned open obediently, and Kisa angled the *Chance* toward an empty cradle.

"Let's make this quick."

For the first time in a long time, Candy felt really afraid—not just the anxiousness of risk or the thrill of danger, but truly, deeply frightened. She had encountered the noh too often to not appreciate their danger, but this felt deeper and more powerful. The nerveless cold spread through her as the towering priestess advanced with measured, malevolent steps. Candy took a deep breath and revved her engines. Cola fired the relic's cannon a second before Candy stomped on the gas.

The multicolored bolt streaked toward the noh as Candy steered the relic toward the cages. The blast struck some invisible barrier and shunted away, vaporizing another noh priestess around the corner. The lead noh moved forward a step, her voluminous sleeves and prayer scrolls twisting in strange winds, and raised her arms. She shouted something in her own language, and the distinctive smell of oil and ozone filled the air. Candy cut hard to the left, skidding and turning erratically, as rifts opened on either side of her path. Several huge noh berserkers flew out. They only narrowly missed landing on her.

She flipped around, the relic's sword hissing as she struck. One of the berserkers died without a sound, cut nearly in half, and two more went flying from the force of the cleave. The last one leapt at her. She managed to cut her rear thrusters and angle upward before it landed. The move drove the relic's chassis into the monster's knees and narrowly kept it from tackling her off of the machine. As it was, she had to release the control yoke and use all her strength to keep the monster's tusks and flailing claws from disemboweling her. She heard Cola shout something, and a colorful blast from the relic's cannon sent the noh tumbling away. She kicked out instinctively, and the relic's right leg moved so swiftly that it crushed half the berserker's body when it connected.

Candy yanked the controls back and drove the relic into a steep climb. She could not go far, and turned the climb into a backward loop, but it gave her space and a chance to survey the field. The two remaining berserkers had gotten to their feet and moved between her and the chee. She pursed her lips and dove at them.

A bolt of red-black esper struck the relic's nose just as she reached her targets. The force knocked her off course, and she watched in alarm as power readings across her panel dipped frighteningly low. The berserkers struck simultaneously but not together. She managed to get her relic's empty hand up to keep one away, but the other knocked her sword aside and clawed toward her. Candy pulled her pistol and shot the noh six times before he fell. She grabbed her controls again and turned the relic's sword on the other berserker just as it pulled free and raised its heavy blade to strike.

She swung the relic back toward the prisoners and saw the scroll-covered noh woman tracing an angry pattern with her claws. Esper flashed in the air, and darkness descended over Candy's eyes. For an instant she felt nothing, and then searing pain ripped through her body like her bones had caught fire. Her vision narrowed, and she thought her eyes might burst.

The pain vanished suddenly, but so much strength had left her that she could only slump back in the flight couch. She realized she was screaming only when she stopped for lack of breath. She instinctively reached for esper to heal her injuries, but she felt so weak. Her relic careened out of control and slammed into the deck plates. Bones broke and skin ripped from her legs as she skidded into the hull beside the cages. That pain felt distant, though, and it troubled her little. She managed to raise her head and saw new rifts open and three demonic, six-eyed hounds come bounding through. She also saw the woman approaching with a careless grace. The hounds fell in at her sides. She pointed to Candy and spoke a sibilant word. The pack bayed and launched toward her.

Cola fired the cannon; it must have been Cola. The first hound fell in a ruined heap of smoking meat and bones, but the other two did not slow. Sparks fell around Candy but no more shots came. The cannon must have died. She managed to will the relic's arm to rise, forcing another beast to change direction around it. But she could do nothing except stare at the fangs of the last monster as it reached for her. Its jaws locked onto her left arm and started to pull. She screamed again, feeling flesh tear away and bones twist and snap. Her weak healing esper faltered before the pain and shock. She reached feebly for her pistol.

Cola shot past her, attacking the beast's rows of eyes with his sharp teeth. The hound let go and reared. Cola barely held on. Candy pushed esper into her wounds as fast as she could, but the energy flowed sluggishly and came from far away. She managed to get her gun into her hand and look up in time to see the other hound latch onto Cola and shake him like a rat. She heard and felt his neck snap. His limp body flew off to the side.

She could barely see past the pain, and both her pistol shots went wide. Then the hounds had her again, one by the shoulder and one on her exposed leg. They pulled. More skin tore and her other leg broke as they ripped her free from her relic. She saw the noh approaching, intoning in her harsh language. Candy recognized the sacrifice for what it was when her enemy raised a black curved blade.

Yellow-white esper whipped out across the noh's path, narrowly missing her. She shrieked and turned toward something Candy could not see. The hounds let go suddenly and vanished. She could hear their growls and sudden cries of pain. She smelled fire, scorched metal, and burning hair.

She reached desperately for esper, her will flailing around inside her until she found the faint connection. The power moved slowly, but she clung to the life it offered. She managed to stop her bleeding, but energy came only in a slow drip, not the roaring rush she needed. Her mind groped around for her cypher and found him after a few seconds, unconscious but alive. She could barely concentrate past the pain, but she pushed what little esper she could command toward him and hoped that it did enough.

The sounds of fighting continued. A moment later, her cypher's face swam into view, his fur matted with his own blood. He produced a bottle of soda from nowhere and forced her to drink a splash of it. Esper flowed from her mouth and throat into the rest of her in a rush. Cola gently put his paws on her neck and warmth radiated out as the bones, tendons, and other connections knit back together. She gasped suddenly, when she could, and gulped down air. When she could swallow, he carefully fed her the rest of the bottle. She could feel her body repairing, the esper mending internal injuries first and then closing her skin. She felt good enough to sob from the pain but only for a few seconds. Then she sat up, woozy, and looked around.

The noh woman and two others in far less ornate, though only slightly more practical, dress retreated before an enormous construct of stone and metal that glittered with esper. A librarian, Candy realized, remembering that several had sat dormant in the *Lucky Chance's* hold. A second later, Mihos landed in her view, and Candy saw Kisa perched precariously on her relic's arched back. Kisa sent another yellow-white whip of energy from her blazing staff to catch the last hound and hurl it into the far wall. It lay crumpled and still where it fell. Mihos slashed out and caught another berserker full in the chest. His body arced gracefully into one of the small rifts that still hung open around the bay. Fiametta sent a stream of fire into the tear, and an instant later it snapped shut almost audibly. Candy turned in time to watch the remaining noh step through the last rift. The tall woman's hateful glare was the last thing any of them saw before that opening also vanished.

Kisa and Fiametta were beside Candy a second later, and both gaped when they saw her.

"You—" Fiametta stammered. "You were . . ."

"You were dead," Kisa said flatly. She shook her head in pure disbelief. "You were true-as-the-Doctrines dead. I saw them nearly rip your limbs off. I was sure you were going to be a bloody pile of parts when we got here." She shrugged, clearly lost for words. "How—I mean, I can take a beating, sure. I don't know a Knight that can't, but this . . ." She shrugged again and gave up.

"It's the first thing I learned to do when Cola showed up," Candy said. Her tongue felt thick, and her words did not sound right in her ears yet. She climbed unsteadily to her feet with Fiametta's help. "Useful trick, but I couldn't keep it up. Something she did to me, some spell." She shook her head and almost fell. "I don't know. It felt like it ripped something out of me. I was so weak. The esper was so hard to use." She coughed, hard and wet, for a moment and finally spit out some blood. "And clearly I'm not right yet."

"No," Kisa said, eyeing her, "but I wager you'll live. Her, though," she said, turning to the chee, "I'm not so sure about."

"Can you do that," Fiametta waved her hands from Candy's wobbling but upright form to the chee's scattered parts, "to her?"

Candy regarded the remains of the robot. "Yes? Maybe? I don't think I can just pull all her parts back together. But if you cut her down and get everything back inside her, more or less in the right places, I can probably get her running again, yeah." She took two shaky steps forward and sank down with her back to the bars. "Just—Just give me a minute or five."

"Fiametta!" someone shouted, and they all looked around to the far cell. Squall knelt there, at the edge of her chains, looking absolutely delighted under the blood and scars.

"Squall!" Fiametta dashed over but recoiled as she reached for the cell door. "What in the empty stars is this? Some sort of dampener."

"Vance is far more cunning than he looks," Squall said, and even in her weakened condition, Candy could hear the ruefulness in the pirate's voice. "He'll also be here any second. Get me out."

"We've got a minute," Kisa said, striding over.

Mihos slashed down with one giant claw and crushed the cell door. Two quick blasts cut the chains, and Squall stumbled out. She pulled the manacles from her wrists and ankles without regard for the torn and bloody skin beneath and threw her arms around Fiametta.

Kisa, smiling, moved into the cage with the chee. "We don't have that long, though," she muttered as she inspected the mess.

"I can help with that," Squall said. "I couldn't do anything before, but I did watch as that—" She bit back several choice words. "That noh priestess pulled Cordelia apart. I know about where everything goes."

"Her name is Cordelia?" Candy asked.

Squall gathered parts up while Fiametta and Kisa moved to cut the chee's chassis down.

"Yes. We spoke a little, when we were both conscious." Squall's seething anger could have blackened and curled the deck plates. "She was a maid and only recently awakened. She was on her way to see M8 when we hit her ship."

"The *Tranquil Wind*," Candy said. "Alliance Security got the report. Small frickin' galaxy."

"And getting smaller all the time," Kisa said. "Okay, let's see if we can't get our friend here working again."

CHAPTER 20

Black Spot, secondary cargo hold

Cordelia sat up. Her optical receptors whirred as their lenses shifted through focus settings. She identified dust motes and dead skin. She blinked and readjusted her optics. She had slipped back into cleaning mode; she must have defaulted to that when she shut down. No, she had not shut down, not really. She remembered it, mostly. She remembered the demon, the woman who looked at her like a thing, the claws that cut her metal flesh like silk. Her limbs still ached and burned where the noh had separated them at the seams. The pain came roaring back. Cordelia's processor cycles spiked, and she felt her cooling system struggle to keep up. Her eyes finally focused, and she saw four women staring at her.

"Um, hello?" she said.

The one in the wizard hat sighed deeply and slumped to her knees. "Oh, thank the gods."

The shortest one, wearing the tattered remains of pirate clothes, smiled with pure, exhausted joy. "I think—I think she'll be okay. I thought she was too far gone."

"No," the one with multicolored hair said with relief. She sat back and smeared the grease further across her cheek while trying to clean it. "The processors never lost power, so her neural network was constantly engaged." A look of horror flickered across her face as she realized the implications of that. "But—Ah. But it means that she couldn't go out completely." She licked her lips.

"Where—" Cordelia stopped. Her projection settings were all wrong. She did the chee equivalent of clearing her throat, running through a range of timbres and intonations until all the values matched her preferences. "Where am I?"

"In pretty deep trouble, not to put too fine a point on it," the human with the multicolored hair said. "Can you access the Interspace Network?"

Cordelia tried, failed, and instantly started to shake. The lack of connection to other chee or the vast, comforting sea of information that cradled each consciousness of her race unnerved her more than the memory of the torture.

"That looks like no," the woman said, clearly concerned. "Okay, we'll work on that later. For now, we—Hey. Hey." She reached over and lifted Cordelia's chin until the chee had to look in her eyes. "Right here. Look right here. Now, you're functional— not right, obviously, but functional. We're going to get you out, but you need to walk and probably run. Can you do that?"

Cordelia blinked as the question filtered through her glitched, panicked processing. She ended the failing routines and nodded.

"Good. Good. All right, introductions." The woman pointed to herself. "I'm Candy. I'm with Alliance Security. The one in the hat is Fiametta, and the tall one with the fuzzy ears is Kisa. They're from the Doctrine. The short one is—"

"Squall," Cordelia said suddenly. She blinked at the small woman and smiled a bit. "I remember her."

Squall beamed and patted Cordelia's hand.

Candy smiled too and stood unsteadily. "Looks like some of those files survived, okay. She's ex-Doctrine," Candy said.

Cordelia detected some reservation or warning in this statement, and she refocused on Squall.

"It's—complicated," Squall said, still smiling. "But I also want you to escape."

"You were—" Cordelia paused to sort through her memory files. They made little sense at the moment. "You were with me. Here. In the cage."

"We were neighbors," Squall said, her smiling fading.

The tall one—Kisa—had not more than glanced in Cordelia's direction since she awoke. Cordelia had not met many tonnerians and was struck by Kisa's feline features and grace. Kisa turned and regarded all of them now. "Listen, ladies, I'm glad we're all so friendly and resolved and such, but we're also on a tight schedule. That monster's going to get some of her friends, and Mihos is detecting large numbers of people approaching this hold from three different directions. We've got to go right now." She strode forward and extended her hand. "It's faster if you ride with me."

"Or me," Candy cut in, her voice going hard.

"Not now," Kisa said. "We're leaving on my ship, all of us, no matter where we end up. We can argue about that later."

Candy hesitated, nodded once, and stepped back toward a sleek, gangly machine that looked like a blend of construction mecha and hoverbike. Cordelia took Kisa's hand. The tonnerian hauled the chee to her feet and indicated a feline mecha that crouched close by, watching the door and swishing its tail. "That's Mihos. He's not friendly, but he likes you. Mount up, buttercup."

Cordelia had no sooner clambered onto the relic than Kisa leapt aboard ahead of her and got the machine airborne. They twisted easily, the mecha matching its mistress's dexterity. Candy and her relic sped off ahead to do a circuit of the hold. Fiametta and Squall moved as fast as they could. Candy circled back to them and seemed to want to put Squall on her relic. Before they could, though, the far bulkhead doors hissed open. Pirates in Golden Vance's livery poured in.

"Hang on!" Kisa pulled Mihos into a looping turn.

They spun through the hold as pistol shots whistled past them. Kisa twisted them onto their left side, so that the relic would take any hits, and aimed for the other bulkhead door. Below, Cordelia saw Candy swing her relic's sword at a group of especially fast pirates closing on Fiametta and Squall. She cut down two and sent a huge, ugly chee sprawling back into half a dozen more.

Something hit Mihos like a meteor. Cordelia heard the relic yowl in pain, and the impact shook loose some of her internal systems. She scrambled to hold onto Kisa, but the actuators in her arms all froze, and she slipped away from the Knight. She fell, tumbling and screaming, until her jump jets engaged—mostly. She stopped falling and started flying and spinning completely out of control. A floating skull cannon in the open doorway fired and hit Mihos again. The mecha spun away and slammed into the far wall; Kisa narrowly avoided getting crushed against the hull.

Cordelia's self-repair routines finally sorted out the problem with her jump jets and got her stabilized. She raced to a catwalk that circled the hold on the uppermost deck and dropped out of the air. Pistol shots pinged off of the decking under her. Her jets had almost no fuel left, and she realized that she had no idea where to find Kisa's ship. She swore, trying to expand her gun. The vacuum extension appeared just fine, but the connections needed to turn it into a weapon simply did not mesh.

"Going to have to get someone to look at that," she said as she rose to a crouch. A quick diagnostic showed that her legs had almost full function. "Okay, so, I do this the old-fashioned way."

An explosion from below drew her attention. She stuck her head over the edge of the catwalk to see that some of the very few crates in the hold had disintegrated under a shot from the cannon. Fiametta and Squall were picking themselves up after the blast, both a bit worse for wear. Candy circled around to cover them, deftly avoiding a hail of corsair fire, and raked her attackers with a parti-colored cannon beam. Candy swung back, her giant sword vanishing in a cloud of esper, and scooped both of the other women into her relic's great hands. She zoomed off toward the cages and twisted around the angle projecting from the left-hand wall to gain some cover. Cordelia rolled back as more pirates flooded into the hold, Golden Vance striding among them.

A boom from below and behind her signaled Kisa's return to the fight. Mihos roared, and Cordelia could track his movement by the great thuds as he bounded across the deck. She glanced down in time to see the cat machine, trailing smoke, duck into the same cover as the others, almost exactly across the entire hold from her. Something below her hissed, but she could not identify that sound.

"You're trapped, my lovelies," Golden Vance called with an esper-enhanced voice. "I've got your ship cut off. You've nowhere to go. But I'm an accommodating man. I'll let most of you leave. The chee and Squall stay with me, though." Cordelia shuddered at the nastiness in his voice.

"Vance," a new voice called out, musical and lilting, "you're a bloody fool."

A new group of pirates, dressed in different colors, approached from almost underneath Cordelia's hiding place. A woman riding a tall, gangly relic adorned with figureheads strode into view.

"You hand over that chee now, and I might decide to let you keep your ship along with your life."

Cordelia slipped slightly back to stay hidden. They thought she was in the corner with the others, she realized.

"Hah!" Vance barked, though he sounded less confident. "This is nothing to do with you, Kate. This bloody mess and idiotic idea of attacking Ulyxis is your fault and your problem. The chee is my prize and my concern." He pointed a blunt, mechanical finger at the Pirate Queen. "By the terms of our agreement, you get a percentage of my plunder, but I decide which plunder you get."

"The agreement also says that you don't make deals behind my back or plot against me," the woman said venomously. "What did the noh offer you, Vance? Did they promise you a fleet?"

Cordelia saw the shock on Golden Vance's face. "How did you know—"

"I didn't," the woman said. "But I do now."

Vance roared. "To hell with you, Calico Kate. And I'll take you there myself."

"Ten of you wouldn't be enough," Kate shouted back, and then she called to her crew. "Gold and grog to whoever brings me that chee alive!"

The two pirate bands whooped and charged each other.

CHAPTER 21

Ulyxis, Forsyth River district

Shock and pulse rifle fire ricocheted off the ruined statuary around Marikan To as she sprinted to cover. The fighting in this section of Ulyxis's capital had turned quickly from ranged sparring to close-quarters brawling, something that berserkers thrived on but she and other Sarva disliked. The Alliance had clearly prepared very well for their arrival, and she cursed the need to search the sector for the artifact instead of scouting this target to learn its weakness. Again.

Shock rounds tore through the remains of the ground cars that had sheltered her a second before. The shots also punched through the two Sarva accompanying her, who had not gotten away fast enough. Marikan To closed her eyes for an instant. With so many prophecies coming to pass in the last two centuries, she wasn't exactly tripping over recruits. Too many felt drawn to the priesthood. But she could take no more time to mourn. She spun smoothly from cover and sent an explosive arrow arcing into the gutted remains of the office tower behind the shock cannon's position. As she slipped back, rubble rained down on the Alliance soldiers. The lack of recruits only makes my duties harder, she thought with a rueful frown.

She scrambled deeper into the damaged city and looked for angles to destroy the Alliance's entrenched positions. The warlord had called for his few berserkers and several of the gigantic, feral war beasts called dahon, along with many of his best warriors, to join him at the House of Speakers. Resistance was toughest there, which suggested to Marikan that he ought to go around, but she felt sure he had a plan. Likely he wanted to confront the mercenary Relic Knight who was holding that position and vaporizing their warriors almost with impunity. Marikan had seen the armored Black Diamond shuttles come down close to that point, which likely meant they had concentrated where they had the best fields of fire. She had expected the enemy's line to break quickly, but the warlord's call meant that it had not. That they fought on with no apparent thought of retreat raised her hackles, though she could not say why.

She sent another enchanted arrow into the first floor of an ornate building with all its windows blown out. Her missile's piercing shriek echoed out of the confined space and sent the defenders scurrying away from the sonic pain. She cursed again when she saw no noh troops rushing to take the building, and yet again when she looked around and saw her friendly lines several blocks behind.

Tahariel slipped lightly into cover beside Marikan To and smiled at her.

Surprised, the noh smiled back. "Where did you come from? I knew you were on-planet but not where." She glanced past the strange woman to the silent, swift warriors in black and bone-white armor flitting into place around them. "Who are your friends?"

"My pinions," Tahariel said, glancing out at the street. "A gift from my superiors for use in unusual circumstance." She grinned. "They wanted to stretch their legs and shed some blood as much as I did."

Marikan To saw a spinning sphere of darkness form in the center of the ring on Tahariel's staff. Wisps of violet and crimson esper whirlpooled around its edges as it grew. The alien stood, rising further on the lift circles attached to her boots, and hurled the black orb down the avenue. It seemed to pick up speed and size as it flew until finally detonating at the far intersection. Screams drifted to them on the flame-tinged breeze. "Where were you, anyway?" she asked as she sank back down. "I was looking before we attacked, but all the Sarva said was that you had another mission." She nudged Marikan To's ribs with a conspiratorial grin.

"So? Spill."

Marikan To sighed, still conflicted about the whole affair, and made a show of looking back for any advancing noh troops. She did spot one of her teams creeping through the rubble half-a-block away and across the street. Random pulse fire pinged around them. "I . . . She shook her head. "I smelled something. A trail of esper. So I followed it."

"Smelled?" Tahariel thought for a second. "That sounds exactly like you. You're a tracker, a huntress. It makes sense that you would not see esper in a traditional sense. So? What did you find?"

Marikan To shrugged and waved at the other Sarva. Vathra To, one of Marikan's more aggressive guthrra, acknowledged and moved her sisters closer. "I don't know. The fact is—" Marikan To hesitated. "It just sounds worse every time I say it out loud. I found something—someone, really—that just radiated esper."

Tahariel whole body came to attention, and her expression turned serious.

"As I think back, she did have some kind of glow, like she shimmered," Marikan continued, watching the street and the approaching noh. "But mostly I could smell and hear the esper. If flowed out of her like water, like she was a fountain."

"A source?" Tahariel asked, her voice taut.

Marikan To looked around sharply at her friend.

"Like a source of esper?"

The Sarva leader hesitated again and then nodded. "Yes. That's a good description, actually."

Tahariel grabbed her upper arm. "Tell me where. That's the artifact, the thing we sought. Tell me where it is."

Marikan To had never see the alien so intent or serious. That alone made her reluctant, but something also called her back to the chee. She stared at Tahariel's eyes for a moment before she felt Lakmi land on her shoulder. Esper flowed from the cypher, and Marikan felt calmer at once.

She smiled lopsidedly at Tahariel. "No. But I'll take you there."

The alien woman blinked twice, caught off guard, and then

nodded with a grin.

Marikan turned and waved Vathra To closer. The guthrra led her team across the ruined street and into cover.

"We need your rift generator," Marikan said.

Her subordinate nodded and unslung the device from one of her huntresses.

Marikan took the generator and began adjusting its settings. "Get your pinions together," she said to Tahariel.

A few seconds later, a rippling, shimmering tear in reality hung before them. The cool smell of the starship's air mixed with the pop and ozone of weapon discharges wafted out.

"We're late to the party," Marikan said.

Tahariel chuckled and followed her through the rift.

Cordelia lay on her back on the catwalk with only the thin deckplate between her and the swirling melee below. This was absolute madness, and it was probably going to kill her. All she wanted was to see M8 and find her place in the galaxy.

Her olfactory receptors signaled something, and she sat up. She sniffed again and identified the scent as ozone and incense. All her processing cycles spiked as she recognized the smell. A sickening, wet tear opened in the air before her.

Cordelia scrambled back as three noh women in the scant robes of priestesses stepped through the rift with their curved blades drawn. They lunged for her. She rolled off the catwalk without a second thought, and her jump jets sputtered to life. She could just see half a dozen or so other rifts opening around the room, and a mixture of male and female noh rushing through into the melee.

Her jets would not stay lit, so she could only partially control her fall. She managed to land on a small knot of Vance's pirates. Though they failed to get to their feet and grab her, she scrambled upright and stumbled clear just in time. She raced through the chaos toward the far corner where she had last seen her new friends, but the roiling fight slowed her. She heard a roar, and glanced left to see Vance lunging for her. She put more people between them, but he tore across the hold like a bulldozer.

Just before he could reach her, a swirl of pirates locked in their own fight swept him away. Esper surrounded Vance as he snarled, and suddenly an enormous chee composed of wildly mismatched parts stood beside his captain. Cordelia shuddered as he followed Vance's pointing finger and shouted command to get her. She tried to push faster through the press of people, but the giant swept away the intervening pirates with horrifying ease. Cordelia felt a metal hand clamp down on her arm. She turned to see the chee's leering, ragged grin nearly on top of her.

More ozone wafted around them, and Cordelia could feel the sudden rush of air very different from the shipboard atmosphere. The giant chee frowned and looked away as another rift opened just behind him. Cordelia followed his gaze to see two women, one a noh with a great bow, dash through ahead of several warriors in strange armor. A vicious-looking bird cypher swooped at the chee's face. He grunted and swatted at it. The noh fired a glowing arrow at close range that took the pirate square in the chest. He staggered. The noh vaulted over three corsairs diving for her and, too fast for even Cordelia's optics to follow, drew and fired again in midair. The arrow spun, trailing red-violet esper, and ripped off the arm holding Cordelia.

Cordelia barely noticed her sudden freedom. Her gaze had fixed on the other woman who came through the rift, an alien of a kind she had never seen. Though almost human, the warrior wore an esper-traced bodysuit and plates of armor tinged with darkness. The alien's pale features held an aching beauty and poisonous evil. She floated on circular condensers that literally pulled the world apart to create lift. Cordelia could see esper motes materialize out of the air and fall into the darkness at the center of the condensers. The chee froze, terrified beyond even her recollection of the noh torture. The woman fixed her malevolent gaze on Cordelia, and a look of pleased astonishment crossed her face.

"Dead gods of the void," she said. "That's it. That's the Source."

Candy bowled through the crowd. She sailed over Cordelia, knocking aside pirates, the noh archer, and the alien horror alike. "Back off!" she shouted, and Cola fired the relic's shoulder cannon. The strange alien raised her staff and deflected the beam. It struck another floating cannon and sliced it apart.

"She is mine," the woman said in a calm, firm voice that filled the bay. "I am a mouthpiece of oblivion, and you cannot stop me."

Candy said nothing. The sword materialized again in her relic's hand, and she charged. The noh archer had regained her feet but now simply dove out of the way. The alien's staff again came up to ward off the attack, and though the relic looked like it could crush battleship armor, its blow never touched the strange woman. Dark esper gathered around her, and she struck with an unseen weapon at the Alliance Knight. Candy deftly avoided the attack and brought her sword around again. Their swift duel shifted away, with the noh archer joining in to aid her companion. Candy split her attacks between them and gave ground.

Cordelia realized that the Knight was drawing her attackers away and scrambled to her feet. She turned and ran smack into Golden Vance.

"You," he said, leering as his mechanical arm latched onto her waist, "aren't going anywhere." The light in his artificial eye glowed balefully.

Then it flickered. A confused look crossed his face. Thick, coruscating bolts of electricity and esper arced over his body. He spasmed, screamed, and released her.

Cordelia stepped clear as the pirate captain fell on his face. She saw Squall, battered and leaning on her staff, approaching with white-hot fury in her eyes. Tendrils of lighting curled around her feet and played across the deck plates, clearing her way through the crowd. Vance groaned and tried to get up, but Squall sent another bolt into him. Small explosions rippled along his cybernetic arm, and he grunted again. Drops of thin blood sprayed from his mouth. Vance fell onto his back, smoke and steam rising from his body. Healing esper wreathed his form, but it had a lot of work to do.

"Oh, no, my lovely," Squall said to him murderously. "We're not done yet." She planted the butt of her staff on his chest. "What say we up the voltage, hmm?"

Electricity coursed into Vance. He twitched and writhed and screamed.

Squall ended the spell and looked at Cordelia. "I'll be a little while here. Run. There's a door behind me, where we sheltered, that leads to the kitchens. Go up two decks and turn to starboard. That way lies Kisa's ship." She sent another jolt into Vance. "Go."

Cordelia ran.

She managed to clear the melee before Kisa spotted her. The tonnerian Relic Knight shouted and sent Mihos plowing through the fight toward Cordelia. The chee waved and ducked around the corner. She saw the hatchway ahead and skidded to a halt in front of it. She struggled with the lock for a second, threw the door open, and glanced back to see a crowd of pirates come barreling around the corner toward her. She leapt through and stopped suddenly as if she had hit a wall. She heard a screech of tearing metal. Pain flooded her. Her vision swam. She turned to look into the glittering eyes of the demon high priestess.

The noh flexed her claws. Driven deep into Cordelia's chest, dripping red-black esper, they hooked onto her frame and internal systems. With a casual sweep of her arm, she flung the chee back into the kitchens. Cordelia crashed into a cooking unit, crumpling part of it and crushing her own hip. More fluids from her barely functioning components spilled out and mixed with the fuel running freely from the cooker. She slumped down on her back.

A lurid red light from open flames lit the deck. Cordelia could see the noh turn toward the pirates coming from the hold and trace a nauseating symbol in the air. The prayer strips adorning her horns rose to stream forward, as if blown by a storm. No, Cordelia realized, they were drawn by a great void. She could hear screaming from the pirates. The noh had consumed them, somehow, and as the prayer strips went slack again, she turned to

Cordelia with an almost ecstatic pleasure on her face.

"I," she said as she advanced with confident steps, "am Zineda, High Priestess of Nozuki the Endless Hunger."

Cordelia tried to flee, but she could manage nothing more than weak scrambling.

"You are a prize that He greatly desires. Though I know not why or for what, I need not know. I know only that He shall have you. And," she held up her claws again. Coolant and lubricant still dripped from them. "I know that you need not be in one piece."

The bulkhead behind Zineda exploded. An enormous chunk of the wall flew free, ripping out part of the decks above and below them. Mihos came hurtling through the gap. Sparks ignited the leaking cooker fuel, and more fires raced across the decking. Zineda lurched forward, driven to her knees by the shockwave, and turned snarling to face Kisa.

"You cannot have her!"

"You talk too much," Kisa replied.

Mihos dove at the priestess. Zineda leapt to the side, and esper shot from her upraised palm. The power caught Mihos in the face, and the graceful relic crashed to the deck. Kisa rolled free and brought her staff up. Yellow-white esper rose around Zineda. The noh grunted and struggled against a force Cordelia could not see. She howled, enraged, but Kisa only smiled. Then Kisa shuddered and swung her staff like a club at something behind her. Cordelia sharpened her optics and saw a small impish creature, like a combination of a snake and a noh woman, race around the Relic Knight and finally sink needle-sharp teeth into her shoulder. Kisa grunted, grabbed the creature, and hurled it away in a spray of blood. Scratch immediately pounced on the other cypher, but Kisa's spell had broken.

Zineda rose on cascades of crimson esper and shouted words in a grating, sticky language. Kisa recoiled as if struck and then collapsed to her knees. Black tendrils of unhealthy energy played around her. Cordelia could almost see the life draining out of her would-be rescuer. She glanced around. She could not move quickly with her damaged hip, and she could not activate her gun. Instead, she rolled to her left and ripped free the fuel line from another cooker damaged by part of the flying bulkhead. She pointed it at Zineda and pressed her thumb to the pumping fluid stream. The blockage added pressure, turning the stream into a spray. Cordelia angled that spray over one of the spreading fires, igniting the fuel, and bathing the high priestess in flames.

Zineda howled again as fire scorched her flesh and consumed her hair. She rolled away, ending her spell. Kisa fell back, gasping. Cordelia tossed the fuel line away, but it twisted, and flammable fluid sprayed everywhere. The flames followed a second later. She beat out the ones on her body, but watched in horror as the fire grew around her. She tried to crawl toward Kisa, but the spreading inferno quickly cut her off.

"No," she mumbled as the heat began to overwhelm her. "No, I don't want to die."

A clanking and clomping approached her with frightening speed, and the next thing Cordelia knew, a robotic arm had hoisted her clear. She looked up to see a battered, bloody Calico Kate smiling down from her relic.

"Just you hold on there, my girl," she said in a surprisingly soft voice. "I've got to grab your friend."

Kate stepped through the flames and scooped up Kisa with the same care she had shown to Cordelia. Without another word, the pirate queen bounded through the kitchen and ripped open a hole up to the next deck. In no time, she had bulldozed her way to the starboard hangar. Cordelia saw a ship, curved and sleek, in one of the docking cradles with its boarding ramp extended.

As Kate approached, two figures appeared on that ramp. Fiametta limped noticeably, and a quick optical adjustment showed her marked pallor. Candy looked somewhat better, though her suit and armor were ripped and scarred. She frowned at the approaching pirate and raised her pistol.

"That's close enough, miss pirate," Candy called.

"Not quite," Kate replied. She tiled her relic's hands forward to show their contents.

Fiametta gasped and rushed toward them.

"No, no," Kate said. "Go get medical cots. Kisa definitely needs one; she got hit by that noh priestess with whatever she does that sucks the life from you."

Candy went white at the memory. She lowered her gun and raced up the ramp.

Kate continued, "The chee will need attention too, so I hope you know a good mechanic."

"Several," Fiametta said. "And her name's Cordelia."

"Is it?" Kate said. "Well that's pretty."

Candy returned, just barely corralling two of the rolling cots in front of her. Fiametta turned to assist, and they carefully moved Kisa first. Scratch settled onto his mistress's legs. Fiametta hooked her friend to the cot's onboard systems while Candy helped Cordelia slide onto the other one.

"Why?" Candy asked Kate as the chee settled in place.

Fiametta turned to hear the answer.

Kate hesitated and finally sighed. "Kisa I owed for warning me about Vance. We're even now. Make sure you tell her that. Her," she nodded to Cordelia and paused. "I'm not—Something Kisa said made me think. If that girl there, Cordelia, really is the Source, and the Calamity really has finally caught us, then all this can't be just about booty and buccaneering anymore. It's got to be about something bigger. Maybe that's what Harker's always been on about, and maybe he's right. Won't stop me from killing him next chance I get, of course." She sighed. "I've done a great many things that most people call evil. I call them that too, if I'm honest. They rarely bother me. But if getting her free helps us against the Calamity, then maybe I've done something good—something to toss on the other side of the scales when that time comes." She shrugged. "Maybe."

"Maybe," Candy allowed. "We need to go."

"So do I. I've a mutiny to put down, after all," Kate said, some of her good humor returning. She turned and launched her relic back the way she had come. A second later, a damaged Mihos limped out of the same opening, casting baleful glances behind him.

"What the black void was that all about?" Fiametta asked as she motioned the relic up the ramp.

"Don't know. Don't care," Candy replied. "Let's get out of here."

CHAPTER 22

Origin Point, Wildspace Sector N.10543

The assault shuttle approached the iron and rock plateau at a terrifying speed. It only slowed at the very last possible second as its energy weapons blasted at likely enemy positions. The landing gear crushed the thick layer of esper crystals that covered most of the asteroid's surface, and the ramps shattered still more as they came down. Malya flew Sedaris out of the ship first, streaking around their drop site in a wide circle. Esper crystals covered nearly every surface, growing literally on top of each other in the lower areas.

"I don't see anybody," she said after her first pass, the comms crackling with strange interference, "but that doesn't mean they're not here."

"Understood," Cross replied.

Squads of Swordsworn and Paragons raced in different directions to grab cover and secure the site. Sebastian's massive relic jogged nimbly into view a second later. Resembling nothing so much as a gigantic suit of armor with Cross perched in the upper chest, the enormous machine wielded a huge mace in one hand and an equally large sword in the other, broken three feet above the hilt. Even Malya, whose connections to the paladins of the Six Peers had always been distant, was impressed by the sight of the Shattered Sword, the artifact for which the Order was named more than ten thousand cycles ago. Cross's recovery of the Sword had sealed his elevation to First, and his use of it now showed how seriously he took this endeavor.

"Get some altitude and keep looking," the paladin said. "We'll get our position settled here and—"

Twisting green render beams crisscrossed the sky, and Malya flipped over to dive between them. It took a few precious seconds for her to realize that they had not fired at her. The attacks had scored the shuttle and blasted off its weapons with the best angles of fire. As she turned upright, she could see the noh gunners behind thin ridges of crystal just above the landing site and probably at their maximum range. They had crouched down for cover and seemed to be adjusting the settings on their huge render cannons. She gritted her teeth and swooped low toward them.

Malya feathered the attitude controls on her relic to slip gracefully through the forest of razor-sharp crystals. Blades extended, she ripped through the noh before they even saw her. Blood splattered across the crystals, and several of them glowed with a lurid light. One of the render guns exploded. Esper-charged crystal shards flew like bullets well behind her. She stayed low, popping up only long enough to identify another noh position. Malya circled the landing zone four times and ripped nearly a dozen gun teams apart before rising again to get a good view.

Pulse rifles flashed along the edges of the iron plateau. In the distance, another shuttle landed and began trading cannon and small arms fire with still more noh. A few of the monstrous warriors had reached the paladins from her ship, but Cross was making short work of them. The six-eyed hounds bounding nimbly through the crystals concerned her more; they navigated the treacherous landscape far better, and there were a lot more of them. She saw the pit crew hustling down the assault ramp. Sarva arrows struck and exploded around them. Malya wrenched Sedaris around toward the source of the arrows and found them well hidden from the landing forces. She dove on the noh archers but only caught two as they scattered.

She aimed Sedaris for the approaching swarm of hounds. The beasts hissed and howled as she approached. Several leapt at her, and Malya had to twist and spin to keep them off. This spoiled her attack, but the pack had scattered and spoiled its charge. She hauled back on the controls for a ragged wingover turn and approached again. She pulled up as the pit crew sent rivets and other mismatched projectiles ripping into the hounds. The creatures kept rushing on, however, and the final few leapt to the rise, only for two wrecker mecha to batter them down. Betty waved to Malya as she passed.

The princess gained altitude in wide circles as the fighting died down. She risked hovering for a few seconds almost directly over the shuttle and scanned the desolate landscape. Mr. Tomn clambered up her arm, staring intently all around and finally pointing with one paw at a dark smear nearly three kilometers away.

"There," he shouted. "That's our destination."

"Are you sure?"

He nodded.

She swung around to get another look. The darkness resolved slightly, and she saw shadows falling across a descending tunnel. She also saw movement.

"It looks like a cave. And there's someone there."

Mr. Tomn nodded again.

"Then we need to tell Cross. Let's get a good look before we go."

She swooped closer and saw the crystal forest below her seem to seethe and move. Hundreds of noh rushed through the defiles and gullies of the scarred asteroid toward the mouth of the cave. She could just make out an impressive monster with blades rising from his armored back and the shadow of what looked like a massive, demonic lion lurking behind him. Another figure floated beside him, slender and feminine and radiating a dark power that might have swallowed the noh without a trace. Malya felt sick to her stomach.

Violet-black esper coursed around the woman as she pointed toward the landing zones. Even from over a kilometer away, Malya fancied she could hear the noh growl. He gestured violently, and the woman floated into the cave, though she did so with an ill-disguised contempt. Then the comparatively slight figures of noh priestesses brought several large devices toward their lord.

Malya's eyes widened, and she turned sharply to race back to her friends. "Rifts," she called over the static-laden and choppy comms. "Rifts!"

She saw some confusion spread through the pit crew, but the paladins snapped to action. Cross strode through their ranks, his relic making sweeping gestures. The Swordsworn began to circle up even as the first sickening tears opened in the air. One appeared a foot above the ground almost directly in front of Malya. Red-gold light spilled from the rip in reality, and she glimpsed an alien architecture of chains and arching bone. Then the berserkers leapt through the rift.

Scores of them raced directly into the paladin's lines, their blood-mad screams filling the thin atmosphere. Malya saw half a dozen other rifts opening. They were surrounded. A tear ripped wide just over the edge of the plateau from the pit crew, away from the first incursion and out of their sight. Malya shouted a warning as she dove in, but they had no time. In an instant, a noh packmaster had driven his hounds into their ranks, and a dozen berserkers literally leapt on top of them.

Malya had no time to think. She kept her blades in tight to avoid hitting her friends and slipped around the outside edge of the roiling melee. Screams rose all around her. The berserkers howled their devotions to Nozuki as they cleaved down the paladins and pit crew. They kept shouting prayers as swords sliced through them and hydraulic spanners mutilated their limbs. Paladins cried their defiance and terror, sometimes in the same breath. One of the wrecker exoframes stumbled as its legs failed. Its pilot tried to keep it upright, but she couldn't compensate for severed pistons. Instantly four berserkers swarmed it. They ripped shattered parts free and pulled hunks of the pilot's body apart. She screamed and smashed two of them to pulp. She was still screaming as the other two broke open her rib cage. Tears almost blinded the princess but she saw well enough to kill the berserkers with her sword. Too late.

Above the screams and cries, Malya heard Betty shouting. Even the roar of the noh could not drown out someone who could shout over the noise of the Cerci Prime racetrack. She rallied the pit crew to her, forming a circle of whirling, wrenching weapons and desperate pistol fire. Lug loomed up over his friend, battering away hounds, until three Hatriya warriors grabbed his arms. Ignoring their injuries, the noh hauled the chee forward, nearly crushing Betty, and ripped his arms from his body in a shower of sparks. Lug wailed, stumbled, and barely managed to miss Betty as he fell. Malya swung in to assist as Betty battered back the warriors with her wrench and inarticulate screams.

Malya's blade cut the Hatriya apart almost casually. Even their armor barely slowed her blows. The attack slowed her, however, and almost a dozen berserkers turned as if answering an unheard order and leapt at her. Their sheer weight nearly dragged down Sedaris. She ducked her head and rolled. The jagged points of broken esper crystals cut at her upper back and shoulders, but they shredded the noh. Their blood soaked her. It pasted her suit to her skin and caked her hair. She pulled up, tucking the relic's limbs in tight, and rocketed into the sky, gasping for breath. The last noh fell away, still shouting praises to his god. She spun again, at high speed, and much of the blood flew away. She still felt nauseous.

As she leveled out, she saw that the battle had settled into chaotic but solid lines. The initial confusion and rush of the noh assault had faltered on the paladins' discipline and experience. Sebastian Cross was clearing away swaths of the bestial hounds with each swing of his relic's shattered blade, blue esper flames dancing on its edge. The attackers had mostly been contained in pockets or pushed to the edges of the plateau, but she could see still more moving through the crystals toward them. The defenders were distracted and disorganized, and their casualties looked horrendous.

Malya swept down, extending her blades, and tore around the edges of the rise, cutting through noh and crystals alike. Enchanted arrows exploded in her wake, and render beams cut the air around her. When she pulled up and returned to the melee, she had turned the dense cover around the plateau into a razor-edged killing ground. She scattered several berserkers near

Cross's position, and the Paragons around him leapt in to finish off the monsters.

"There are more approaching," she called to the First as she pulled up near him.

Cross nodded, dispatching his last opponent. "I'm not surprised. I am surprised at how many there are, and how organized their defense is proving. Whatever else he may be, Kasaro To is earning his reputation as a formidable opponent. Where have you seen the rifts?"

"Not rifts," she replied. "They're approaching on foot. I don't think they're trying to kill us." She rolled her eyes at his incredulous look. "I mean totally destroy us. I don't think they have as many troops as we think they do. I think that, if they can't push us off this rock, they're going to try and keep us right here."

He frowned. "Keep us from where, I wonder."

"There's a cave." She turned and pointed. "Maybe three kilometers off. That's where the noh are coming from. I think they're using underground tunnels to get close. I saw some warriors moving in the crystals near here but not in the open ground between here and the cave."

"Makes sense," he replied, nodding. "And you think that the cave is our objective?"

"I do. So does Mr. Tomn." They all looked at Rook. The knightly cypher pulled his lance from a noh that had been trying to rise, wiped the blood from the weapon, and nodded.

"All right, then," Cross said. "We need to get to the cave. But first, we need reinforcements. I'll call Harker. Let me know what else you see."

Malya nodded and swept back into the fight.

CHAPTER 23

Marianne, Origin Point

The ship shook and wrenched. Harker could feel her shuddering and straining, and he willed her to hold together. The lights failed across the bridge amid the scream of klaxons and the shouts of the crew. Independent power supplies kept the consoles functioning, but the overhead holodisplay flickered and vanished along with the illumination, drenching them all in cool blackness.

"Gravimetric distortion astern, Captain," Digby called. "Good and strong this time."

"What gave you the first clue, Mr. Digby?" Harker replied sarcastically.

"We're nearly past its edge," she said, and he distinctly heard her mutter, "jerk," as she turned away.

He grinned despite himself, and then held his breath with the others as the distinctive, dreaded sound of shearing metal echoed around them. The hull hissed and popped twice, and then the lights returned.

Harker settled back into his command couch and consulted his still-fuzzy monitors. "Steady as she goes, Mr. Digby. I have the damage reports here. Give me a situation report as soon as you have one."

Explosions lit the blackness outside the main viewport. Harker looked up in time to see black-edge wreckage spinning away in three directions, trailing fire and venting oxygen and violet esper. Another shadowy shape loomed ahead and starboard, and he watched the *Marianne's* secondary plasma batteries rake through the darkness trying to hit it.

"Sooner would be better," he added.

"Aye, Captain," she said, a little distracted.

He hid his concern as he scanned the damage information. Not bad, considering, he decided. They would need time in drydock—probably extended time—to fix the keel and reseal the hull, but she would hold together for a while yet. He smiled again, gently caressing the worn arm of his command couch.

"Sir," Digby said.

He looked up at her. She was pale under her normally ice-fair complexion, and he glanced immediately at the ragged dressing on her abdomen. It needed changing, but he let her continue.

"We've lost the *Gorgon's Eyes*. She's not wrecked, but her engine's completely gone, and she's venting air like a cheesecloth."

He narrowed his eyes, and she needed nothing else to understand his question.

"No, De la Garza says they have it under control, but they're out of the fight."

"And Captain Estaban?"

"Dead, sir." She took a moment to breathe. It clearly hurt. "Lost in the attack that took their engine."

Harker nodded, and the silent prayer for a spacer lost in darkness immediately crossed his mind. "What else?"

She shrugged, which also clearly hurt. "We seem to have managed to establish the perimeter around the asteroid that you wanted, and the alien ships have not gotten through. I don't know how long we can hold them, however."

"The battle is not won," Harker said as the overhead display returned, "but it is—"

"Meaningless," came a soft voice, liquid on the vowels and long on the consonants.

Water burbled through her armor as Soliel drifted forward. Her wide-eyed cypher climbed up onto Harker's command couch and looked at him with the 'she's-in-one-of-her-moods' expression the captain had come to know so well.

"The balance here is about to shift; I can see it in the currents," she said, staring past all of them at the blackness outside. "We will turn the tide to us in space. But it does not matter. Only the fight on the asteroid truly matters. The paladin knows this, and you will too in a moment. That fight is on a knife's edge as we speak. Whoever can even breathe on the scales may tip them."

Constanza Digby sighed. "Now is not the time, lady. Speak plainly."

Soliel shook her head. "I can only say what I see."

"Some parts of that are clear enough," Harker said. He rubbed his temples. His eyes closed, and he had to fight to reopen them. "Mr. Digby, prepare landing parties. All able hands. We'll leave a skeleton crew and the walking wounded to hold the perimeter as long as they can."

Constanza seemed about to protest but ultimately held her tongue and nodded. "Aye, aye, Captain. And where will you be?"

"Where he's needed," Soliel said firmly. She kept staring at the stars as both of the other officers stared at her.

"Which is . . . ?" Digby prompted.

The comm on Harker's couch chimed. The captain signaled for quiet as he accepted the call.

Sebastian Cross's harried expression resolved in front of them. "Captain Harker. I can honestly say I'm pleased to see you still alive."

"And you, my lord," Harker replied. "But I doubt that's why you called."

"Indeed not, Captain. We are pressed to our limit here; there are far more noh than we thought possible, and our casualties have been high. Kasaro To is master of the Kyojin berserkers, after all. We require reinforcements—any and all that you can spare."

"I understand, my lord. We have already begun preparations. Unfortunately, while the battle here moves slowly in our favor, it remains a near thing."

Cross hesitated for a second. "If you feel that you cannot personally lead your troops, I understand. We have identified Kasaro To as commanding our opposition, along with a creature matching your description of the Herald. I will not question your insight or grasp of your duty, but another Knight's strength would stand us in good stead down here."

Harker rubbed his lips. "I appreciate that, my lord, but—" He paused as Soliel put her smooth, cool hand over his.

"Sometimes, you must follow the esper," she said softly.

Harker blinked at her open, warm expression. For an instant, he had not seen her face or heard her voice. For less than the beat of a heart, he had seen another place in a distant time and remembered galaxies long dead and old promises that still lived.

"Where do you need to be?" she asked.

Harker swallowed and took two breaths to control his voice. "I will join you on the surface, Lord Cross. We need a few moments to gather our forces and embark." He paused, considering. "And I need to find someone to take over coordinating this battle."

"I can manage this fight," Soliel said with easy confidence. "Go. I shall finish up here."

Digby's mouth dropped open. "Now wait just one minute. You don't know anything about fighting a ship, let alone coordinating a fleet."

"I don't need to." The witch placed her hand on the first mate's shoulder. "I have you to fight this ship and command the rest." Her eyes had gone black. Brilliant pinpricks of light burned across them like a starry night. "I can see it all and tell you where they will strike. You will be able to stop them."

"My—" Harker hesitated and licked his lips. "Lady Soliel, are you certain?"

She smiled as if she had just received a plate of her favorite dessert. "Of course. You have already done the hardest work. Space is just another ocean, and that is my home." She blinked, her eyes clearing, and she touched his arm. "Go. The fight is down there, my captain, not up here."

He took a breath and nodded. "Mr. Digby, you have the ship and the fleet. Follow Lady Soliel's direction and keep the aliens away. Send the order for landing parties to all commands."

She nodded.

Harker turned back to Cross. "How long can you hold, my lord?"

The paladin frowned. "As long as we must, but I pray you, do not dawdle."

"Tell them to home in on the paladins' landing zones and set down at any one that has defenders and a flat space. They have fifteen minutes at most."

"Thank you, captain," Cross said and cut the link.

"Be—" Digby hesitated and then saluted Harker. "Be careful, Captain. Take no prisoners."

"Aye, aye, Mr. Digby." He grinned and grabbed up his cloak as he strode away.

He had given his crews fifteen minutes, but his own attack skiff slid into the thin atmosphere only eight minutes after the order.

"Lock onto Lord Cross's position," he told the pilot as he flipped on the comm. "For better or worse, that's where the heaviest fighting will be. Captain Morteen, follow us in."

The grizzled commander had barely acknowledged before render beams began snaking up at them from the surface. The assault skiffs slipped and danced around the ragged attacks, and the wide swings gave Harker a broader view of the battles.

"There," he said, pointing through the armored viewport. "Just beyond them, do you see that?"

"Looks like noh moving through the crystal," the pilot said, swerving again.

"Exactly. Bring us around over that movement." He turned and strode back to the assault compartment. "Ready, lads and lasses?" he called. "We're dropping straight on top of 'em!"

A rousing shout rang back at him. Moffet arched an eyebrow but grinned all the same.

"Nothing like getting stuck in," he said.

She shook her head. "Someday, captain, you'll get stuck in somewhere you can't get out of."

"Yes," he agreed, smiling back. "But hopefully not today."

The skiff slowed, turned slightly, and the indicators switched to yellow.

"Stand by," Harker called.

The bottom doors hissed open, the gravity dampener fields

engaged, and the lights turned green all at once.

"Go, go!" the captain shouted and leapt through the nearest opening.

The dampener fields slowed his descent, and Harker angled to come down nearly on the shoulders of a surprised Hatriya warrior. The noh raised his weapon, but Harker casually batted it away and let momentum drive his sword through the monster's chest. He shot down two hounds preparing to leap at his crewmen and turned to see three berserkers racing forward. Their howls nearly deafened him. He shifted left, trying to keep all of them from reaching him at once.

Then the first one stumbled and fell on his face. Blood pumped from wounds in the creature's neck. Moffet briefly flickered back into reality to slip her blade behind the knee of the next charging monster. She slashed three times as it fell, and the noh gurgled as its lungs filled with its own blood. The third berserker swung its heavy blade at her, but Moffet had already disappeared again. She appeared between eye blinks inside the noh's reach and rammed her sword up under its chin. The reaver's eyes glazed over. Moffet neatly stepped aside as her victim fell.

She grinned again at Harker. "Someday. But not today."

He raised his sword in salute and turned back to the fight. The corsair's surprise assault had scattered the noh formation, slain the Hatriya coordinating the attack almost instantly, and quickly overwhelmed the scattered survivors. Harker rallied his people and shouted them forward, pushing around to the right side of the landing plateau where he had seen still more movement. They quickly came upon several groups of berserkers and hounds held in check by more warriors. Suppressing fire from the paladins kept them waiting. Harker understood their reluctance to rush over the dozen or so meters of crushed crystals between them and their enemies. He suspected that the group they had just destroyed was to provide a diversion for these creatures here, a diversion that would never come. With a shout he charged forward into the noh.

The berserkers rose and countercharged with a roar, the

hounds scattered, and warriors wisely used the confusion to fall back. The paladins quickly shifted to more precise shooting. Harker cut down two as they got close. He shot several hounds when they paused to feast on crushed human remains wearing rags in his ship's colors. With gritted teeth, he pushed his people forward until the last noh had fallen and the hounds fled. Then they turned and hurried up to the cheering defenders.

Sebastian Cross personally lifted Harker to the plateau. "Good to see you, captain," he said with a broad, tired smile. Iron-rich rock dust and crystal power caked in the blood streaked across his relic, some of it from the paladin.

"Good to be here," Harker replied. "We feared you might leave little for us to do if we waited much longer." He nodded to Malya, equally disheveled and regarding him with a tired stare.

Cross actually smiled at the terrible quip, and Harker took that as the clearest sign yet of the paladin's fatigue. "Sadly, there's much yet to do." He pointed nearly over Harker's shoulder. "We believe that our objective lies within that cave. Our cyphers have both identified it the destination for all the esper flows on this asteroid. Indeed, we think this region of space has been repurposed to direct esper to that point."

Harker nodded slowly, still inspecting the distant smear of darkness. "That makes sense of why they would choose an asteroid of a certain density and dimensions and drag it into a stationary location."

"We also know that virtually every noh in the sector is between us and there," Malya said, her voice hoarse. He glanced at her, concerned, but she ignored the expression and pointed down. "We think there are tunnels leading to the cave."

"Then we should find them. I dare say it's better than trying to cross that killing ground." He glanced up to see his cypher circling closer. "Caesar, my friend, locate the nearest tunnel entrance."

The creature cawed and rose quickly.

"We're not all going to fit through those tunnels," Malya said.

"We need not," Jeanne Romee said. She stepped over broken bits of noh armor as she approached. "If we locate a way to the enemy, you must take it. You and Lord Cross and the good captain here. A few of the Paragons may accompany you, but it is you three who have the best chance of success."

"I agree," called Isabeau. The Purifier moved with surprising grace considering the obvious wound in her side. Though blood stained her skirt and sword, and her emerald green hair was matted and singed, she had lost none of the quiet calm and confidence she had displayed on the battlecruiser. "A smaller team has a better chance of success, if you're all Knights. If we occupy their attention here, they won't be watching for you."

"Now just a cold minute," Malya cried. "We're getting slaughtered out here. They'll just keep throwing attacks at us until they overrun each landing site. We can't just—"

"Sit here and wait for that, no," Isabeau said, nodding. "I've already sent orders to consolidate here. There's several other landing sites holding their own—we seem to have caught the brunt of the attacks. They're packing back onto their ships or striking off across the crystal fields. Some will be here momentarily, and the rest whenever they can." She grinned and settled her sword across her shoulders, appearing to enjoy this. "We came all this way so that you could stop the Calamity. You need to get in and do that. We'll make sure you have something to come back to."

Malya drew breath to argue, but Jeanne cut her off.

"No, princess. She's right. We'll hold this ground and their attention." A surprising, almost fanatic glint came into the young Paragon's eyes. "I swear it."

"And she," Sebastian Cross said, "is the one who holds against all odds. If Jeanne swears it, it will be so." He glanced at his subordinates and both nodded to him.

Harker could feel the shift in the air, the resolution now that decisions were made and courses set. It almost felt like the moment that the sails bellied with air, or the main drives engaged, and the ship began to move.

Malya turned to Harker, eyes wide. "We can't just leave them. We're barely holding on with two Relic Knights here. If we leave, they'll be cut apart."

"If we stay," Harker said, "then we will fail. All of us will die for nothing."

Malya choked on her next words. She stared at him for a second, and he saw her tears well. She closed her eyes and let them run silently for a second before nodding. A sound rose in Harker's mind. On instinct, he cocked his head as he concentrated, and the sound resolved into the voice of his cypher. He saw Mr. Tomn and Cross's cypher Rook both come to attention, also listening.

"Caesar has found the nearest tunnel entrance. There are a few noh just inside it, but they should be no problem." He grinned. "Come. Let's finish this."

Kasaro To watched the ripple of explosions spread across his forward lines and frowned. He would soon run out of hounds. He needed to attack again, but he had not yet moved the remaining berserkers into position. With the asteroid's strange esper patterns throwing off the rift generators—or so the wayfinders had snivelingly assured him—and his ships still engaging the pirates above them, he had little choice but to use the tunnels for the approach. The reports from his Hatriya of the increased difficulty controlling the madmen even while still drugged concerned him; perhaps whatever the Herald was attempting here really was unbalancing everything. He shrugged and hefted his weapons. He would join the fight and see it ended, no matter the distractions.

One of the priestesses beside him suddenly convulsed and choked. Her eyes rolled back, and her face went slack. Kasaro To turned toward her rigid form and waited. Her lips moved, but it took a moment for sound to come forth. When she did speak, the voice of a male noh warrior drifted from her lips. "Anointed One. We have lost contact with the warriors at the end of the southwestern tunnel. They seem to have been attacked. We also cannot see any evidence of the Knights that formerly defended the plateau."

Kasaro To frowned. Sebastian Cross's gigantic relic was

difficult to lose track of.

"The southwestern tunnel system is the largest one we have mapped," the voice continued, "and we fear that the Knights and perhaps a small force are using it to infiltrate our lines."

"You have done well to inform me," he said. "Continue as you were. I will deal with the Knights."

"As you and Nozuki will," the warrior replied.

The priestess gasped and collapsed.

Kasaro To waved to one of the other priestesses. "Send word to Homumi To to take his berserkers down the southwestern tunnel. Tell him that we suspect our enemies are there and to kill all that he finds."

The priestess nodded but hesitated before leaving. "Anointed One, that is a small force. If the Knights are indeed coming that way, Homumi To likely cannot stop them."

"Then he is not worthy to serve with me," Kasaro To replied, setting his weapons on his relic. He reached for the last pieces of his armor.

"But Anointed One, if the Knights continue up that tunnel, they will reach the caves where the Herald awaits."

He paused. "Yes, they will."

"She said she must not be disturbed." The priestess's consternation amused him.

"She did say that, yes."

"But lord, if they disturb her, they may disrupt the ritual."

"The Herald has made it more than clear that she can take care of herself. I see no reason not to take her at her word. If she cannot, then she also is not worthy."

"But interrupting a ritual may cause it to fail regardless of the practitioner's worth. It has nothing to do with strength."

His amusement faded. "I am Kasaro To, Chosen of Nozuki and Anointed of the Hydra God," he said a little wearily. He grew tired of repeating his credentials. "I am His messenger among our people, the incarnation of his will. What I do, I do not only with His blessing but as a reflection of His own true desires. Is that understood?"

The priestess nodded. "Of course, lord, but—"

With only a flicker of consternation, Kasaro To struck. His tetsubo connected with the priestess's chest, collapsing her ribcage and rupturing nearly every organ in her torso. The blow had such force that she cracked the rock wall behind her when she struck it.

He looked at the next priestess in line. "Did you hear my commands?"

The other priestess nodded firmly, her face a carefully blank mask, her eyes fixed on his.

"Then go and see my will done."

She nearly fled from his presence, and Kasaro To smiled.

CHAPTER 24

Origin Point, wildspace

Malya frowned at the crystals that threw more shadows than light through the tunnel. The esper crystals grew almost as thickly underground as they did on the surface. Even with Sebastian's relic battering them down with easy sweeps of its massive mace, they still made agonizingly slow progress. The noh they had killed at the tunnel entrance and the group of Hatriya and berserkers that had come barreling into them a few minutes ago had not helped matters.

She floated just behind the two men, keeping an eye on the path behind, while all their cyphers scouted the route ahead. She drummed her fingers on the side of Sedaris's saddle. Every moment they spent slogging through this mess meant more lives lost above. She still could not believe the ease and willingness Jeanne and Isabeau had shown in volunteering to stay, fight, and die for nothing more than to buy the Knights time. The whole idea made her sick, but she could not deny the necessity. That was what sickened her the most.

"Sacrifice is the way of all life," said a calm, melodious voice from below her. She glanced down to see Rook. The paladin cypher leapt easily onto her relic and climbed with simple grace to stand on her control yoke. Though he seemed to have no face and, thus, no expression in the shadow of his armored helm, he radiated reassurance, solidity, and wisdom, not unlike his Knight. "All life ends, but a life that ends in service to another is never truly gone. They live on in the lives they have touched. We are the sum of all the lives—simple and complex, humble and great— that have gone before us. Some died only to give us nourishment;

others died to give us hope and opportunity. And we," he glanced at Cross, "die so that others may live safe and free."

"Let's hope it doesn't come to that," she replied and revved Sedaris's engine.

Rook looked questioningly at her and she winked back. He jumped clear of her relic as she rose a bit higher and edged next to the paladin.

She tilted slightly to see both of the other Knights. "I'm going to run ahead."

"We don't know what's there," Cross replied, looking up. "Even Caesar can't see very far through this gloom."

"I know, but we don't have the time for too much caution." She smiled with more confidence than she felt. "Trust me. Turn around. Harker, get behind him."

"What are you—?" The pirate stopped when he saw Sedaris's blades extend while the relic's limbs tucked in. "Oh."

Cross clearly got the hint as well, because he twisted his relic mecha around and crouched to shelter his body and Harker's.

Malya eased backward, building up thrust without releasing it, and aimed just slightly to the left of the paladin. Mr. Tomn bounced into view, leapt from the other relic, and landed on her control yoke. She had not seen her cypher this pleased in a long, long time. She ducked down until she could just barely see over her handlebars, began moving green-blue esper through her relic to repair any damage, and rocketed forward.

Sedaris raced past the other knights and barreled into the crystals along the tunnel floor. She flew through the razor-sharp forest like a cannonball through glass. Her blades lead the way, and she slowed only slightly as she encountered resistance. Crystals shattered, smashed, and a few outright exploded behind her. She shifted her esper away from repairing or healing nicks and cuts to simple, pure speed and began to twist gently on the control yoke. She moved so quickly that the shrapnel and shockwaves vented their fury on the crystals around them rather than her. Mr. Tomn guided her around bends in the tunnel, protrusions in the cave wall, and stalagmites that loomed suddenly from the ground. Neither of them noticed the four strange, shadow-shrouded figures until they had sped well past them.

Malya and Mr. Tomn shared a quick glance, and she pulled Sedaris into a looping wingover, speeding up one of the tunnel walls, across the ceiling, and down the other side in the opposite direction. Crystal shards rained down behind her like a shower of razor blades. She angled to widen the path of shattered crystals, but when she spotted the figures again, she moved to intercept. They had turned toward her, clearly tracking her, and one on her right raised its arms.

Sedaris jerked, as if it had struck deep mud, and Malya nearly flew over the handlebars. She grunted as she slammed forward and aimed a red-green esper bolt at the figure. Closer now, she could see the figures more clearly in the strange, sickly blue light falling from many of the nearby crystals. Her attack struck the target in her chest and burned cleanly through her light armor, black bodysuit, and the porcelain flesh beneath. She died without a sound, falling back into the esper shadows around her. Her body never hit the ground.

The other three women attacked in unison. Black bolts of violet-edged esper crackled into Sedaris, ripping through its armor and savaging its systems. Mr. Tomn shrieked piteously as one of them scorched across his fur. The smell of burnt flesh and hair filled Malya's nose. She gritted her teeth against the searing heat and raced toward the nearest attacker. She swung sharply left a little too soon, so the woman did not duck away, but the relic's right arm shot out further than seemed possible. Its blade sliced the pale alien completely in half, though the shadows swallowed her too.

Suddenly, the esper drained away from Malya. She felt heavy, as if the gravity had tripled, and Sedaris turned sluggish. Mr. Tomn wailed softly. She turned to see one of the witches extending a hand toward her, the fingers clutched and squeezing empty air. Malya's breath caught in her chest and came only slowly. Energy poured out of her like water from a spring—she could almost see it. Sedaris stalled and faltered, stuttering toward the ground.

Motion caught her eye, and Malya turned to see the other alien leaping up. The flowing cloth draped about her reached impossibly forward. The lengths of fabric stiffened as esper infused them. The princess desperately wrenched on her control yoke. Sedaris's arm barely rose in time. The alien's hardened robes struck the relic and gouged deeply into its armor. Before Malya had time to recover, the alien's richly embroidered sleeve shot out like a whip. Malya managed to duck, but the attack sliced across her exposed shoulder. She felt blood welling out and running down her back. The wound burned. She tried to pull Sedaris free, but it had lost too much power. Mr. Tomn, pale as a ghost, fell from behind her as weak green esper rose from him toward her injuries. The witch floated closer, blood dripping from the edges of her robe.

Gunshots rang out, and the alien died. Her eyes rolled up as she collapsed, and the shadows took her body. The last one, still draining the princess's life, turned at the sound but too late to avoid Sebastian's attack. His relic's mace caught her cleanly and sent her broken form flying into the dimness of the cave. They never heard it land.

Harker raced to Malya even as she felt her power and strength returning. She looked desperately around for Mr. Tomn and found the cypher standing up, wobbly, his color returning. Warmth settled over her then, and she saw esper rising to surround her. Cross moved his relic back just a bit, to give her space, and she nodded in thanks. She focused her native power then and felt her wounds closing. "Thanks. What were they?"

"Alliance Security calls them void witches," Sebastian Cross said. "We've only a few recordings of them, all from other galaxies. You're the only person I know of who has survived a fight with them."

"I know of a few others who have," Harker said, "but not many. Soliel is the only other one I've ever met. And I've never even heard of anyone surviving four of them."

"It means we're close," Cross said, staring down the passage.

They heard a squawk from above, and Harker raised his arm

for Caesar to land on. The bird chittered at him for a second.

"Indeed we are, Lord Cross," the pirate said. "Two turns yet, Caesar says. Are you fit for this?" he asked Malya.

She took a deep breath and nodded.

Harker climbed onto the lowered arm of the paladin's relic and gripped its superstructure tightly. "Let's not keep them waiting."

Candy locked Kisa's medical cot into one of the infirmary's docking bays. She took a second to figure out which of the cot's hook-ups plugged into which of the bay's ports. She finally jammed the cords into what looked like the most likely spots and hoped for the best. The cot's displays all turned green and the wall displays synched up. She figured that was the best she was going to get and turned to hook up Cordelia. That went faster, now that she had the general idea, and she locked the cots in place before heading for the bridge. The *Lucky Chance* shifted under her feet and Candy stumbled along the hallway, but she took it in stride. A small price to pay for finally getting out of here for somewhere reasonably safe, she decided.

Fiametta didn't look up as Candy entered the bridge. "The hangar doors are still open."

"Thank goodness for small favors," Candy muttered as she slid into the copilot couch. "What do you need me to do?"

"Watch those secondary monitors. That's the tracking. We're still cloaked, but we can always get hit or rammed by accident."

"We still haven't talked about where we're going," Candy said, trying to sound casual.

"I guess 'anywhere but here' isn't a good answer, is it?" Fiametta sighed as she focused on maneuvering out of the docking bay. "Look, I know your objections, but I would have suggested Catermane for a variety of reasons."

"We're not—" Candy stopped as her brain processed the last statement. "Wait, 'would have'? Why aren't you suggesting it?"

Fiametta's face was drawn and looked washed out in the

yellow light from the displays. She clearly had to concentrate on flying, and Candy started feeding sensor data to the pilot's panel to help. But the tightly controlled emotion in Fiametta's reply did not all come from the tricky maneuvering. "It—It sounds like Catermane is completely overrun."

Candy blinked; she had no response.

"The report came in while you were in sickbay. Black Diamond—or at least that bastard Leopold Magnus—has mounted a full-scale invasion."

"An invasion," Candy said, still trying to process the fact. "Of the Doctrine capital world. That's idiotic. It's a violation of the Rakert Treaties; a blatant act of war."

Fiametta shrugged. "I said he was a bastard. Anyway, that option's completely off the table."

Candy paused, considering, and finally laughed with some bitterness. Lights flashed across her panels, and she turned her attention back to them. "Well, I would have suggested taking Cordelia to Ulyxis. Seems like that's not such a smoking hot idea either."

Fiametta laughed harshly and flipped the *Chance* over twice to avoid a disintegrating pirate ship. "This would be easier if we knew more about the Source."

"I know everything I need to know for now," Candy replied, focusing on a series of disturbing readings. "The Source is a chee named Cordelia, and that's what matters. Frankly, she's been 'studied' enough."

"Agreed," Fiametta said, and wrenched the controls to send their ship spinning away from a dozen fighters in a rolling dogfight. "We still don't have a destination. We need someplace to hide, heal, and figure out what to do next."

"We need to get lost, preferably in plain sight," Candy said. "And we better do it fast. It looks like that paladin battlecruiser's sensor package is better than we thought. I think they're tracking us."

"What? How?"

"Don't know, but they've got sensor beams falling all around us. They don't have a fix, but they're close."

"Mother of Night," Fiametta muttered, and swung the *Chance* hard to port to avoid an expanding ball of debris that had been a corsair boarding ship. "We need a destination, now!"

"I don't know," Candy shot back. "I mean, if you needed to disappear but still be connected to what's happening and have access to medicine and whatever else, where would you go?" She blinked and stared at Fiametta as the obvious answer rose in her mind.

Fiametta stared back with clearly the same thought in her head. "So bloody obvious," she muttered as she swerved again. "Excellent services, huge crowds that are mostly strangers, and I even have a few favors to call in there. Get me that course."

"Copy," Candy replied automatically and called up the preset from the navigation computer. A silent explosion lit them all in angry red light for an instant. "Does this tub have any guns?" She turned to look into the silence and found Fiametta glaring at her.

"It's not a tub." Fiametta jerked her chin behind them. "Dorsal and ventral mounts, but I can't shoot them and fly at the same time. They're routed to a common panel in the secondary control station, though. The big round room."

"Got it," Candy replied. The course confirmation came up on her display. She punched the accept icon and then bolted back for the weapons control. The round meditation room lay about twenty meters and half a deck behind and above the bridge. She made it with only a few bruises from Fiametta's fancy flying. Kneeling on one of the overstuffed cushions, Candy took a few seconds to bring up the weapons displays.

Her eyes widened, and she grinned involuntarily. "Gods of our fathers," she whispered.

Fiametta chuckled over the internal comms. "I thought you'd like that. However lucky she may be, Kisa does prefer to stack the deck."

"No kidding," Candy replied, skimming the displays. "Rapid-fire pulse cannons. A macro-load rail rifle with extended targeting. Hydrian implosion missiles? Are those even legal on civilian ships?"

"Not in the Alliance."

"I promise not to tell," Candy said, awed. "Oh, I take back everything I said about this ship."

"Good. Now clear the road. There's a lot between us and the acceleration run to slip space."

Candy adjusted the fire controls and fed in the expanded sensor data. Her heart sank. "I'm not liking this, Fia. Even with these marvelous toys, I don't think we can shoot our way clear."

"Well, try."

Candy sighed and tapped the nearest two targets, things the computer tagged as some sort of unknown heavy fighter. Neither Alliance nor paladin, and therefore a bad guy, she decided. Fast and maneuverable, the computer estimated it had only a forty-four percent chance of hitting the craft. Candy removed one target and set both pulse cannons to fire on a single ship, but that only upped her chances to sixty-two percent. At that rate, she figured, they would destroy three of the four fighter craft in their immediate vicinity, but the last would see them and probably end it. She tapped the Fire icon anyway.

The strobing flashes of pulse cannon fire raced away over her head. A second line of energy bursts appeared from under the ship. In an instant they converged on the alien craft, and though it flipped over with almost impossible nimbleness, the shots caught and shattered its wings and engine housing. The other three fighters turned toward the source of the unexpected attack. Then all the fighters vanished in balls of expanding gas and burning oxygen.

Candy looked disbelievingly at her display. The computer said that a cluster of hyper-speed rail gun slugs had torn the craft apart. "That's capital grade anti-fighter weaponry," she muttered and, on instinct, looked up through the armored glass roof.

The paladin battlecruiser had come uncomfortably close. Its point defense batteries sprayed down the areas around the *Lucky Chance* with nickel-iron slugs moving at what would be escape velocity on any habitable planet. A dozen fighters and small attack craft vanished in an instant. The comms crackled beside her panel, and she heard a calm, professional voice.

"Doctrine vessel, this is the *Inexorable Justice*. You are clear for slip run. Good luck."

"What just happened?" Fiametta asked.

"Once again, I don't care," Candy replied. "Punch it." A second later, the ship lurched forward, bucked hard, and forced its way out of reality.

CHAPTER 25

Origin Point

Sebastian Cross led the way down the tunnel and moved boldly. In short order, the passage widened into an enormous chamber. Malya honestly could not believe that the asteroid could accommodate such a space without collapsing. Blue-white light fell softly across the vast space and glinted off of polished stone walls. The reflections had an unhealthy sheen to them that made Malya vaguely nauseous. The cathedral ceiling peaked dozens of stories above them, its features only dimly visible from the weak lights and pulsing veins of esper that ran through every surface. All six esper types flowed through the room, hundreds of rivulets of each type twining and swirling around the others but never mixing. Her eyes followed these paths and saw that the esper moved to the rhythm of a staggering heartbeat toward a huge, ornate device of arcane and malevolent design at the lowest point of the chamber.

The device looked like nothing so much as a round mirror clutched by six spidery talons. Each of these black claws pointed to the distant ceiling, and a halo of one of the esper types glowed faintly around them. She could make out ribbing and strange couplings beneath the disk that suggested bones and veins and the dried husks of dead things and somehow still seemed to writhe. The surface of the disk had the same sickening gloss as the walls, which lent it the glint of a mirror or still water. Diseased yellow-green oils slid across its surface. Esper motes drifted away from the talons and collected into a roiling blue-black above the disk. Each of the six colors shimmered briefly across its surface before vanishing inside, subsumed into black.

Malya could not look at the device for long without getting dizzy. She tore her gaze away and focused on the angelic figure floating between them and the machine.

She was almost divinely beautiful, even at this distance. Clad in violet-tinged armor, with alabaster hair spilling from her near-featureless battle helm, she turned slowly on arcane wings of esper. She turned a distant, almost disinterested look on the three knights, and for an instant, Malya felt like a girl again. She was looking up at a woman who was everything that the princess wanted to be; powerful, distant, accomplished, untouchable. Everything she had felt when she saw her first racer. She shook her head, snapping out of it, and saw the other two drawing back much the same way.

"You have succeeded where I thought no one could," the alien said. Her warm voice carried to the entire chamber. Her distant indifference made Malya feel like an object instead of a person. "Congratulations. Your reward is oblivion."

"That," Harker managed after a ragged breath, "is Amelial, the Herald of the Void."

The alien cocked her head at this, and her eyes widened slightly. Had she been human, she would have looked impressed. The esperic ball behind the Herald pulsed twice, and the Knights shuddered as a wave of poisonous energy swept over them. Mr. Tomn wailed softly. Malya forced her eyes back to the device and saw the esper flowing faster.

The Herald smiled slightly at their pain. "Well done," she said to Harker. "Few ever learn so much of us if we do not choose to tell them. It will avail you nothing. The gate is opening. The Void Reaper approaches, and with him comes the death of the Last Galaxy." She turned lazily back to the rapidly pulsing esper and raised her arms. "Rejoice, for you shall be among the first to die." At her gesture, the ball of esper doubled in size, pulsed once, and then collapsed to a concentrated mote almost too small to see. That mote exploded. The collected esper washed across the room and struck them all in a freezing wave of corruption, entropy, and chaos. Malya's vision went dark.

When she could see again, she discovered that the surface of the mirrored disk had gone utterly black. No reflection raced over its face; not even light escaped it. It seemed to have gained depth, but she could see nothing within it. She pulled her gaze away, dizzy, and fought down the feeling of falling headlong into that pit.

"That is the Calamity," Harker shouted. He pointed to the disk without looking directly at it. "Nothingness; Darkspace. A universe devoid of life, of light, even of matter. That is what will become of everything if we don't stop them now."

"That is what will become of everything no matter what you do," said a rich, pleasing male voice.

Malya blinked and looked back at the machine. A shape, grey and vague like smoke, drifted out of the disk. She could not understand why she had not seen it there before. It rose into the chamber and shifted into a twisted, humanoid form. She saw the suggestion of wings, of arms, of robes across its slim body. Something like a cloud of hair trailed behind as it moved toward them.

"Futility is the definition of life," the voice continued, pleasant and warm. "What you see here is the answer to that futility; nothingness. The perfect dark, the original being of all things. The void, unspoiled and undiluted." The voice seemed to come from all around them, though they all looked at the smoke.

"Don't let it touch you," Cross hissed.

"You have done well, my Herald," the voice said, focused away from them this time. It had lost some of its echo.

The Herald bowed her head. "It is my honor, my lord. And my pleasure."

"And mine as well. Now, let us begin the final work."

"Are you going to talk all day or get on with it?" Harker shouted.

The Herald glared at him, but the voice laughed. It definitely sounded more solid. The smoke, however, broke apart and swirled around them. "Patience, Captain Harker. There is much to do, but it must all happen in its own time. Yes, we know your name, though for all your desire and tireless effort, you do not know us. All your sacrifices and pain could not discover what you most wished to learn. Now, when it no longer matters, I will grant you that wish. I am Harbonath."

The small hairs on the back of Malya's neck rose, and she whipped her head around. She saw a shadow in the smoke, like someone looming out of a fog. A huge, skeletal humanoid relic appeared behind her. Bound in its ornate ribcage stood a beautiful man. His porcelain skin and perfect features accentuated the malice in his eyes. He wore a black-and-white armored bodysuit similar to the Herald's.

When he saw Malya watching, he winked at her. "Be careful what you wish for."

Too late, she saw that the relic had its arm drawn back. Too late, she realized that it had summoned a massive scythe. She screamed and reached out; too late. She could not stop it. The blade seemed to hiss through the thin air, leaving a bone-numbing chill in its wake. Harker had an instant's presentment, and he twisted away, but the scythe still raked him across the body from shoulder to hip. Harker sobbed and flew back from the force of the blow. Blood splattered out. It instantly pooled into droplets in the low gravity and formed a thin skin of ice. Caesar screeched and plummeted to the floor. Black tendrils of esper like silk cords trailed from the pirate's body. Yellow-gold esper flowed from him up those trails and coiled around the scythe. Harbonath sighed in obvious pleasure.

Without a word or shout, Sebastian Cross raced toward Harbonath and swung with his mace. He struck hard enough to shatter starship armor. Harbonath grunted and went spinning away. Cross swept the Shattered Sword down through the black tendrils, and the blue fire along its blade broke the esperic connections with an audible snap. The pirate gasped and shuddered. Caesar picked himself up and hopped over to his Knight. Malya saw green-white esper flow from the cypher to enshroud the captain.

"Princess, the gate!" Sebastian moved between her and the now upright Harbonath. "Destroy the gate."

She wrenched Sedaris around to face the shimmering black disk. Mr. Tomn bounced up and grabbed onto one of the relic's maneuver fins. Rook leapt and clung to one of her forward stabilizers. She shot him a surprised, questioning look. The paladin's cypher responded with a calm nod, and a sense of reassurance washed over her. She fired her thrusters, but the Herald moved to intercept her. A blue-violet energy blade flickered to life in her hand, haloed with void-dark esper. Malya set her jaw and increased her speed.

The black halo spread up the Herald's arm to encompass her entire body. It pulsed rapidly for a few seconds as Malya closed the distance and then burst outward. The protective fields around her relic shimmered ever so slightly at the passing of the energy, but the machine registered no damage. And then she realized that damage did not matter. The Herald had already moved between her and the gate. The alien's blade drank in the weak light around them, and the princess could feel it leaching her esper. Nothing she did, nothing she tried, would get her past Amelial and her vampire sword. She was not fast or strong enough to succeed; none of them were. Even Cross was struggling against Harbonath, and this was only the vanguard. The armies of oblivion would march through that disk from their endless abyss; bitter angels of the void come to snuff out existence, and nothing anyone could do would stop them. Futility overwhelmed her.

She shuddered and shook with sobs as she surrendered to the terror and despair. She felt Mr. Tomn strengthening Sedaris's defenses, but it would make no difference. They all would be cut apart like every other galaxy—like everyone who had opposed these aliens. She could not get enough air, though she gulped it down. Her blood-stained, sweat-soaked bodysuit clung to her clammy skin as tears streamed over her cheeks.

Then Sedaris stuttered and barrel-rolled left. The spin almost threw her off, and when they came upright, she saw the Herald floating behind with a look of frustrated rage. She had attacked,

Malya realized, and her relic had acted of its own volition to save her life. And it had; the blow had missed.

Almost at once the cloud in her mind vanished. The aliens could be defeated. Harker's people had been killing them in space. They could be stopped, and no one had a better chance than these three Knights, right here, right now.

She felt Rook place a hand on her calf. "This is what you were born to do," he said. "Go, and fear no darkness."

Esper from Mr. Tomn flooded into Malya along with adrenalin. She grinned, turned Sedaris, and raced back toward the Herald. The relic's arms extended, and its sword glittered with esper. Amelial raised her sword to guard, but Malya leveled her weapon and sent a blast of pink and gold esper into the alien. The blade seemed to split the esper, shearing away some of the attack's destructive power but none of its pure force. The Herald tumbled end-over-end, shrieking, as the princess pulled up and changed her attack angle.

Amelial regained control almost immediately, esper pouring from her wings, and streaked back the way she had come. Malya saw the second when the alien realized that the princess was not where she had been. She recognized the instant when, because of their combined speeds, the alien would have no chance to dodge or even react. And she saw the look in Amelial's eyes when she realized that too.

Mr. Tomn poured esper into Malya and Sedaris, bringing them to impossible speeds. The Herald's desperate twist and swing at the racer seemed slow and clumsy. Malya ducked easily under it and drove her blade through Amelial's stomach. Power coursed along the weapon and burned at the alien from within. Amelial screamed. Blue-white light streamed from every seam in the Herald's armor until it cracked and shattered. Her wings cut, her mind overwhelmed, her body broken, Amelial tumbled away from the princess and slammed into the cavern's rocky floor.

Malya glanced over to where Sebastian Cross and Harbonath still fought. Both relics were damaged; Cross's mecha was deeply scarred and trailed smoke. The Void Reaper's machine, however, had lost an arm and he lacked something of his former swagger. He glanced over as the Herald fell, and an angry, frustrated growl echoed from him. Malya recognized the duel for what it was, Sebastian buying time, and turned Sedaris around. She winked at Harbonath and sped toward the gate.

"No," Harbonath shouted, barely audible behind her. "No, you will not deny me!" A shock wave rippled past her, and she risked a glance behind. The Void Reaper had sacrificed one of his relic's legs to land a blow that threw the paladin across the cavern. Harbonath fired his immense thrusters and raced after Malya. For a sinking instant, she though he might catch her. Then the skeletal relic shuddered and stumbled, as if it had reached the end of its tether. Behind, she saw Sebastian Cross, his relic on one knee, extending his hand as if clutching the Void Reaper. The alien machine strained, but the paladin pulled it backward inch by inch.

Red-gold esper laced with black rippled across Harbonath's relic like water on a force shield. Cross's psychic bonds snapped. The paladin grunted in pain, and the Void Reaper rocketed toward Malya. He would be too late, she saw. She turned back and found her goal just below her. A quick pull on the handlebars turned Sedaris into a sharp skid and brought her in a tight circle around the circumference of the disk. Thin, foul-smelling trails of wispy gray esper, like steam rising from a hot spring, drifted lazily up from it. She stared down into the darkness.

It looked infinite, like a tunnel, and she knew that it was. The gate had opened, and it connected this galaxy to . . . somewhere cold and alien. It did not look like anything at first, but then she saw distant energies like lightning. The energies reflected on the shapes and forms of an irregular landscape. Even this emptiness, then, held something. As she watched, that something moved. It took on definition and scale and finally intent. Ghost images like the smoke that had brought the Void Reaper drifted closer and quickly became clear enough. She recognized humanoid shapes in ordered rows, soldiers moving with drilled precision and inhuman grace. Others floated around or near them, discernible only by the shadows they cast in the smoke. She felt cold, and a terror clearer than the Herald's illusion swept over her. This was an army, an alien army, and they were coming to murder the galaxy.

Malya shook her head and turned from the approaching enemies to the means of their arrival. The gate seemed solid; she could see no moving parts from this angle. Even the writhing and twisting of its lower systems seemed like a consequence of the gate's function rather than a key to it. She cast around for anything that might be a point of weakness. Mr. Tomn leapt down and hovered just above the oily surface and searched frantically. They could all feel the Void Reaper bearing down on them.

One of the gray wisps shifted and curled around her cypher. A small, thin creature materialized behind him. Its white robe matched Harbonath's armor, and its cruel scythe mirrored the one his relic bore. The thing seemed surprised to find Mr. Tomn there, but before the rabbitlike cypher could react, the grim imp swept its blade through his body.

Mr. Tomn only whimpered—Malya howled. The connection between them vanished in an instant, as if someone had turned off a faucet. Pain and weakness from the psychic backlash raced through her whole body. She focused long enough to see Mr. Tomn fall past the gate toward the cavern floor, his body fading as he went. From her left, she heard Harbonath laugh, almost cackle, and saw tendrils of black esper edged in gold swirling about him like dust. Cross was on his feet and running, but he would never reach them in time.

The superficial damage on the Void Reaper's relic vanished. "Well done, my cypher," he called to the imp. He moved more swiftly, and his voice had renewed strength. "Now, princess," he shouted as he closed, scythe raised, "for you."

Gunshots rang out, and Harbonath staggered. He turned slightly and a bullet coated in yellow esper caught his relic in the left side. The ribcage snapped closed to shield him from the blast, but the strike drove him off course.

Harker lowered his pistol. How he had crawled this far, or

found the strength to raise the weapon—let alone summon an esper attack—she could not guess. He looked too pale to even still be conscious.

Caesar streaked in at the robed imp and clawed at it. It hissed and swung its scythe with little effect. Green healing esper rose around her instinctively, and she dove toward the pirate.

"The gate," Harker called, so weak she could barely hear him. "Nothing else matters. The gate."

She pulled up so sharply that Rook barely held on. He climbed up to her handlebars as she replied, "How?"

"The talons," Harker said, weaker still. "They condense and transfer esper. Break them."

"But you—"

"Can't," he said. "So you must." His eyes flicked to the side, where Harbonath was back up and charging. "Only speed matters now, princess."

She nodded once, tears back in her eyes, and fired her thrusters. Sedaris whipped around and shot forward like a bullet. Another glance showed her that the Void Reaper would reach the gate just an instant after she did, and she opened her throttle all the way. It was not enough, she could tell, and with the connection to Mr. Tomn lost, she had no more energy to give. A thick haze hung over the disk like morning mist, and she knew that at least some of the enemy would materialize in a few seconds. She deployed her blades, hoping to destroy one talon at least before he struck. She looked back and saw Harbonath moving faster than she would have thought possible, raising his scythe. Blood flowed from a wound on his head, but his smile betrayed only exultant joy as his scythe began to swing.

Rook rose and leapt from her handlebars toward Harbonath. With a speed only possible through esper, the cypher moved into the path of the scythe. Blue light wreathed his armored form, and then he seemed to collapse into himself. With a thunderclap of displaced air, Sebastian Cross stood in his cypher's place. Malya barely had time to duck under his massive relic.

As she rose and looked behind, she saw the paladin's head

slightly bowed and his hands together in prayer. His relic had the Shattered Sword drawn up before it as if in salute. She heard the Void Reaper's hiss an instant before his blade struck the great Knight. The scythe punched through the shielding around the mecha with ease. It struck the Shattered Sword and, for the briefest of seconds, hesitated. Then the Sword exploded apart into four distinct pieces. Two flew past Harbonath and lodged into Sedaris's rear armor. The scythed pushed on and ripped through the relic's heavy armor until it pierced the paladin within. It struck him just below the sternum and sank to the haft before it stopped. Cross made no sound or motion.

Harbonath roared in triumph. "Hah! The twice-Shattered Sword! Little good will it—" He stopped as he pulled on his weapon, but it did not budge. He pulled again, and then wrenched on it with all his relic's might. "No! What is this?"

Sebastian Cross's eyes opened, too slowly, and Malya could see their light going dim. He looked past his murderer to Malya. "Princess," he said in his quiet, commanding voice, as if they stood in sunlight with all the world before them. "The gate."

Malya drove Sedaris forward without another thought. The energy around her blade flickered weakly. Without Mr. Tomn, she felt like she had lost a lung, but she feared more that she would not be able to break the talons. A haze like that from which Harbonath had emerged had gathered over the disk and continued to grow. She was running out of time.

Then Caesar settled on Sedaris and squawked. A thought entered her mind, a point of failure in the machine's stone. She angled down, and struck the first claw below where it held up the disk. The impact nearly threw her from the relic, and she had to struggle to keep control and get her speed back, but the machine shuddered. She swung around and saw a similar fault in the next tine. She sped up, hope flaring in her heart, and suddenly energy raced along her blade. This hit sheared cleanly through the stone, and through the next talon, and the next.

The whole disk shifted and began to slip. The conduits and connections below the gate began to whip like a wounded snake.

She cut the last two supports, and arced up over the lip of the disk. The smoke above its surface began to form into a half dozen of the malevolent aliens, but inside the gate's blackness, the distant army had lost its definition and its cohesion. Indistinct figures milled around and seemed to flee from her.

A wail rose through the chamber, thin and high and chilling. One of the newly arrived aliens, its face shrouded by a deep hood, spread esper wings and charged at her with a clipped shout and a burning sword. She twisted and dove again. The image within the abyss wavered as the Void Reaper kept screaming denials, and then cracks appeared across the disk. With a sickening tear, the surface split, the oily fluid drained away, and the abyssal hole in the world vanished.

Malya flew beneath the failing structure, guided by the most tenuous intuition. She saw brief movement, a flash of white fur against the slick black mechanisms, and reached down. Mr. Tomn raised a paw and caught her arm as she raced by. The connection returned, surging back as she fed him esper. She pulled up as they emerged into the dim light, and turned toward Cross. The disk slipped again behind them, and the whole gate machine collapsed. As it fell, so did Sebastian Cross. The Void Reaper's scythe sprang suddenly free from the paladin's body, which could only mean that his will no longer held it. His relic fell like a stone and smashed on the cavern floor. Even as this speed and distance, Malya could see that the Knight was dead.

Caesar squawked again. Malya glanced up and saw the angelic monsters diving at her. As she turned away, Malya saw movement on the cavern floor. Harker raised his pistol yet again. He fired once at her pursuers and then collapsed. Caesar whined piteously.

"Not both of them," the princess swore though gritted teeth. "Not all of them. Not today." She swung around and grounded next to the pirate. Mr. Tomn helped her hoist him up and drape him across the back of the relic's saddle, wedged in place by the shards of the Shattered Sword sunk into her armor. With a kick and a roar, Sedaris rose again as the aliens came within range of their strange weapons. She dodged easily. Harbonath stood, desolate, over the wreckage of the gate. "Not today," Malya shouted and raced from the cavern.

CHAPTER 26

Origin Point

Kasaro To watched with mounting frustration as another wave of berserkers died among the paladins. "How much ammunition do they have left?"

The priestesses around him said nothing and kept their fearful, respectful distance.

How many berserkers did he have left? The thought struck him as odd the moment it entered his mind, and he could not recollect having asked that question before.

He summoned a priestess without looking. She approached no closer than the edge of his vision.

"Contact the ship. Tell them to prepare dahons, and get Rashinma To. I wish to speak to him about the beasts he has remaining."

She bowed and hurried off.

He growled again, frustrated, as he watched the last of his warriors die or fall back into the blood-soaked forest of crystals. "Nozuki take them all," he muttered. "We must—"

A wave of heat, like opening the door to a furnace, swept over him. It flowed from the cavern, and as he and the priestesses turned toward it, they all heard a soft wail drift from deep within the asteroid. The heat passed, and Kasaro To licked his fangs. The air tasted different but he could not say how. "What has—?"

A tall priestess convulsed as if an enormous hand had caught her in a crushing grip. She struggled to breathe for a second and then arched her back and rose two feet into the air as if lifted by her breastbone. A nimbus of red-black esper surrounded her, and the voice that issued from her mouth sounded like nothing in this universe.

"My servant," the voice said mildly, echoing from the stone. The esper crystals around them vibrated to its strange intonations, and many of them instantly cracked.

Kasaro To dropped to one knee. For the first time in more cycles than he could remember, he felt afraid. He knew that voice. "I am here, O Endless Hunger."

The voice of Nozuki, who had never spoken directly to him outside of the ritual chambers of the blessed temples, slithered around the jagged surface of the asteroid. "My servant. You have failed."

Kasaro To felt sick; genuinely queasy for the first time since Azi had appeared to him. He looked up at the suspended priestess. "Great Nozuki, I beg you, no. I have not driven the paladins from this rock yet, but I—"

"You have failed," his god repeated, each word falling like a stone. "The Knights of this galaxy have penetrated the inner chamber and prevented the Herald's ritual from completing. You were to guard her, to stop them. You have failed."

"Coiled One, no, I—"

"You contradict me?"

Kasaro almost said 'no' before he caught the word on his tongue. He swallowed. Sweat broke out all across his body. His arms began to tremble. "Great One, please understand. She insulted me—us. She denigrated you! She boasted so much of her great strength and the prowess of her people that I thought she could defend herself. We kept them from the chamber as best we could, but—"

"You lie." Nozuki's voice stayed mild, which made the indictment all the stronger. That cut through Kasaro as no weapon ever had, for he knew it was true. "You think I do not know all that has passed here, all that you have done and thought?"

"She was weak!" he shouted desperately. "She was weak and unworthy of you. She deserved destruction if she could not win with her own strength."

"Her worth is not for you to judge. Your place is not to know my mind or to claim your desires as my will. Your place is to do as I command. You have failed."

Instinctively, Kasaro To tried to rise. He reached for the priestess as if he could clutch his god's hand and beg still more. The possessed priestess moved with divine swiftness, however, and touched a fingertip lightly to the Relic Knight's brow. Every nerve in Kasaro's body seemed to catch fire. He howled in agony and writhed away from the fingertip. His muscles clenched as if trying to rip free from his bones. The pain passed in a few seconds, but his body continued to shudder and spasm.

"You must atone," Nozuki said a moment later, when Kasaro To could again process the words. "And you shall. There is yet value in this lonely, forsaken place, so here you will remain. You will drive the paladins from this rock, as you always should have done. You will secure the asteroid for our allies and guard it, as you always should have done." The Coiled God's voice dropped impossibly deep so that it vibrated through every organ in Kasaro's battered body. "And you will not fail me again."

The priestess collapsed in a heap beside the Knight, gasping for air. They lay together on the powdered crystals and cracked stone, twitching. Kasaro To recovered first and struggled to his feet. Blood seeped from a dozen cuts under and around his armor, and leaked from his ears and mouth. He spit and wiped his lips clean.

Azi appeared on his shoulder and fed him healing esper. Kasaro felt a few bones knitting back together. He desperately wanted to kick the unconscious priestess, still shaking on the ground before him. It would help nothing, he knew, and held back since Nozuki would be watching. He struck the cave mouth with his tetsubo instead, cracking the stone further, before leveling the weapon at the terrified priestesses watching him.

"One of you get me the ship. Now. Our god has commanded, and we obey."

———•———

Malya flew as fast as she dared, glancing back every few seconds to see that Harker's comatose form remained wedged in place. Each time, she saw that Mr. Tomn and Caesar had a firm grip on the fallen pirate. Each time, she thought he looked worse. She wondered if she would know if he died. She thought so, since she reckoned that Caesar would vanish with his Knight's life. It occurred to her only when she extended Sedaris's blades to cut down a trio of noh warriors near the tunnel's mouth that she did not know that for sure. It seemed logical, but logic, she reflected, had been conspicuously absent lately.

She soared into the brightness of open air and climbed through the thin atmosphere with undisguised relief. She had barely noticed the claustrophobia of the tunnels and caves until it was gone. She banked quickly, dropped, and flew low over the crystals toward the landing zones. The blocky, battered shapes of the assault shuttles loomed up. She rose a bit higher so as not to surprise any twitchy paladins with pulse rifles.

Almost at once she saw Betty waving. The landing zones were a true, grisly horror; bodies from both sides lay across the crystals. Blood shimmered on the rocks. Malya saw Jeanne and a junior paladin jogging over toward Betty and the clear space beside the pit chief. All of them wore field dressings, the junior paladin with his right hand bound into a fingerless mass of dirty cloth. Malya set down with limited grace and discovered that she had started to cry again.

Everyone looked exhausted. "What happened?" Betty asked and seemed to realize the question's inadequacy almost instantly.

Malya shook her head. "Later. I'll tell you everything later. First thing first, we need a medic for Captain Harker."

The junior paladin nodded and touched a comm in his ear.

"Second thing is that we succeeded. The device is destroyed, and whatever those bastards were trying to do failed."

"What was it?" Jeanne asked. She glanced around, clearly looking for someone. She finally fixed on the racer Knight with a grim expression. "What were they trying to do?"

"They had set up some kind of, of gate; like a direct pipeline to the abyss. They were trying to bring through an army of those bitter angels."

"There are more of them?" Betty looked stricken. "A few showed up here in the last attack, some troopers and a weird construct. They vanished when the last noh died, but I don't think we killed more than two of them." She swallowed hard, and her normally unflappable calm looked close to coming apart. "They almost killed Lug. Twice."

"Is he—?"

"He's okay," Jeanne cut in. Now that she looked more closely, Malya could see the young Paragon's nerve dissolving almost before her eyes. She was a Peer of the Shattered Sword, however, and kept focused. "You stopped them, though."

Malya nodded. "And destroyed their gate, or at least damaged it enough that they'll get no use from it for a good long time."

"You've done better than that," came a voice from Jeanne's feet. Her lion cypher Gallant bounded from around her legs and leapt onto Sedaris's front panel. "We could feel the shift here. The esper wave rolled over the entire asteroid."

"Is that what that was?" Mr. Tomn asked. "We were a bit busy at the time."

Gallant nodded. "Undoubtedly. Feel the flows."

Mr. Tomn closed his eyes and swayed ever so slightly, like a reed in a river. His eyes snapped back open a second later and the biggest grin split his face. "He's right. He's right! The flows have shifted. It must have been backlash from breaking the tines and collapsing the disk. They can't channel esper into the device properly anymore, even if they can repair it." He bounced again and again. "It worked! We did it!" Malya's smile at her cypher faded as she looked back at Jeanne's fixed expression.

"And Lord Cross?" Jeanne asked in a soft, barely controlled voice.

Mr. Tomn stopped bouncing and looked instantly chagrined.

"He—" Malya's voice failed her. She saw two paladin medics and the green-haired Purifier approaching at the run. She swallowed, took a deep breath, and started again. "He—He fell.

Saving me. Somehow he—Rook was with me, while Sebastian fought another Relic Knight. He called himself Harbonath, the Void Reaper. He broke free from Cross and would have caught me before I could get to the disk."

Betty's eyes went wide at the thought that anyone could catch the princess.

"He—Sebastian—teleported, I guess. He traded places with Rook and took the blow meant for me." She finally looked Jeanne in the face.

The young Paragon had turned ashen and tears streamed unnoticed over her cheeks.

Malya added, "He did it to save me. He made it possible. I'm so sorry."

"He's dead?" the Purifier asked. Malya could only nod. The paladin swallowed and blinked her eyes clear. "I—I see."

The paladin medics had likewise come up short, stunned by the news, but the Purifier drew herself up, smacked one on the shoulder and whistled piercingly through her teeth. "Go on. You've got work to do." She looked back at Malya. "He died saving your life and allowing you to finish the mission. That sounds exactly like him. We're—"

Jeanne collapsed beside them. Her knees unlocked and she just sank to the stone.

The junior who had accompanied her knelt instantly to grab her shoulders and keep her upright. "Jeanne," he said. "Jeanne, come on."

The young Paragon made no response. She stared straight ahead.

The Purifier swore, her green braids whirling as she reached down and started to haul Jeanne up. "Not now, not now, not now," she muttered. "We've lost the best of us. We won't lose all of us." She turned to the junior paladin, now nearly bone white from his wounds and all he had just heard. "Casteen, get her up and out of here. Give me your comm first."

He awkwardly removed the device with his uninjured hand and pulled on Jeanne again.

The Purifier—bloody, battered, burnt—had a look of resolved calm as she took a second to settle the comm in her ear. "Attention all Shattered Sword commands. This is Purifier Second Isabeau Durand. Command override four delta green. I am assuming control."

Malya felt it before she saw it, the shuddering pause that spread across the Peers like a wave as the message sank in. She looked around and hundreds of armored figures half rose or shuddered or turned to look toward this landing zone. Their First, their talisman, the warrior who had defined them, was dead. Training and devotion took over almost at once, but the sorrow and shaken confidence was palpable in the air.

"All commands begin a phased fallback," Isabeau went on. "Ships will lift immediately on boarding. We're done dying here." She switched channels and sent the recall out on the corsair frequencies as well.

Malya turned to help the medics lift Harker from her relic and lay him on a collapsible stretcher. Caesar settled onto his Knight's bloody abdomen, healing esper rolling off of him like water. "If we can get to the *Marianne* quickly," the cypher's voice reaching her mind weakly, "I believe I can save him."

She saw the medics start, surprised, and look at the cypher. "You heard the bird," Malya said, hopping that they had. "Move like you mean it."

"With a will, people," Isabeau shouted and then called over her shoulder. "Casteen!" The junior paladin had barely gotten halfway to the assault shuttle with Jeanne and looked back, concerned. "When you get in, tell the ships that we'll need pickup under fire. Tell Captain Corvan that we're withdrawing the fleet to one-point-five AUs and to coordinate with the pirates."

The young man nodded, hesitated, and frowned at her. "That's standard blockade distance."

"Yes," Isabeau replied, her eyes hard and her jaw set. "We're not letting these bastards out of our sight." She turned to Malya. "Get your people aboard. We'll go straight to the *Marianne*. If you have any way to warn them, do it. And don't dawdle. Ramp goes up in three minutes."

Betty raced off to get the crew.

Malya nodded, slid off of Sedaris, and turned to Mr. Tomn. "Get this thing aboard. I'll call the ship." She glanced at Harker. "And see what you can do for him."

The lop-eared cypher grunted and started the relic forward. Malya turned fully around once and then directed her gaze to the highest point on the landing zone, just behind the edge of the assault shuttle's hull. Light glinted off of the barrel of a rifle, almost like Rin winking at her. Malya actually smiled and tapped her own comm. "Come on down, Rin. We're leaving."

"About bloody time," the sniper replied. "Did we win?"

"We'd better have," Malya said, "considering the cost."

The *Lucky Chance* slipped easily into the sheltered landing bay. Candy sighed, relieved in a boneless way, like every muscle had uncoiled at once. Even this unglamorous part of Cerci, first and greatest of the Alliance's recreation worlds, had never looked so good to her. Ekona City did not have the most sophisticated port facilities on the planet, she reflected as she watched the scored and scorched concrete bay walls rise around them. But it did have the virtues of isolation and customs officials that accept almost anything you tell them. A few nimble cranes and gantries extended as they settled onto their landing struts.

Candy glanced at Fiametta, who had slumped in the pilot's couch as the cooldown sequences ran automatically. "You okay?"

The wizard shrugged. "Mostly. Ask me again when we get a better idea of Kisa's condition—and Cordelia's, of course."

"Fair enough." Candy unstrapped and stretched. They had dropped out of slip space further from the system than most ships did so as to not project a slip shadow on their approach. The nine hours of constant flying, however, had worn them both down to nubs. "So what's your plan from here?"

Fiametta rubbed her face. "Well, the Doctrine's footing this bill, whether they know it or not. We need to make repairs and then get away from this ship. It stays here, quietly, in case we have to bolt quick. That won't be possible if anyone connects us to this ship, so we need to hide somewhere well away from it." She swiveled the chair around and eyed the Alliance Security agent. "What are you planning to do?"

Candy rubbed her neck. "The Source is too important. I need to find a secure channel and report in, but there's no way I'm leaving Cordelia."

Fiametta nodded. "Good." She smiled at Candy's raised eyebrow. "It would have been out of character for you to take off now. And frankly, we can use all the help we can get."

"Speaking of that, you said you had some favors here you could call in?"

Fiametta's face fell slightly. "Yeah. I suppose I should."

"That's not a ringing endorsement," Candy said.

Motion on the dock below them caught her eye, and she turned to see a motley group approaching the *Chance*. Some were clearly ground crew, but four of them had the tidy, polished appearance she associated with officials. One of them seemed vaguely familiar.

"Well, the ones that would be the most useful are also the most, um, thorny."

"Criminal?"

"Oh yeah." Fiametta chuckled. "And even though he owes me, I doubt he'll repay the favor without getting something out of it. That's just the way he does business."

"Well, we've got company coming now, so let's get the docking squared away." Candy brushed down her ship's coveralls. She had ditched her body suit and Alliance uniform, as both were damaged beyond repair, but though the coveralls were clean, they hung on her like a burlap sack. They felt like one, too.

Fiametta led the way down the boarding ramp, Candy just behind, and Cola scampering around her feet. The cypher had been in an increasingly good mood throughout the trip, and Candy wanted a private minute to pin the little critter down and find out why. Not likely to happen soon, she thought ruefully as they stopped and waited for the dock officials to arrive. The ground crew began scattering around to inspect and lock down the ship. The four she had pegged as suits aimed right for the women at a reasonable pace. Candy frowned, still trying to identify the leader, and she noticed Fiametta stiffen.

"What?" she whispered to the red head.

"Can't be," Fiametta muttered. "What in the empty void is he doing here?" She turned as if fiddling with something on her belt and muttered, "How could he have known we were coming, and to this port? This isn't anywhere near his usual haunts."

The party stopped a few paces from them, and the man in front bowed. Candy had not expected that. His ash-blond ponytail fell charmingly over his left shoulder, and he grinned widely as he straightened back up.

"Fiametta," he said in a smooth baritone voice. "Good to see you again."

"Asger Faust," the wizard replied. "What a surprise."

"For me too," Faust replied, "whether you believe it or not. I honestly was here on other business, but when I heard that the *Lucky Chance* was on approach, I just had to come see you." He shrugged. "I thought you'd be coming to see me sooner or later anyway."

Candy stopped trying to hide her stare. She glanced from Faust to Fiametta and back, her eyes going wide.

Fiametta noticed and grinned without humor. "Oh, of course. Asger Faust, whose reputation you doubtless know, this is Candy, special agent at large for Alliance Security. Candy, Asger." Fiametta started, and gazed down to see Cola tugging on the wizard's robe with an indignant expression. "Oh, ah, of course. This is Cola, Candy's cypher."

Faust bowed to Candy, though not as deeply or as long as he had to Fiametta. "Charmed, of course. Always an honor to meet a Knight. These," he gestured to the two men and the woman behind him, "are my associates. So, what brings such renowned persons to my corner of the galaxy, aside from recreation, of course?" He looked past them. "And where's Kisa?"

"That's part of why we're here," Fiametta said firmly. "Faust, I'm calling in my favors." He blinked and his face turned serious. "Kisa needs medical attention, and I've got a chee that badly needs patched up. She was—" Fiametta took a deep breath. "She was eviscerated by the noh."

Faust's jaw dropped, and one of his companions blanched.

"We fixed her up pretty well, but we need to make sure she's okay. And then we all need to hide."

"From whom?"

"Everyone. Asger, this is very important. Until we figure out what kind of trouble we're in and how to fix it, we need to disappear." She shrugged. "This seemed like the best place."

Faust nodded slowly, considering. "All right. Yes, of course I'll help you; I owe you. But it will be tricky."

"We can cover the cost," Candy began, but Faust waved that away.

"I did not say costly, Lady Knight. I said tricky, and I meant exactly that. Cerci is not so peaceful as it was even just at the beginning of this cycle. We can shelter you while you make repairs, but perhaps Catermane is a safer place to hide."

Fiametta shook her head. "Not anymore. Black Diamond has invaded."

Faust chewed his upper lip for a second. "So it is true. Very well. I'll do what I can. Stay here tonight. I'll have something ready by dawn and more permanent arrangements made soon after." His smile returned. "It'll be, by no means, the best accommodations on our fair world, but should any of you choose to take in a race now and then—"

"Just get us off the grid, Asger," Fiametta said.

"Of course," he replied, bowing again. "I'll send word by dawn."

"I don't like this," Candy muttered as the gangsters walked away.

"Me neither. But I don't have a better idea."

Candy fumed but shook her head. "Me neither. Come on.

Let's get out of sight and check on the patients."

CHAPTER 27

Origin Point

Marikan To felt strange. The portal that Tahariel had opened bore only a passing resemblance to the rifts of the noh, and the passage through it had felt wrong. She found that she missed the smell of spice and ozone, the ragged and rippling edges. This had appeared as a black shadow, almost invisible unless she looked straight at it, and seemed almost reflective at the horizon. And it was cold. Breaking its plane had felt like plunging into snow, and the brief instant she spent between here and there had stolen all her breath. She panted for a few seconds as they stood in the cave, lit only dimly by thick-growing esper crystals, and got their bearings.

Tahariel patted the noh on her shoulder. "Sorry; should have warned you. That's a rough passage for someone not used to it. Especially when going this far."

"Where are we?" Marikan hated the reedy sound of her voice in this low atmosphere.

"An asteroid. It has no name," Tahariel replied, turning to inspect the passages out of their small chamber. "It needs none." She pointed to one that seemed like all the others. "That way. I can smell them." She sniffed, as if to emphasize the point, and wrinkled her nose. "And other things. Something's wrong."

"Well, yes," Marikan To said, straightening up. She still felt like she couldn't quite fill her lungs. "That's why we're here, after all."

Tahariel made a face but acknowledged the point. "Well, something else, then." She beckoned, and Marikan To followed the elegant alien down the narrow tunnel. They wound through the rock in a darkness broken only by scattered blue-green esper crystals. Other crystals crunched under Marikan To's feet or cracked and fell when Tahariel's armor smacked into them. Lakmi flew ahead, while Cupid fluttered around behind them.

They could hear the arguing and shouting well before they entered the larger passage. The new tunnel had clearly been modified, its sides widened and smoothed with high-energy tools, and its surfaces selectively cleared of most esper crystals. Tiny patches had already begun to grow back. The smell of ice and iron wafted strongly into Marikan To's nose, and her head turned automatically to follow the scent. It led toward the sounds of angry voices. She shared a look with Tahariel, and they both rolled their eyes but proceeded on.

The chamber they entered staggered Marikan To. It seemed to rise impossibly high, and every esper type pulsed through the veins in its walls. More aliens from Tahariel's species worked in the space. Some picked over the remains of a wrecked device that Marikan To could not look at for long without feeling dizzy. A compact and powerful figure in a deep hood stood with the Herald off to one side. Marikan To thought that the Herald looked bad; clearly injured, but something beyond her wounds had done her harm.

The center of the room, however, was the knot of figures making all the noise. Marikan had recognized Kasaro To's voice well before she had entered the great chamber, but she had not gotten a sense of his towering rage until she saw him astride his relic and bellowing. The half dozen priestesses accompanying him stood in a nervous semicircle behind him. The figure he berated sent an involuntary shudder through Marikan To. Tall, almost human but clearly alien, and beautiful even to her sensibilities, the regal man stood encased in a skeletal relic that brought him nearly to Kasaro To's eye level. He chilled her, though, and as she inspected the figure with a mixture of appreciation and discomfort, she shuddered again. She felt Tahariel looking at her and turned to her friend.

"I didn't expect that from you," the alien said, thoughtfully.

She didn't sound condescending or pitying, just curious; as if she had learned something interesting and filed it away for later. "Come on. Let's get this over with."

"You cannot lay this at my feet," Kasaro To said, clearly repeating himself and tired of it.

"If you had held the line, as you were charged to do," the alien replied with a steely calm, "we would not now be in this situation. I don't see how we can lay that blame anywhere else." Marikan To bristled at the smooth tenor of his voice. Her skin crawled slightly.

"If you were even half the warriors you claim to be," the Kasaro snarled, "you would have prevailed."

"Against three Knights, two of them Relic Knights?" The alien Knight actually chuckled. "You had the resources of two dragon ships and not only could you not stop them from getting in, you could not even overrun the landing zones of a paltry few paladins, pirates, and *some pit crew*. We understand our own limitations, slave master, as any good warrior does. We would not have asked for your assistance if we had not required it. Count on that."

Something pulled at Marikan To's attention, like half-heard noises or fleeting shadows at the corner of her eyes. Tahariel shot her a questioning glance, but the Sarva shook her head.

"It seems that is all we can count on from you," Kasaro To declared, obviously clamping down on his anger. "You have given us precious little beyond arrogance and orders since this so-called alliance began. I see no reason why we should not take our people and depart this place. You deserve to deal with this on your own. In fact, I fail to see why we should do anything but attack you on sight."

The man clearly had a cutting remark or thinly veiled threat ready for this statement, but Amelial chose that moment to step forward, supported by the hooded alien, and drop her head in a bow. Even that much obviously caused her pain, and that pain came through clearly in her voice. "Lord Harbonath, I have news."

Harbonath took a deep breath. He never broke eye contact with Kasaro To. "Proceed, my Herald."

Amelial licked her lips. "The gate is repairable, but perhaps not fully. We require replacement parts that must be brought from—That must be brought in. That is not the core problem, however. It seems that, as the gate was active when the racer Knight damaged the tines, the esperic backwash has disrupted our alignment."

Now Harbonath's eyes widened and glanced over to his servant.

"None of us noticed in the heat of the battle," she said, frowning. "But I have checked several times since, and we have definitely shifted. The esper flows are no longer properly formed here."

Harbonath glanced at the hooded alien supporting the Herald. The figure nodded. "It is so, my lord," he said in a gruff, almost comforting voice. "I've examined the gate device myself."

Marikan To shuddered and turned slowly to inspect as much of the cave as she could. She finished the turn to see Tahariel staring at her. "What is it?" Her friend whispered.

"I don't know," Marikan To replied, nervous and shaking her head. "I feel—I feel like we're being watched."

Tahariel looked concerned but did not get the chance to ask more as Harbonath's curses echoed through the cavern.

"No. No, I won't accept that," Harbonath cried. "We have too much prepared, and our timetables are rigid."

Kasaro To broke into a slow grin at the aliens' consternation, but a strange halo was forming around him. It vanished as Marikan tried to focus on it, but she saw it spreading over the priestesses too.

Harbonath seethed and rounded on the hooded figure. "Mikhal, detail a team to take new measurements. We will realign the astroid to the new patterns."

Mikhal shook his hooded head. "We cannot, my lord. The flows have shifted widely. We would have to reorient almost three full lightyears of material to—"

Kasaro To's laughter cut him off. The halo deepened. "You're saying that this failure has cost you your entire plan?" He laughed again. "This asteroid is useless to you now? Hah! Then I see no reason for any of us to remain."

"My master," Amelial said pointedly, drawing Harbonath's gaze from the noh. "This is a setback, nothing more. We have planned for such contingencies. This has only delayed us. Regrettable, yes, but not catastrophic. This galaxy has gained time, and with the Source revealed, they have gained opportunity. They have not gained victory. We have other chances to deny them that. Other locations exist for the Nokrian Gate to draw—"

"No!" Harbonath shouted. "No, everything is planned from this point, down to the placement of the Discord. We cannot—"

"You have failed," Kasaro To interrupted, intent on drawing matters back to his argument.

Rage twisted Harbonath's features but only into a more impressive form, almost majestic. Before he could speak, Tahariel stepped forward and dropped to a knee. Marikan To almost knelt too—it just seemed the obvious thing to do when addressing this alien—but managed to resist.

"My Lord Harbonath," Tahariel said, her voice soft but echoing through the chamber all the same. "The situation is more starkly changed than you realize." She looked up at his porcelain features. "The Source has not simply appeared; it is fully manifested and in play. And our enemies currently possess it."

Harbonath's face fell. Marikan To saw the other aliens go, if possible, even paler than normal. She shook her head. Tahariel's words sounded wrong. Marikan understood what her friend had said, but she could not make any sense of the actual words.

Amelial took a shaky step forward. "Is this true?"

Tahariel cocked her head as if asking why her mistress would doubt her but nodded all the same.

"This is too soon. The Source should not have come into the full expression of its nature yet. This has happened too quickly." The Herald took a moment to catch her breath. "Explain."

Tahariel hesitated and glanced at Marikan To. The noh thought it was the first time that she had seen her friend unsure. She shook off her unease for a moment and stepped forward while

Tahariel's eyes narrowed.

"There is much we do not know," Marikan said. "But shortly before the noh and corsairs assaulted Ulyxis, I found and followed an esper trail through our fleet." She took a breath and watched the aliens' reactions carefully. "I discovered one of the machine people, the chee, imprisoned on a pirate vessel. To my senses, she seemed like a fountain or a spring that poured forth esper of all kinds in an endless stream."

Everyone except the other noh clearly recognized this description. Harbonath looked dismayed but hid it well. Amelial's eyes widened and a desperate air settled over her bearing, though desperate for what Marikan could not tell. Mikhal's carriage shifted slightly, coming up straighter as if in the presence of divinity.

That thought made Marikan To still more anxious and she faltered. She took a steadying breath and looked at Kasaro To, knowing he wanted to hear this. "I did not know what I had found, so I returned to the *Hydra's Will* and informed High Priestess Zineda." Kasaro To's eyes flashed. "She was interested but not concerned and dismissed me to prepare for the battle. I do not know exactly what happened then, but when I found Tahariel on the surface and told her of my discovery, she insisted that we go to that ship immediately."

All the alien worthies nodded approval of this. Kasaro To frowned more deeply.

Marikan To licked her lips. Something about the whole conversation bothered her, but she could not pin it down. "I do know that, when we arrived, the pirates had already turned on each other, I think fighting over that chee, and High Priestess Zineda was there with several of her acolytes. I learned only later that she had been torturing the chee to understand her nature." She shrugged. "We fought to claim the chee, but Alliance and Doctrine Knights shielded her escape. Lady Zineda apparently caught up to them, but the Relic Knight Calico Kate turned on her, betraying our alliance, and rescued the chee."

She faltered again and hung her head. "That's all I know,

though I don't know what it means." She shuddered as a wave of nausea washed through her. Revulsion, like she had smelled the foulest thing imaginable, settled in her stomach. She knew that the feeling had not come from her.

"It happened as she says, Herald," Tahariel said. "I fought, but the chaos was too great and our enemies too many." She broke eye contact and deflated somewhat. "Between that failure and the setback here, our plans have unraveled."

Marikan To choked. The words grated on her; their clipped and sharp sound felt alien to her ears and cut through her mind.

"Hah!" Kasaro To barked, though the laugh sounded forced. "All your plans lie in ruins, all through your own weakness." He spit on the stone, but Marikan To shuddered and fell to her knees. In his words, she had heard the clue that she had missed thus far. She clutched her arms around herself, and Lakmi landed on her shoulder, cooing in distress. Everyone turned to look at her.

Marikan To glanced at the aliens and then looked imploringly at Kasaro To. "My lord, listen to them." She saw his eyes darken and pushed on. "Not what they say, but their words. Listen to your own. We are speaking nohkuzu, a language none of them know."

Tahariel nodded in agreement and immediately frown as she realized what had happened.

"And they are speaking a language I've never heard," Marikan said. "We do not know their speech, Lord Kasaro To." She felt more frightened than she ever had. "So why do we all understand everything that is said?"

Every noh priestess in the chamber twitched in unison. They jerked upright, made small, choked noises, and rose as one into the air. The halo Marikan To had seen blossomed forth around them. She smelled spice and the tang of ritual unguents. She began to shake. She could feel Him rising through her like bile. Then the voice of her god bellowed from all the priestesses and throughout the chamber.

"I have let you speak freely, so that you may reveal your failure. The Source is found and lost, by my servants."

Even the aliens staggered. Kasaro To fell from his relic but managed to land on his feet. Marikan To felt a force like fire stab into her chest.

"Tell me that you have not spoken falsely, Marikan To," Nozuki's voice echoed around and through her. "Swear to me the truth of your words."

The Sarva stuttered. She could barely breathe, but a panic that had nothing to do with the lack of air clutched at her. "Lord Nozuki," she stammered, "I do swear." The pain eased slightly, and breath rushed into her lungs. She gasped. "I swear that all I have said is the truth as I know it." Tears burned down her face. A red haze had narrowed her vision. She clutched at one slim possibility that she found buried in His words and snatched another lungful of air. "My mind. Look into my mind if you doubt my word."

The pain eased still more, and the voice lost its edge of controlled rage. "I doubt not your word, for you have never failed in your service. But I must know all, even that which you may have forgotten or neglected."

The fire sliced into her head like a blade. She could see nothing. Pain ripped from one temple to the other. Blood dripped onto her lips, and she realized that it came from her nose. She thought she might have screamed. She held the memories she had described foremost in her thoughts, clutching them desperately, and harboring only the faintest terror that He would probe too deeply.

Nozuki did not. Just seconds later, the pain vanished completely. Marikan To collapsed forward on the cave floor, tears and blood and spittle mixing on the stones. She felt Tahariel grabbing at her shoulders, but the gratitude at that contact faded behind what she suddenly needed to know. She rolled up to see Kasaro To. The Relic Knight clearly could not tell where to look and turned to face as many of the priestesses as he could. The Coiled God's voice washed over them all again, and Marikan began shaking uncontrollably.

"This is not treachery. This is incompetence from one of my

greatest servants. This will not be borne."

"My lord Nozuki," Kasaro To cried. "I will return at once and exact your righteous vengeance on your failed slaves. I will erase this stain on Dragon Fleet To with the blood of the guilty. I—"

"No," the Hydra God said. His voice had lost much of its malice.

Marikan To managed to sit up. She wiped tears from her eyes to clear her vision. The blood had stopped, and she ineffectively tried to clean it from her lips with the back of her hand. She smiled at Tahariel as the void witch helped her stand. The alien smiled back, her expression wry.

"No," Nozuki repeated. "You will remain here and assist your allies as they require. Much can yet be accomplished here, and they must be protected." Kasaro To's face fell, but he said nothing. "I will deal with my wayward priestess. Come forth, Marikan To. I have work yet for you to do."

Marikan took two unsteady steps forward but found her balance returning quickly. "I live only to serve."

"Yes," the Endless Hunger said. "A lesson others are about to learn."

A gigantic rift opened before her, the kind only the largest devices fixed on the greatest dragon ships could have managed, and even then for less than a minute. She smelled the familiar scents of home and felt the welcoming warmth blowing over her skin.

"Proceed."

Marikan To stepped gingerly through the tear in space and nearly slipped on the smooth decking of the *Hydra's Will*. She recognized the bridge spaces immediately, though she stood behind the warlord's throne. The rift had attracted attention from the crew, and she saw wary, unsure faces approaching. She glanced back to see the priestesses in the cave collapse, gasping for air, and Tahariel hesitantly waving goodbye. Then the rift snapped shut with a sharp bang. Marikan turned to see Mamaro To standing and staring back over his seat. Zineda stood at his side, outrage coloring her features.

"What is the meaning of this, Sarva?" the priestess began. She clearly meant to continue, but something in Markian To's expression stopped her.

"Oh, my lady," Marikan To said without thinking. "I'm so sorry."

The indignation on Zineda's face dissolved into confusion and then fear. An instant later, the dragon ship shuddered around them. The air stagnated suddenly and then vibrated with Nozuki's presence. They all felt it, and none doubted what it was for even an instant.

"My slaves," the Hydra God said. "I know all that has transpired. I know of your attempts and of your failures."

Panic edged into Zineda's expression and the confusion spread to Mamaro To.

"Those responsible must answer for the latter."

Zineda turned from the Sarva to the warlord. She started to speak, but a bright light erupted from below her. She rose, as if pulled on wires, and a fire-red glow haloed her form. With barely a shriek, she seemed to implode, her limbs snapped and her body crushed as it flowed inexorably through a narrow rift. She vanished. The light faded.

The voice returned. "She held the greatest prize of all, my prize, in her claws and let it escape. Seek it now, for your lives. Seek the chee called Cordelia. She is the Source of all that will come. And now, because Kasaro To has also failed me, you must race to find her. Do not fail me again."

The pressure lifted almost instantly as the divine presence disappeared. Everyone on the bridge took another few seconds to start breathing again, however. They all looked to Mamaro To. The warlord continued to stare at the space where Zineda had vanished. Markian To thought that he looked more sad than chastened. Finally, he shook his head and barked, "Back to your stations. We've neglected our duty too long." As the crew scrambled to obey, the warlord turned to Marikan To. "Well, huntress, it seems you've a new mission. How soon can you begin?"

Malya stood in the darkened cabin and watched the flashes of battle recede. The *Marianne* and its surviving corsair companions were withdrawing under cover of the paladin corvettes and two newly arrived destroyers. The dragon ships had fallen back, both badly damaged, and now only the strange aliens stood between the asteroid and the surrounding fleets. She heard soft movement and the quiet murmuring of water as Soliel moved to stand beside her.

"Captain Harker is stable," the corsair Knight said. "I believe the esper your cypher contributed is responsible for keeping him alive this long. Caesar could not have done it alone." She nodded in clear, grateful thanks.

"You're welcome," Malya said. She turned back to the armored glass viewports. "So what happens now?"

"Now? Hmm." Soliel considered for a moment. "I do not know your paladins as well as you do, but I imagine they will not abandon this place when they finally have their enemy before them."

"Indeed we won't," Isabeau said. Malya turned to see the Purifier—her wounds tended and hair bound around her head—stride stiffly into the cabin. "We have already begun establishing a cordon. When more ships from the Order of the Red Shield arrive, we'll have a proper blockade and begin the siege works." She nodded toward the distant asteroid. "Their gate is down, you said, which means that they can't move people through it at all or only very little, if they can repair it. Either way, if they want to break out of this area, or rescue their people here, they're going to have to do it the old-fashion way." She smiled only slightly. "For all the mysteries here, that one we understand. That one we can handle." She took a deep, steadying breath and turned to fully face Malya. "We've had word from Ulyxis."

The princess froze. Sudden trepidation gripped her and sent shots of cold fear radiating out from her stomach.

Isabeau's widening smile somehow did not dispel that. "Your family is fine. The attack was repulsed, though Hauer suggests that it was stopped rather than repelled. Of course, that's how Hauer thinks." She shrugged, smiling. "He believes that something separate from the fighting on the surface happened to cause the noh and pirates to retreat. There was some kind of falling out, apparently. Several pirate bands turned on each other, some attacked the noh, and then the whole thing fell apart."

Malya sighed, and only then realized that she had been holding her breath. "Gods of our fathers, some good news. Is Hauer all right?"

She nodded. "Banged up, but he wouldn't have it any other way. Apparently, the Black Diamond troops held their ground like champs. He singles out One Shot for particular praise, though that's about what I'd look for from a Relic Knight."

Malya slumped against the armored viewport and scrubbed at her face. "Oh good. I guess—I guess I owe my father a note."

Soliel looked at the princess strangely, and Isabeau quirked an eyebrow at her. "I'd have thought a visit at least, but it's your family, I suppose," the paladin said.

Malya frowned a bit until she saw Mr. Tomn glaring at her. "Yeah, yeah. I just, you know, don't want to go back there. I'm afraid they won't let me leave." She shook the feeling off and straightened up. "Any idea what made the bad guys leave?"

"No," the Purifier said, turning thoughtful, "but Hauer suspects it had to do with an incident in orbit. A Doctrine ship was operating, cloaked, up there during the battle. Some kind of rescue mission. They pulled someone or something off of one of the pirate flagships and escaped the system. The attack seems to have fallen apart around that mission." She shrugged. "Apparently, Fritz, One Shot's cypher, had tried to pull her out of the battle to assist in the rescue, though that's out of character for him. When that didn't work, he suddenly changed his mind and insisted that they help the Doctrine ship escape. He said something about keeping the Source out of enemy hands."

Both cyphers went rigid at that and turned toward Isabeau. She stared back at them warily. The cyphers exchanged glances, and Mr. Tomn nodded.

"The Source has appeared," he said, and it sounded like a

pronouncement. "The Calamity has come."

"What? I thought we stopped the Calamity," Malya nearly shouted.

"No," Mr. Tomn replied quickly. "Not exactly. We have delayed it, though. Our enemy isn't destroyed, and they're still interfering." Soliel's cypher nodded. "But now we have time."

"For what?"

"To do this properly," Mr. Tomn said. "The Source is a conduit for esper, the valve that will let it flow into the universe from the void. Whoever controls the Source can determine which kind of esper is favored, which kind predominates." He pointed from Malya to Isabeau. "Creation, Law, et cetera. If the wrong people get it at the wrong time . . ." He let the thought hang. "Because we fought here, because we won, there's time."

"So," Malya said slowly, "the fight's not over?"

"No," Mr. Tomn said, and he sounded genuinely sad. "It's just getting started."

"Gods of our fathers," the princess muttered and turned back to the stars. "I really needed that vacation."

"I know," Mr. Tomn said, patting her leg. "Me too. But now, at least, we have an honest chance at victory."

Malya took a deep breath and let it out quickly. "Right. Well then, let's get going."

Never miss a Future House release!

Sign up for the Future House Publishing email list:
www.futurehousepublishing.com/beta-readers-club

Connect with Future House Publishing

Facebook.com/FutureHousePublishing

Twitter.com/FutureHousePub

Youtube.com/FutureHousePublishing

Instagram.com/FutureHousePublishing

About the Author

Christopher Bodan is a freelance writer, editor, and full-time dog caretaker. He lives in Seattle with his wife, their aforementioned dog, and more electronics than he honestly knows what to do with. They don't have enough games, though; they can always use more of those.

If you liked this book, I'd love to hear.
Reviews keep me writing.
Find *Darkspace Calamity* online and leave me a review.